FAMILY AFFAIRS AT ORCHARD COTTAGE HOSPITAL

LIZZIE LANE

Boldwood

First published in Great Britain in 2024 by Boldwood Books Ltd.

Copyright © Lizzie Lane, 2024

Cover Design by Colin Thomas

Cover Photography: Colin Thomas

The moral right of Lizzie Lane to be identified as the author of this work has been asserted in accordance with the Copyright, Designs and Patents Act 1988.

Every effort has been made to obtain the necessary permissions with reference to copyright material, both illustrative and quoted. We apologise for any omissions in this respect and will be pleased to make the appropriate acknowledgements in any future edition.

A CIP catalogue record for this book is available from the British Library.

Paperback ISBN 978-1-80483-445-9

Large Print ISBN 978-1-80483-446-6

Hardback ISBN 978-1-80483-447-3

Ebook ISBN 978-1-80483-444-2

Kindle ISBN 978-1-80483-443-5

Audio CD ISBN 978-1-80483-452-7

MP3 CD ISBN 978-1-80483-451-0

Digital audio download ISBN 978-1-80483-448-0

Boldwood Books Ltd
23 Bowerdean Street
London SW6 3TN
www.boldwoodbooks.com

1

MARCH 1931

'The women's quarters are in the east wing and men in the west wing. Depending on their ages, children are quartered separately for lessons and in the dormitories when asleep. They are allowed one hour in the morning with their parents and half an hour in the evening before bedtime.'

'What about the married quarters? Where might that be?'

Mrs Tuffington, the workhouse matron, drew in her hairy chin as a duck might just before emitting a loud quack.

'As in any other such establishment, men and women are confined to separate quarters regardless of whether they are married or not. Consider what would happen if it were not so,' exclaimed Mrs Tuffington with a laugh that sounded as if it were caused by a tickle in her throat. 'More babies would likely be born should we allow conjugal arrangements, and then where would we be? Overpopulated with even more of the dissolute and parish poor, Mrs Devonshire. That's what!'

'I see your point.'

A few weeks ago, she'd asked if she could have a copy of a certain birth certificate. The answer had been a terse, no. 'Such information is confined to staff only. Many babies were adopted and the adoptive parents have the right to privacy.'

'What about the babies and the mothers who bore them?'

'Girls who fall into wicked ways have no rights.'

That's what she'd been told. It was sheer luck that she'd heard about their need for someone to work as a member of staff, an opportunity she'd jumped at.

'Right.' Mrs Tuffington heaved a sigh that seemed to proclaim satisfaction that the woman she'd employed to assist with workhouse admin and other duties as yet to be confirmed understood the rules. 'Now,' she said, her shoulders as angular as a set square, 'let us proceed.'

With the opening of a door came the sound of a crying baby. So too did a milky sour smell and a hint of ammonia. On entering the room, she espied the source of the ammonia in a bucket containing soiled nappies.

'Four small babies under six months old are looked after here. Eight toddlers up to four years old in the next room. It will be your job – yours and Miss Simms – to feed, bathe and change them. Miss Simms?'

A whey-faced young woman of about seventeen years old looked up from laying a swaddled baby alongside two others in a shared cot.

Mrs Tuffington indicated the new employee. 'This is Mrs Devonshire.'

The cowed-looking young woman gave a quick nod.

'Mrs Devonshire will be assisting you with general duties when needed and taking care of record keeping. She will do all the writing that needs to be done.'

Miss Simms swiped the back of her hand across her runny nose. 'I don't need no 'elp.'

'Of course you do, Jane Simms, and don't you be so cheeky.'

Hand in front of her mouth, Mrs Tuffington whispered, 'She can neither read nor write. Been here all her life. Gave up her baby and there'd been nothing for her in the outside world.'

The new employee, Mrs Devonshire, made no comment, but her heart bled for the poor girl. How had she felt about giving up her baby?

She forced herself to bury her true feelings. 'I have to say that I much appreciate you taking me on.'

Mrs Tuffington sniffed dismissively. 'It's the least I could do. The war made far too many widows and I can't think how difficult it must be to manage on just a war pension. And, anyway, your grasp of words and figures will be of great advantage.'

On the outside, Mary Devonshire smiled humbly and muttered how very pleased she was to be here. Inside, she was doubly so. So impressed had Mrs Tuffington been with her figures, words and general aptitude that she'd taken her on without further ado. She hadn't even checked her credentials or asked for references, for which Mary was doubly grateful. All Mrs Tuffington saw before her was yet another woman – in her fifties and left destitute by the carnage of the Great War. Better still she could take over the general administration of the workhouse besides assisting the truculent Jane Simms with the babies and toddlers.

'I'm so pleased you applied for the position,' Mrs Tuffington said.

'I must admit to being a little nervous. Being of the age I am...'

'Nonsense. You've a few years yet before retirement. To my mind, older people are far more reliable employees than younger ones. Such as her there,' said Mrs Tuffington, dropping her voice whilst her eyes travelled in the direction of Jane Simms. 'I do believe you will do us proud, and we will have a long and worthy working relationship.'

'I'm sure we will,' returned Mary Devonshire, which was an outright lie. For a while, this place would serve as a refuge from the outside world whilst she investigated a subject that was closer to her heart. Henry Devonshire, a man she had married in haste and certainly repented at leisure was dead and buried on the other side of the world in Australia, a country she'd been obliged to live in whether she'd liked it or not. The man responsible for her exile was no doubt long dead by now, but Henry was not. Thankfully, there were thousands of miles between them.

After a tour of the sad little world of destitute people with nowhere else to go, Mrs Tuffington took Mary Devonshire down into the cellar, where the archives of years gone by were stored in canvas folders. Her heart skipped a beat at the sight that greeted her.

'You won't often need to come down here. Now and again, we are asked for past accounts by the Board of Guardians and when you need to archive the records of those who are no longer with us: those whose fortunes have improved and the others – those who have left us and entered heavenly portals.'

Mrs Devonshire eyed the shelves containing the records of past years and past inmates of the establishment. Each year was clearly identified. So were the manner of the records. Her jaw clenched when she saw the section labelled 'Births'.

She commented that the records went back a long way.

'Yes. Those at the end there are the oldest archives. Hence the papers curling around the edges. I'm sure a mature woman like you will have no trouble filing and finding the things you need,' trilled Mrs Tuffington, flicking her fingers over dusty files lined up in crumpled rows along the shelves.

'I'm sure I'll cope very well indeed.'

'Just one thing.' Mrs Tuffington adopted a serious expression. 'At no time do you give out details of babies born here who were subsequently adopted, so to anyone who comes asking for birth certificates, et cetera, the answer is always no. Is that clear, Mrs Devonshire?'

'Yes.'

Mrs Tuffington beamed with pleasure. 'I'm sure you'll settle in no time at all.'

No time at all. The words rang inside Mary Devonshire's head. Time, some said, was a great healer. But it wasn't for her. She still hurt from what had happened all those years ago when she'd been brutally separated from her child and forced to travel to the other side of the world. It might have made a difference if she'd been blessed with more children, but she hadn't. No children and an unhappy marriage to a violent man who'd almost killed her had caused her to consider what she wanted from life. There was only one answer. She had to go back. She had to find the child who had been taken from her. Getting this job was the first step in her quest. Whether she would be successful or not was neither here nor there. She was back in the country of her birth, and somewhere – as yet she did not know where – there was a child who had grown into womanhood. Somehow she would find her daughter.

2

NORTON DENE, SOMERSET

March 1931

Doctor Frances Brakespeare was sitting at her desk in her office at the Orchard Cottage Hospital in the Somerset town of Norton Dene, a country town, the land around it scarred with coal mines and quarries. She was writing new copy for the leaflets that would advertise the women's clinic, wondering if she was brave enough to mention advice on family planning. She'd seen so many women back in London and here, in the town of Norton Dene, their health impaired by too many pregnancies. Many of those women struggled to feed families of four, six or more children. And yet who could deny them their natural urges, for some the only pleasure they had in life?

Susan, who looked after record keeping, reception and typing letters, knocked at the door and without waiting for her to answer brought in the most beautiful bouquet.

'You have an admirer,' she said in her usual jovial fashion.

'I know I do,' said Frances, putting down her pen and taking the bunch of flowers in her arms, consisting of spring flowers, daffodils, tulips and fluffy, frothy stuff that she didn't quite recognise. The handwriting was a different matter. She smiled as she read the words that broke her concentration and brought a smile to her face.

Doctor Brakespeare.

These flowers are by way of a reminder that you have been resident doctor at Orchard Cottage Hospital for a whole year. Congratulations. You've stayed the course and I for one am very glad that you have.

Love, both heavenly and otherwise, from the Reverend Gregory Sampson, vicar of this parish – and your greatest admirer.

His message brought a smile to her face. Her time working at a large London hospital seemed a lifetime ago. She'd thought at one stage that it was the place she always wanted to be, but had been fired because she'd dared to speak up for herself to a male colleague. As fate would have it, Izzy Brakespeare, her beloved benefactress who had taken her from the workhouse and brought her up, had died around the same time. Greater dismay followed when she'd received a letter from solicitors representing Mrs Beatrice Trinder, Izzy's sister, to vacate the premises forthwith. As a result, she'd ended up jobless and homeless.

Fate had further lent a hand when her attention had been drawn to a position at the Orchard Cottage Hospital in the Norton Dene. Wheels within wheels, in the form of Izzy's old suffragette friends, had worked behind the scenes to land her the position. One of them was Lady Araminta Compton-Dixon – more informally called Minty – and a Deborah, one of Izzy's friends from London.

From the moment Frances had arrived from London, the

Reverend Gregory Sampson had been her staunchest ally and friend. He'd also asked her to marry him, though pressure of work had prevented them setting a serious date.

'We'll get around to it,' she'd said to him. 'But first I need to make my mark at the hospital.'

He'd responded that she'd made her mark with him but that he was prepared to wait.

She'd thrown herself into being resident doctor at the Orchard Cottage Hospital. Some people in town had baulked at the prospect of a female doctor. Others thought her a breath of fresh air. She'd made changes, she'd modernised, and she intended carrying on doing so. She'd set up the mother and baby clinic shortly after she'd first arrived. Now she had plans to take it a bit further, which were both modern and bound to shock in such a traditional small town. Family planning advice was likely to be contentious, but something about the flowers arriving and Gregory's message had suddenly lifted her confidence.

She'd discussed it with Gregory the night before over a very fine dinner and a glass of wine fermented from elderflower.

'Family planning! My goodness, Frances, you're certainly going to set the cat among the pigeons. I'm not sure this town is ready for the ideas of Marie Stopes.'

Frances had thrust her chin forward in the determined manner that Gregory was getting used to – loved, in fact. 'Women need more information on what they can do to prevent pregnancy if that is their wish and I intend giving them that information. Marie Stopes has opened a clinic in London and is particularly keen to help the poor escape the grinding poverty that comes with having too many children.'

'I understand that, but can't you be just a little more subtle?'

Perhaps it was his tone of voice, or perhaps the comforting

way he was kneading her shoulders, but her feisty determination became less vibrant.

'And tell people to control their natural urges? Or to practise methods a Catholic priest would insist on? Odd, seeing as they've vowed celibacy.'

'Right. You've got the mother and baby clinic up and running and the town's got used to that. But family planning. I'm not sure some here are ready for it.'

'Especially the church.'

'The church per se might, but opinion varies from bishop to bishop and vicar to vicar.' He'd grinned. 'You know my stance. I agree with what you're trying to do. I'm just saying tread carefully. Take it slowly.'

It had been his idea to have leaflets printed for circulation at the clinic rather than paste big notices outside the town hall, the hospital and the post office.

'Keep the mother and baby clinic posters up and give out the new leaflets about family planning to the mothers who attend. Doesn't that make more sense? Nobody getting upset?'

She'd admitted that he was right. 'I wouldn't want to cause a riot.'

'Absolutely.'

She'd smiled at the thought of his method of persuasion, surprised that the calming power of his massage had made her change her mind. 'Massage,' she'd said with a sigh of satisfaction, 'could well become a healing force to be considered for the future.'

Last night had ended on a high note, a kiss beneath a sky of stars and a deep sleep that had lasted until the dawn chorus began out in the garden.

Turning her attention back to the copy for the leaflets, Frances wrote and rewrote the valuable information she thought would benefit the women of Norton Dene.

'Norton Dene. Are you ready for this?' she muttered to herself. This town was such a different place to where she'd grown up and settling in had been something of an ordeal. She'd steeled herself to fit in even though the town was so different to London and the life she'd lived there.

London had seemed the heart of her world, both the hospital where she'd trained and hoped for advancement, plus the excitement of living under the roof of a highly intelligent and unwed woman who had held amazing parties attended by clever women who discussed politics, social conditions and international responsibility on the part of the most widespread empire the world had ever known.

She'd enjoyed those years, the colour, the energy and the love of a confirmed spinster for an abandoned child. Had she ever wanted to know the identity of her natural mother? The question had never seemed that important. She had Isabelle, who she'd both admired and loved.

A confirmed spinster and suffragette, Izzy, whose full name was Isabelle Frances Brakespeare, had rescued her from likely destitution and made a concerted effort to encourage her to become whatever she wanted to be.

'This is only a man's world if women allow it.' It had been one of her favourite sayings.

Frances could see her in her mind's eye, pacing up and down the drawing room, her clothes businesslike, almost bordering on masculine, the smoke from a French or Turkish cigarette trailing from between her fingers, a black silk bow tied at the throat over a crisp white shirt.

Her strident voice still rang like a bell in Frances' head. 'Just because you're a woman doesn't mean you have to be a wife and mother. This is the twentieth century. You can be anything you want.'

There were hints in some of the things that Izzy said, some second-hand titbits from her friends. One of them had suggested that Izzy was a female Professor Higgins and Frances, her protégée, had been groomed to fulfil Izzy's ambition to be a doctor. The person who'd dared to suggest such a thing was never invited to the house again.

Yet the idea persisted that Izzy had wanted to break the shackles of female serfdom that had inhibited her life and blaze a trail in the medical world. For some reason that was never explained, this did not happen.

Whatever the truth was, Frances had adored her and tried to be everything Izzy had wanted her to be.

She could remember saying, 'I'm your little girl and I swear I'll make you proud of me.'

Something about that comment had made Izzy take a deep intake of breath. Frances had been young at the time but still she had perceived a sudden draining of Izzy's sizzling energy, coupled with a haunted look in her eyes.

And then it was as though she'd woken up from a deep sleep, jerked back from her inner world to the everyday normality of familiar surroundings. The haunted look was vanquished with sudden laughter, a merry quip and flighty movements from chair, to piano, to books and conversation confined strictly to the moment. The mask of a woman who radiated confidence and tough independence was pulled back in place.

'I knew when I picked you from all the others that you would make me proud.'

Her explanation had been flippant and somewhat dismissive, which led Frances to believe that she hadn't been telling the truth, that there was some other reason, but then, she'd been a child.

She could have been wrong, and besides, her curiosity was for simpler things.

'Was it sunny that day?' Frances had asked. 'Did I cry when you brought me home?'

'I don't remember,' Izzy had returned somewhat curtly.

'Was it a very long time ago?'

'Too long to worry about.'

Frances had remembered feeling disconsolate. She'd so wanted to not just know the details of her past but to *feel* it.

Izzy had noticed the sudden silence, the dropping of her trembling chin. 'Sweetheart,' she'd said softly, her fingers combing through Frances's hair. 'The past is a foreign place. Water under the bridge. Never to be revisited. No regrets.'

Yet Frances had sensed there were regrets, ones that for whatever reason Izzy refused to utter – at least not to Frances.

There was one more question Frances had dared to ask.

'Do I have a daddy?'

Izzy's face had turned white, and the haunted look had turned black, so it seemed that her pupils filled her eye sockets.

The question remained unanswered. Izzy had changed the subject. Frances couldn't recall as to what. Just a jarring U-turn.

Even now, after all these years, Izzy had the capacity to crowd her thoughts. Sometimes it was little things that barged into her mind and became big ones.

She had thought to ask whether Izzy had a father, but her adoptive mother tended to fend off any questions regarding her family. In all the years they'd been together, the Brakespeare family had never visited. Neither, as far as Frances knew, had Izzy visited them. Even two or three years ago when a letter had arrived informing her of her father's death, Izzy had held firm. When Frances had asked if there was any particular reason she didn't want to pay her respects, the answer came sharp and quick, the tone brittle and bitter.

'He doesn't deserve respect. Certainly not from me.'

Her eyes had glittered like cold diamonds and in that unique moment she seemed to shut the world out, to withdraw into herself. It felt to Frances that she was licking wounds, although she had no idea what those wounds might be, only that they appeared to run deep – deep enough to breed hatred of monumental proportions.

It came as a great shock when Izzy died. The whole world seemed to crumble around her. Worse still, her death had come at the same time as Frances had upset a senior doctor at the hospital and been dismissed. Nowhere to live and no job. It seemed that tribulation piled on tribulation and Izzy's sister, Beatrice Trinder, was not helping matters. This business about evicting her from the house she'd grown up in was downright vindictive. But why? Frances couldn't help but feel as though the woman wanted to make her life as difficult as possible and for no real reason. All she could think was that when alive, Izzy had slighted her in some way.

No matter how deeply she thought about it, her fine eyebrows slanting over her deep-set grey eyes, there was no valid reason why Beatrice Trinder should hate her so much. Whatever the reason the woman gave no quarter. She'd even tried to snatch the little car Izzy had given Frances when she'd passed her finals. The little car was imperative to a doctor moving to the country and Beatrice herself could have no use for it. But that was the way it was. Izzy's sister seemed dead set on making Frances's life as difficult as possible.

Although a dismaying occurrence at first, losing job and home turned from a tragedy into a triumph. It seemed by chance that the opportunity at the Orchard Cottage Hospital in Norton Dene had beckoned her to apply, although latterly she had a sneaking suspicion that friends of Izzy might have had a hand in it, especially Lady Araminta Compton-Dixon, lady of the manor and driving force on the committee of the cottage hospital.

Izzy, her ladyship and several of their friends had been members of the Women's Social and Political Union, commonly called the suffragettes. Younger then but feisty, the brave souls who had fought so fiercely for women's rights in the past were still a sisterhood, the ties born in a time of struggle as strong as ever. Friendships made in youth had become friendships for life.

Detaching herself from her thoughts, Frances concentrated once again on perfecting the copy for the leaflets on family planning. Reluctant at first, she had to accept that Gregory was probably right about not plastering posters in prominent places. Give the good people of Norton Dene time to adjust. The world was changing, and the attitudes of the past were being slowly, but determinedly, overridden.

The present title of the leaflet sprang out at her. FAMILY PLANNING.

Her lips moved soundlessly as she read it through.

She asked herself whether it was pitched at the right level? Was it attention-grabbing? Would it attract the outrage of those of a more narrow-minded disposition, such as the church and various women's groups?

Holding the end of the pen between her teeth, she reread the heading. Family Planning. She said it out loud before deciding it didn't really say enough.

Tipping her head back, she closed her eyes and thought through a few options.

MODERN CONTRACEPTION

BIRTH CONTROL

A WOMAN'S PLACE

PLANNING FOR CHILDREN
A WOMAN'S WORLD?

She let the pen drop from her hand. It was hard to decide which of these titles – if any – would shout what was on offer to those desperately in need of limiting their families whilst not upsetting the more conservative residents of the town.

So much was good about Norton Dene and her new life, but there were still prejudices that must be overcome, the clinging to the past replaced by the new ideas that would take them into the future. To many people, the idea of controlling the number of children they had was alien, something else they could dislike about the modern age. There would be no point telling them that Mrs Annie Besant, a member of the Malthusian movement of the late nineteenth century, was one of the leaders of the birth control movement. Along with Charles Bradlaugh, Annie Besant published a physiological treatise in 1876 entitled *Fruits of Philosophy*. Some other great reformers of that time were also firm supporters of birth control, a means by which the health of the nation could be improved. The health of the British Empire depended on healthy people to maintain its credibility.

Marie Stopes, and her husband, Humphrey Roe, had opened the first birth control clinic in Holloway, London in 1921. Frances felt in awe of this woman but also it was a challenge to her own capabilities. Norton Dene wasn't London, but the problems of women struggling with large families was national not local and like this stalwart of the movement, she wanted to help the poor as well as those who could pay.

Such a lot of thinking! For now, she needed a break before her brain burst.

After filling a blue and white jug with water, she began arranging the sweet-smelling flowers, smiling at the thought of her first meeting with the Reverend Gregory Sampson. Hair as golden as a sun god, his expression had consistently wavered on a smile. It had struck her at the time as the look of a man who seemed constantly bemused with the world, a unique look in more ways than one. Never had she met a minister of any church without the slightest trace of dryness to his sermons or a hint of gloom and doom on his face or the threat of damnation in his words. But hellfire and Brimstone were not Gregory's style. He exuded infectious joy in his job and everyday interaction with people and the world at large. In short, he had the capacity to make religion part of everyday life, not just for Sundays.

Never had she envisaged herself as a vicar's wife, but the possibility was there and although it was early days, the future looked promising. So long as she could continue to be a physician, that is. So far, no objection had been raised.

Flowers arranged to her satisfaction, Frances gathered up the leaflets and placed them in the top drawer of her desk. Once everything was tidied away, she reached for her stethoscope. Next stop the children's ward. Then the women's ward. Then the men.

Outside her office, she turned to the staccato sound of stout shoes to see Sister Edith Harrison bearing down on her.

The ward sister came level before glancing tellingly down at the fob watch hanging on her breast. 'I was wondering where you'd got to, Doctor,' she said, letting the watch drop back onto her chest.

'Goodness. Is it that time already?' Frances said it with innocent aplomb after taking a cursory look at her wristwatch.

'Ten minutes past.'

'What would I do without you to keep me on my toes.'

She said it cheerfully whilst hiding the mirth in her eyes by marching on ahead, her face firmly forward. Sister Harrison was more than a trifle overbearing, but in Frances's opinion, it was better to feed her self-importance and make her feel valued. Being convivial and eschewing a little praise helped maintain hospital efficiency and professional interaction. The staff worked as a team. It didn't do to let personalities get in the way.

They stopped at the small alcove at the entrance to the children's ward. It was routine for the ward sister to run through the cases needing attention that day.

'We have a new patient who I think you should see first.' She passed Frances the record card for the new patient.

'This card looks incomplete,' she said, flicking it over onto the reverse side just to make sure she hadn't missed details such as name and address.

Sister Harrison marched on, a picture of starched uniform and clipped efficiency. 'It's all we have.'

Of the three boys in the children's ward, two were getting over scarlet fever. These two would be allowed home soon.

Along with Sister Harrison, her face devoid of expression and as stiff as her apron, they attended the boy admitted only that morning who lay alone behind a drawn screen.

The smell of carbolic mixed with that of pungent filth.

Frances wrinkled her nose, which Sister Harrison noticed and commented on.

'He's been given a wash. Once he's well enough, I'll have him bathed, but as you can see, he's currently in no state to be interfered with too much. I've had his clothes incinerated. They were infested.'

'Judging by the state of him, he needs complete rest.'

If it hadn't been for the purple and yellow bruising on his face, the boy's pallor would have matched that of the starched pillow. One eye was half closed and his cheeks were sunken. His body was wraithlike beneath the bedclothes, his arms patterned with bruises and burns.

Bile rose from her stomach. She'd seen beaten young boys before back in London.

'He's not given a name or address?'

'No. We've asked, but he won't answer.'

'Did he come here alone?'

'Someone found him and brought him in.'

'Well, we can't have that, can we.' Frances smiled down at the tousle-haired boy. 'I didn't catch your name. Can you tell me what it is?'

He blinked just the once, as though surprised to see her there. After that he turned away, staring blankly at a spot in the screen not quite covered by the green material.

Sister Harrison had found him some clean and rather washed-out pyjamas from the store they kept for those who didn't own any nightclothes.

After a brief scrutiny of his wounds, Frances tried again, 'You look as though you've been in the wars.'

A nerve flickered beneath one eye where a yellow frill encircled a purple bruise. There were bruises down the side of his face, a particularly large one sitting like a Victoria plum on his cheekbone.

Frances composed herself. This wasn't the first child she'd suspected the subject of severe and prolonged beatings. London was full of them. So too, it seemed, was Norton Dene.

She took a deep breath before addressing Sister Harrison. 'Let's take a look at his chest, shall we?'

Sister Harrison's adept fingers rolled up the lad's pyjama top into thin folds as high as his collarbone.

Frances took shallow breaths as she placed the stethoscope in various places over the lad's prominent ribs, which, like his face, was liberally dotted with bruises.

Doctor and nurse exchanged knowing looks over the boy's undernourished body.

'Right,' said Frances with soft reassurance. 'We're going to turn you over, so I can hear what's going on in your lungs. Sister Harrison?'

One on one side and one the other, they gently turned the boy onto his belly. He did not protest and stayed silent. They rolled up his pyjama top again to the level of his shoulder blades.

Frances swallowed the sharp intake of breath that threatened and exchanged a tight, outraged look with Sister Harrison. There were weals across the boy's back. Some were relatively new. Others were a mixture of yellow and violet, a sure sign that they were older.

Even once he was lying on his back again, he made not a murmur, neither did he look at them but kept his eyes partially closed. It was, thought Frances, as though he was falling inwards with nothing for company except his thoughts, which were likely as bruised as his body.

Taking a fountain pen from her breast pocket, she entered her diagnosis on the record card.

Unknown boy. In my estimation possibly nine or ten years old. Multiple contusions, cuts and grazes. Evidence of broken ribs. Malnourished. Partially healed and fresh weals across his back. Possibly the result of being beaten with a whip or cane.

Feeling sick to her soul, and so wanting to cuddle him and tell him all would be well, Frances leaned over him. 'Don't worry, young man. You're in hospital. Nobody's going to hurt you. I won't let them. Neither would Sister Harrison. Would you like some food?'

He didn't answer.

She turned to Sister Harrison. 'Get some brought to him anyway,' she said softly.

'Yes, Doctor.'

'Do we know who brought him in?' whispered Frances.

'Mr Locke from the Goose and Gander Inn. He found him curled up behind the beer barrels.'

'Did he give a name for the boy?'

Sister Harrison shook her head. 'No. Left him here and shot off like a hare fleeing the hounds.' Her tone was disapproving.

Frances frowned. 'Let's ask him again, shall we?'

'I doubt he'll tell us.'

'We'll try anyway.' She leaned closer to the expressionless face, noted the tangled unwashed hair. 'We don't know your name. Would you like to tell us what it is?'

The same question received the same answer, that is total silence, plus an unwillingness to turn his head and look at them.

Frances sighed. 'Well, let's get him cleaned up and comfortable, shall we?'

'Yes, Doctor Brakespeare.'

Sister Harrison had shown a caring side to her nature, which made Frances think she was breaking through to a softer centre. 'You can call me Doctor Frances, Sister Harrison. Everyone else does.'

The middle-aged nursing sister held her head aloft and sniffed. 'I'm not everyone else.'

Being snubbed like that left Frances speechless but reminded her that it took all sorts to make a world. Including Sister Harrison, who had old-fashioned attitudes, at least in her professional life. In private, if rumour and what she knew herself was anything to go by, she had male friends. Simon Grainger, son of the lessee of the Orchard Quarry, had been one of those she'd dallied with. He'd since left town and was living in the village of Monkswell overseeing the quarry he'd tried to get Ned Skittings transferred to. Ned Skittings was married to Nancy, sister of Lucy Daniels, both nurses. Following an accident at the quarry when Ned was badly injured, even before he was healed, Simon Grainger had contrived to have Ned take a job at Monkswell Quarry in the Forest of Dean on the other side of the River Severn. It came to light that Simon had been negligent and caused the accident and Ned was witness to it. When this was found out, it was Simon who ended up in the quarry.

It wasn't beyond belief that Sister Harrison was missing him and, in a way, who could blame her. She lived alone with her mother and that was a good enough reason to enjoy a little social life on her own account.

After completing her round of the men's and women's wards, Frances's thoughts went back to the boy, his injuries and where he might belong. Who knew, it was possible that a family was missing him – though not much of a family if his injuries were anything to go by.

'Perhaps Lucy – Nurse Daniels – might know who he is,' Frances suggested.

'She'll be in shortly. I'll ask her then, but I don't hold out much hope,' returned Sister Harrison through tight lips. 'Everyone knows everyone else in this town. If none of us know him, then I'm afraid that's the way it will stay.'

'Not a gypsy child perhaps?'

'No. The gypsies haven't been around here for years and when they do, it's in one of the surrounding villages, not in town.'

They came to a stop at the end of the sleeping boy's bed.

'Unless he wandered or ran away.'

They'd spoken softly and the boy gave no sign of having heard them.

'Has he eaten?'

'Some soup.'

'Good.'

'And with Nurse Daniels' help he'll be having a bath tomorrow.'

'Gently,' said Frances. 'Go gently with him.'

'Of course.'

'I want to find out who did this. I'll phone the police.'

'They won't do anything.'

'I think they should be informed. You never know.'

At the end of the day, her office still smelled of flowers and their colour brightened the room. For a moment, it felt as though time had rewound itself and Frances was seeing the flowers and reading the card all over again. But hours had passed since they'd arrived and tending to patients and writing medical notes had taken over.

The identity of the young boy who had endured several beatings over a period of time was uppermost in her mind.

A phone call to the town police station had proved fruitless. They'd had no reports of a missing child but did promise to send someone along to look at the boy and take notes.

Her next thought was that Gregory might know the child. It was a long shot but worth asking anyway.

The phone at the vicarage rang four times before he picked it up, his rich baritone reverberating down the line.

'The Reverend Gregory Sampson here, St Michael's Vicarage. How can I help you?'

'Gregory. It's me.'

'Whilst on duty at the hospital? Goodness, I am flattered that you've taken time out to phone me.'

'Don't be facetious. I have something very important to ask you, though first I should thank you for the flowers.' She fingered one flower of pale blue. 'I love the smell of spring flowers. They're very calming. And at the present time I am in great need of calming.'

'That's why I chose them. Beats the smell of lavender furniture polish every time! Though my housekeeper Mrs Cross wouldn't agree. I think she'd wear furniture polish as perfume if she could.'

Frances laughed loudly at the very thought of Mrs Cross dabbing lavender furniture polish behind each ear. 'You're lucky to have her. The vicarage wouldn't be half as spick and span without her.'

'Only teasing.'

'I know you are. Thank you again. They really are lovely.'

'I'm glad you like them.' His voice softened into gentleness as well as affection. 'I was going to cook for you tonight.'

She laughed. 'You're always cooking for me. I must have put on eight pounds since I moved here.'

'You're a picture of health. The bloom of the countryside is on your skin.'

His words of affection were flavoured with amusement.

'I'm going to say no to your kind invitation – or at least partially.'

'Now that is confusing. Are you accepting or not? Or are you going to eat half and take the other half of the meal home|?'

His jokiness brought a smile to her face, and she imagined that he was smiling too.

'I thought we might go to the pub.'

'The Cross Hands?' He sounded greatly cheered. 'I cannot refuse. Their cider is terrific.'

She barely suppressed a chuckle before she informed him

that they were not going to his favourite local. 'I have other plans. I want to go to the Goose and Gander.'

'Really?' He sounded greatly surprised.

'Have you been in there yourself, Gregory, for pleasure or the business of saving souls?'

'I've always tried not to. It's not the most salubrious establishment in town. Why do I get the feeling you have a specific reason for going there?'

'Because I *do* have a specific reason for going there. I don't have time to speak to you now, but perhaps later, when you're downing that second pint of cider – or whatever.'

'I will bend to your will and give into temptation.'

'I want to speak to the landlord there. He brought in a patient – a young boy so thin, and dirty, I'm surprised he's still alive. No name. No address. He's a mass of bruises and he's been beaten. I want to find out who did this to him. If you don't wish to accompany me, I'll go by myself.'

'No. You won't. I'll be your guardian angel.'

3

LONDON

Breakfast was finished at the Trinder house in Islington and Arnold Trinder had given his wife a quick peck on the cheek before leaving for his job at the stock exchange in the heart of the city of London.

Beatrice Trinder, who had been born Beatrice Brakespeare, was similar in features to her late sister, though lacked Izzy's dynamic exuberance. Instead of a face shining with relentless energy and zest for life, Beatrice had a bitter twist to her narrow lips and a stiffly determined demeanour as though she had constant battles to fight in a world that showed her little regard.

She couldn't remember their mother who had died when they were young, but she did remember and had worshipped her father. He'd been her entire world and she'd so wanted to be his favourite, but that position was reserved for her sister, Izzy. It was Izzy who'd received demonstrative affection. Izzy the lively one who'd made his eyes shine with a love she'd so wanted him to show her, Beatrice. She'd done her best to win his love whilst he was alive, but it hadn't happened. Not really. But now, after his death, she would prove that she was the daughter who had loved him unconditionally, the one who would honour his name in any way she could. He might not be privy to her steadfast loyalty, but she would know and she would be content – at least that was what she told herself.

A polite knock at the dining-room door preceded Annie, the parlourmaid, a silver tray in hand on which lay the first mail delivery of the day.

Beatrice searched through the small pile, placing those addressed to her husband to one side. Amongst them was one addressed to herself; one she had been waiting for. This was a letter she wanted to read alone.

'Thank you, Annie. You may go.'

'Yes, ma'am.' The girl hesitated. 'Mrs Trinder, I wonder...' Her voice was hesitant, which immediately put Beatrice on her guard.

Her brows beetled; her eyes were glassy.

'What is it you're wondering,' snapped Beatrice.

Annie nervously knotted her hands behind her back and crossed the fingers of her right hand. 'There's a stale half a loaf in the pantry. I wondered if I might give it to the hurdy-gurdy man at the end of the road...'

'No, you may not! Tell Cook to make a bread-and-butter pudding from it. You know I abhor waste. The hurdy-gurdy man can buy his own.'

'Yes, ma'am.'

Eyes downcast, the maid left the room.

Outside the door, unseen by her mistress, Annie poked out her tongue and muttered, 'Mean old bitch!'

The maid wasn't wrong. Beatrice had a deeply covetous streak and was not inclined to be generous. The letter she'd received from the firm of solicitors who acted for her in all matters pertaining to her family would be testimony to that. Or so she hoped – if they'd done their job right.

Letter in hand, she headed for the study, where the air smelled of stale cigar smoke and gold-spined books glinted in the semi-gloom.

After closing the door, she sat behind her husband's desk, picked up the brass letter opener and sliced open the envelope. The paper was thick and stiff, and the letter was handwritten, which pleased her no end because it meant they'd taken time, which in turn conveyed their respect for a woman of means, a woman of good family and commendable status.

Dear Mrs Trinder,

As per your instructions we made enquiries as to the present whereabouts of Doctor Brakespeare, your late sister's adopted daughter…

The term 'adopted daughter' caused Beatrice's bottom lip to curl downwards exposing her clenched teeth. Reference to adoption, allowing a workhouse waif into the family, grated. Addressing her as doctor, a qualification she regarded had been bought with Brakespeare money, set her teeth on edge.

Taking a firm grip on her grinding teeth, she read on.

We can confirm that she is still in the town of Norton Dene, where she holds the position of resident doctor at the cottage hospital…

The term 'cottage hospital' immediately struck her as amusing, a contemptuous amusement like a cat hissing through sharp teeth. Cottage hospital. Like a poor man's hovel but with more beds. If this upstart had been practising her craft at a London hospital, she might have been impressed – though possibly not.

Nothing this person could do would either impress or soften her attitude.

'Cottage!' She laughed out loud before her jaw tightened and she gritted her teeth and read on. This woman, this detritus from a workhouse and a common working girl, had been educated at her sister's expense. The very thought of her gaining professional status was infuriating. Without the Brakespeare money and name, the girl would probably have become a domestic servant, a barmaid pulling pints, or a shabby little person working twelve hours a day in a factory. Or she could have become worse, a street urchin, a whore selling her body for her daily bread. That was what she should have been, and would have been if it hadn't been for Isabelle's overly generous disposition.

A deep-seated resentment boiled within her, alongside a conviction that she was better than anyone else, a person of class and respectable to the core. Nobody could persuade her to be generous of spirit towards the urchin from the workhouse. People in the workhouse were of a feckless nature, which was why they'd ended up there in the first place. Never mind the heart-rending lamentations and cries for help. Beatrice had no time for any of that. In her opinion, they had only themselves to blame.

The question of her sister's adoptive daughter smouldered inside. She was like a dog with a bone, she couldn't let go of it, couldn't stop it ruling her days and her nights.

Her husband's kiss that morning had helped smooth over the argument they'd had the night before when she'd declared that the workhouse child's mother must have been of low morals to have ended up giving birth there.

Her husband had countered that she couldn't know the circumstances and therefore should not condemn either the child or the natural mother out of hand.

Beatrice had retaliated with angry indignation. 'I don't care about the circumstances of the child's birth. She is not entitled to my family name.'

'You married me. You're no longer a Brakespeare. You're Mrs Arnold Trinder.'

Livid and furious, she'd thrown a teacup at him and shouted that she'd been born a Brakespeare. What she was now was of no consequence.

'You're going through with this,' he'd said whilst touching his forehead where the teacup had landed.

'Yes.' She had gone on to tell him in no uncertain terms what she wanted to do and how she'd set the wheels in motion by instructing her solicitor to trace where the adopted guttersnipe was living. Never would she address the usurper as doctor. She was not of their class. Most certainly below the salt! 'And then I will instruct them to petition for her not to use my sister's name. It doesn't belong to her.'

'Are you mad?' He'd stared at her in disbelief whilst preparing to dodge anything thrown in his direction.

Beatrice had reacted as though her insides were made of ice, her face rigid with a cold anger that made him wonder why he hadn't seen this lack of compassion when he'd first married her. *Love is indeed blind*, he'd thought to himself but felt helpless to stand his ground.

'It's my family name,' she'd repeated, her lips twisting over her small, pearl-like teeth.

Arnold had made another attempt to placate her, a hopeless task but one he felt obliged to do. 'But she was only a child, and your sister was of a charitable disposition.'

'*Charitable!* My father would turn in his grave. He was charitable. Many was the poor girl he took in and had trained in domestic duties.'

'He did indeed,' Arnold had said, a slightly cynical look on his face. His wife was unaware of her father's reputation and seemed unaware that many young maids had been dismissed from their positions. He'd heard the rumours. Was party to the tales of young girls taken in then turned out onto the street to live with the disgrace of an illegitimate pregnancy.

He'd liked Isabelle, Beatrice's sister, not that he'd known her for that long. She'd moved out of the family home and into a house provided by her father in Carwell Street. He'd bumped into her a few times in town, had even drunk tea with her. Their conversation had referred in only a small part to her sister, and when her father was mentioned, she'd clammed up, her face hardening and a fierce look in her eyes. Basically, he'd considered Isabelle a good person. As for the child who was now a doctor, wasn't she entitled to the Brakespeare name even though she was adopted?

The argument from last night was still with him as he walked into Threadneedle Street along with a whole army of bowler-hatted gentlemen, the tips of their umbrellas tapping a steady rhythm with each footstep.

He'd tried one last time. Just one last time. 'Please reconsider, Beatrice, at least out of respect for your sister's memory.'

'Pah!'

He shook his head. That had been it.

Back in Trinder Street, Beatrice made the same exclamation. 'Pah. Pah and poppycock.'

She did not believe in being charitable. Charity, she believed, should be kept at a distance and even if such people did arouse sympathy and one was inclined to donate a little largesse, such people should never be invited into the house and certainly not be invited to join the family.

Her mind was made up. She would instruct the solicitors to inform the subject of her hostility, Doctor Frances Isabelle Brakespeare, to relinquish her name. Surely it couldn't be too difficult to change it to something else – anything so long as it wasn't Brakespeare.

This was yet another step in distancing the family from the usurper. Beatrice's ire and determination had started long before her sister's death when she'd visited the house and collected those things she believed belonged to the family. The house belonged to the family of course. Her widowed father had insisted it was Isabelle's as long as she lived. That in itself rankled. Why hadn't he given her, Beatrice, a house? Just because Arnold Trinder was a man of means and could buy his own didn't mean that an extra property wouldn't have come in handy. But her father had not bequeathed her a house or the money to buy a second one or something bigger than the one they currently lived in. But that wasn't really the point. Izzy had always been his favourite, the one who'd received hugs and applause for being clever, elegant and listening attentively to the stories of his youth, the Battle of Omdurman when he'd been promoted to colonel, the lights of Paris and his visit to the Moulin Rouge. Beatrice had blushed at his tales of Paris, his rather risqué descriptions of the girls, the dazzling lights, the creamy thighs...! She still blushed at those descriptions, whereas Isabelle had laughed, her face bright with fascination.

There were many tales of the people he'd encountered in foreign lands whose ways were different and sometimes quite exotic. His eyes had blazed when he'd told those stories and his cheeks had become flushed whilst his hand played with Izzy's silky hair as she had looked up at him in rapt adoration.

Her sister had been his favourite. There was no doubt about that. She'd revelled in his attention, whilst Beatrice had hovered in the shadows, the lesser child, neglected, glum and bad-tempered. She had fretted even more when father and daughter repaired to the library, the two of them alone, laughing behind closed doors, which after a time became pregnant silences. To Beatrice, it seemed as though they were sharing secrets that she was not party to, which had hurt and angered her.

It was after Isabelle turned fourteen that things changed. The girl who had fizzed with electricity became withdrawn and avoided her father, refused to go into the library with him, and although it was impossible to lock her bedroom door, she placed a chair behind it.

The situation pleased Beatrice no end. She would seek her father out minus her sister and although she did go into the library with him, there was no laughter, not even silences, just short discussions about school. In all, he had seemed distracted, uninterested in her life, though she'd tried her best to engage him. No matter how much she had tried to ingratiate herself with him, though, he didn't hug her as he had her sister. Sometimes he looked at her regretfully, even with pity.

Beatrice had accepted all this, told herself that in time she would be the one he counted on. She was always there for him, although, regardless of the change in Isabelle's new and more aloof manner, he still didn't treat Beatrice the way he had her sister. There was none of the intimacy she had been so jealous of. He kept her at arm's length, his eyes sliding in Isabelle's direction whenever he sighted her, sat across from her at dinner. Sometimes he knocked on the door of her room but got no answer. Beatrice suspected her sister was pretending to be asleep, a moment she, Beatrice, took advantage of, skipping up to her father and slipping her hand into his.

It was a few months after their first party with adults that, with her father's consent, Isabelle drank half a bottle of champagne. Beatrice wasn't sure what happened after that, although she recalled her running off into the garden and her father striding across the lawn calling her name.

A few weeks later, at age fifteen, Isabelle had disappeared from the house. Beatrice was told that she'd become ill and had been sent away to Brighton to convalesce. 'Miss Isabelle has a stomach problem,' the housekeeper had said. At no point did the motherly looking woman meet her eyes. She was also told that she'd be away for some time.

A loving sister would have been worried about her, would have asked more questions, but Beatrice did not. Izzy being away meant that she would be the single recipient of her father's attention. He was hers at last and she would do anything for him.

As for Izzy, she did indeed come back for a while but was very much changed. The old exuberance was no longer there, but Beatrice perceived hatred in her eyes and all of it directed at their father. Something had occurred between father and favourite daughter, but she couldn't guess what. Perhaps her sister had fallen in love with someone totally unsuitable, which had led to scandalous behaviour, hence the reason she had been sent away for a time. She felt a kind of revenge at the thought of it.

As the distance between Izzy and her father increased, Beatrice had done her best to fill the gap. She'd loved the smell of him, cigars, damp tweed when he came home through the rain and had forgotten his umbrella. Everything about him gave her immense pleasure, but still his eyes had followed Izzy, who rarely spoke and cried into her pillow at night in the room they shared.

On the infrequent occasions her father did entice Izzy into the library, and then only for a matter of minutes, there was no laughter and little conversation, except for one particular night. Beatrice had overheard her father and sister in the library. Isabelle was screaming at him hysterically, shouting that it was the very least he could do after forcing her to give away...

Beatrice hadn't caught the rest of what was said and didn't ask. All she knew was that when Izzy came storming out of the library, her sister was close-lipped, red-faced and there was a fiery look in her eyes. Her father had looked overly distressed as though he couldn't believe whatever it was her sister had said.

Soon after that, at her own request, Isabelle went away to finishing school in Sussex, run by a woman called Anne Goldman who had a daughter named Deborah. Beatrice had expressed her envy. 'I wish I was going. You're so lucky.'

Izzy had glared at her. 'You're such a silly goose, Beatrice Brakespeare, but yes I suppose it would suit you, smooth off the rough edges so that you bag yourself a suitable husband.'

Beatrice had looked at her with round eyes. 'But isn't that what you're going for?'

Izzy had laughed a brittle, bittersweet laugh and shook her head. 'No. All I want is to get away from this house and from HIM!'

After finishing school, Isabelle had completed a two-year college course in medicine. At the end of it, aged twenty-one, she'd come home only briefly, stormed into their father's library and slammed the door behind her. There was no shouting as such, but there were firm words that somehow seemed to form an ultimatum. Shortly afterwards, their father provided Isabelle with the house in Carwell Street.

Beatrice had asked him why her sister was not proceeding with her studies and perhaps qualifying as a doctor.

He had stared at her as though she wasn't there, before saying, 'She hates the sight of blood.'

Beatrice rarely saw her sister again. Neither did they speak of her – in fact, it seemed at times as though she'd never existed. This situation suited Beatrice. She was happy to fill the position of single child, only daughter, following him round the house like a lost puppy. At long last, she had her father to herself. She'd been his loving daughter until the day he'd died.

Years before his death, long after she'd taken up residence at Carwell Street, Izzy had written to her father stating her intention to adopt a child. On reading it, he'd had trouble catching his breath, mouth hanging open, eyes wide with shock.

Beatrice had grabbed the letter from him. Her jaw had dropped when she'd read it.

And I have a suitable child in mind. The mother was once in gainful employment, but her employer took advantage of her youth...

'She's disgusting,' Beatrice had shouted, determined to defend her father no matter what. She'd always hated her sister. Now her hatred increased fivefold.

Receiving no response from her father, she'd taken it upon herself to consign the letter to the fire, where it curled and blackened, consumed by the flames.

'How could she bring a stranger, a guttersnipe, into our family? I swear at times that my sister is deranged.'

It was from that moment that her father's health began to go downhill and there was nobody else to blame but her sister.

That was years ago now and her father was dead and so was her sister. The house in Carwell Street had been reclaimed and sold, the money placed in the bank. The family home just off Russell Square had been retained and let out to a gentleman and his family and formed a good part of her nest egg. She was the only beneficiary of her father's will, a Brakespeare by birth although a Trinder by marriage. Her very soul bridled that someone should carry the family name who was not connected by blood. The child her sister had taken from the workhouse was a usurper. She had no right to the Brakespeare name and Beatrice, being the way she was, had no intention of letting her keep it. To her mind, it dishonoured her father's name.

Setting the letter from the solicitors to one side of the desk blotting pad, she took a piece of paper headed with the Trinder name and began to write.

Dear Sirs,

I thank you for the work so far carried out. I have no real curiosity regarding this creature. My main purpose is to retrieve my father's name from someone who is not entitled to share it...

4

NORTON DENE

Terraced cottages built sometime in the eighteenth century leaned against each other like old men on rickety legs. At the corner of Mutton Street, the brick-built Goose and Gander pub looked barely able to stand. Its walls were lopsided thanks to the old mining seams beneath its questionable foundations, laid sometime in the late eighteenth century. Window frames had twisted out of shape, the lintel above the door was higher one side than the other; in short, the whole building looked in imminent danger of collapse.

The sign above the pub door was faded, the paintwork weather-worn, so it was difficult to tell the original colours or whether the pair of white fowl depicted were what the sign decreed they were – a goose and a gander.

They'd opted to walk to the pub rather than take the car.

'I need to prepare what to say,' Frances had said.

'And I need to prepare myself in case I have to fight our way in – or out,' said Gregory, who'd opted to discard his dog collar this evening and dress casually smart in flannels and corduroy jacket.

On the plus side, the night air had put roses in their cheeks and had given Frances time to give Gregory the details about the young lad whose wounds could only have been inflicted by a violent hand.

'And this was where the boy was found,' said Gregory, his eyes raking the dangerously quirky building.

'Yes. The landlord found him in the backyard among the empty beer barrels.'

Gregory grunted. 'Was he telling the truth, do you think?'

'You mean he was lying and that he was related to the boy?'

'That's about it.'

When Gregory shrugged his shoulders, Frances noticed how broad they were and sincerely hoped they would give a solid impression that he could take care of himself. On reflection she decided that although he had fought in the bloodiest conflicts in recent history, he was not a violent man although his strength was there if need be.

The Goose and Gander was not a pub they'd ever visited, but she had heard of its reputation, which was far from good.

Gregory's hand cupped her elbow, a reassurance she much appreciated. Although she was doing her best not to show it, entering the Goose and Gander was unnerving.

'Just the look of this place gives me goosebumps,' Frances murmured.

His voice whispered into her ear. 'Understandable. We've entered the battleground for the Salvation Army – but only when they're feeling brave enough.'

When Gregory pushed open one half of the double doors, a soup of smells blasted their senses. Stale beer, tobacco, unwashed clothes and unwashed bodies. The air inside was thick with smoke from pipes and cheap cigarettes. The floor beneath their feet was in turn sticky or gritty – thanks to spilled beer on the one part, coal dust and aggregate on the other. Walls that had once been cream were yellowed with nicotine and the ceiling sloped towards the bar, where seven feet became six feet and lumps of plaster bulged like giant blisters.

Dark figures in crumpled clothes and greasy caps, shoulders hunched, huddled in small groups, or leaned on the bar with one arm, the fingers of their free hand gripped around the handle of a pewter or glass mug. Faces grimy with sweat and ingrained with dirt stared at the newcomers, their eyes wary and challenging.

Frances avoided meeting those looks, instead weighing up their surroundings. Had the boy known this place? Had he lived here, in which case the landlord might be lying?

Gathering all her courage, Frances made an effort to put a brave face on it, stepping forward ahead of Gregory. A woman might possibly make more progress than a man. A woman was less threatening.

'Good evening. I'm looking for the landlord.'

Their expressions were openly hostile, but she swallowed her apprehension, held her head high and searched the belligerent expressions in the hope of spotting a response.

Her forthright and commanding attitude swept two or three times over the grimy-faced patrons, until suddenly a man who stood leaning on the bar straightened. The top of his head brushed against the ceiling. He had a fleshy face, a broken nose and his cheeks were a spider's web of broken veins.

'You ain't allowed in yur,' he growled.

'And why might that be?' Frances asked sharply.

'In thur,' he said, jerking his stubbled chin at a door on which the word 'saloon' was written in crackled gold lettering.

'I don't see...'

Gregory grabbed hold of her arm before she had chance to say any more. 'In here,' he said, opening the door of the saloon bar and pushing her through. 'Men only in the public bar.'

'Really?' Never having been a regular pub patron, even back in London, Frances was ignorant of the norms of a licensed establishment. If that was the case, then so be it. She swallowed her pride. 'Well, I can't say I'm that put out.'

She looked around the oddly shaped room, which somewhat resembled an octagon. A large timber beam had been forced into the gap between floor and ceiling in the far corner where three old women sat playing dominoes. Just as in the public bar, they eyed their arrival with hostility. Likely as not it wasn't often a stranger entered the Goose and Gander.

Gregory looked for a bell on the bar but didn't see one. He turned to the three women, who had not yet turned their full attention back to their game. 'Ladies. Could you tell me how one orders drinks in here before I die of thirst?'

'Knock three times on the counter,' said one of the women. Loose lips smacked in front of her toothless mouth before she added, 'Loud. As though you means it.'

Gregory exchanged a brief glance with Frances before bringing his fist down on the bar – three times – as instructed – sending a clutch of bottles and beer glasses on the back bar clattering merrily.

The woman who appeared behind the bar looked surprised to see people who were too well dressed and too clean to be regular customers. A half-smoked cigarette dangled from the corner of her mouth, the ash almost as long as the remains of the cigarette. For a moment, Frances thought they'd be shown the door.

'Can I 'elp you.' When she spoke, the ash from the cigarette fell onto the counter, where it fluttered like fine snow from the draught coming through the ill-fitting windows and doors. She didn't bother to brush it aside but left it there to congeal into a porridge with spilt beer slopped from glasses and tankards.

'Good evening, madam. Is the landlord around?'

It was Gregory who asked.

At the sound of his voice – not a local voice by any means – the woman behind the bar pulled in her chin and looked at them as though they were lost souls and had entered hell when they should rightly have been in heaven.

'Who wants to know?'

Frances had got over being apprehensive and was becoming impatient. The thought of the battered lad gave her the courage to continue. 'My name's Doctor Brakespeare. I'm from the Cottage Hospital. I believe a young lad was found on these premises by the landlord, and he very kindly brought him to the hospital. Do you think I can have a word with the landlord, please?'

The woman's eyes narrowed on either side of a thin, long nose as she thought it through. There followed a decisive stubbing out the remains of her cigarette. 'I s'pose so.' As she went looking for him, her voice could be heard somewhere deep in the premises. 'Fred!'

'He's out back,' somebody shouted out to her, probably from the public bar.

There was the sound of a lavatory flush being pulled from the private quarters behind the bar.

Frances and Gregory exchanged glances.

The woman shouted again. 'Fred. There's a doctor from the 'ospital yur to see you.'

Heavy footsteps and a few swear words were followed by a shadow blotting out the lights behind the bar, a shiny hairless pate bumping aside the overhead light bulb, a face half hidden in a copious black beard.

The landlord was enormous. Frances judged him to be over six feet tall and almost three feet wide. His bulk filled up the space behind the small bar, which was at least a quarter of the size of the public bar.

His eyes shifted from Frances to Gregory. He had a wary manner, but Frances also got the impression that he wasn't a man to cross. She judged he had a hot temper that for now was under control. They needed to tread warily.

He fixed a warning look at Gregory. 'Good evening, Doctor. What can I do for you and your lady wife?'

'I'm the doctor,' said Frances, slightly irritated by his assumption.

'And I'm the vicar,' said Gregory, his voice as friendly as his smile. He tapped at the ordinary shirt collar and tie. 'Off duty tonight. Do you think we could have a pint of cider and a small sherry whilst we talk? And one for yourself of course.'

That, thought Frances, *is a good move.*

Gregory had a natural ability to placate people. Any reluctance to engage in meaningful conversation was instantly quelled.

'Very Christian of you, Reverend. Don't mind if I do.'

Frances waited for the drinks to be served and paid for. The sherry glass was wiped with the tail end of a glass cloth before being filled with sherry. The cider glass looked a bit smudged, but if Gregory had noticed, she supposed he didn't care. The landlord poured himself a pint of cider. Half of it went down his throat before anyone had chance to take a taste of their own.

'Your good health,' said Gregory and they all raised glasses, the landlord's glass only half full.

The taste of the sherry brought Frances to the conclusion that the bottle of sherry had been imported around the time of the Napoleonic Wars. It was incredibly tart, which led her to the conclusion that he didn't get much call for anything except cider and beer.

Gregory seemed to be relishing his pint of cider.

Frances asked the question she was aching to ask. 'Fred. I

much appreciate you bringing the boy in. I think he might have died if you hadn't.'

'Christian thing to do,' said the landlord whilst throwing a bemused smile at Gregory now that he knew he was a vicar.

'Thank you. He was in a bit of a state, but whether it's from his ordeal or otherwise, he seems in a bit of a daze. We've no idea of his name or where he lives. Is it possible you can enlighten me? Do you know anything about him?'

He shook his head. 'Never seen 'im before in me life. I'll tell you 'ow it was. I was taking out an empty barrel and 'ad just got to the back door when I 'eard a bit of a thud. Went outside and found 'im lying among the empty barrels. Saw 'ow he was, chucked 'im over me shoulder and marched up to the hospital. That's about it.'

'You carried him all the way?'

'No other way of getting 'im there without wasting time.'

Frances smiled and thanked him. 'You certainly did your good deed for the day. He will live but has told us nothing. Not even his name.'

The landlord swiped at a dew drop hanging from his nose, then swigged back the rest of his drink. 'Looked like a bundle of rags, 'e did. That's what I thought at first. Just a bundle of rags somebody had thrown round the back of the pub.'

Frances imagined the scene. 'He was very neglected. Very thin and very bruised.'

Fred poured and tipped another glass of cider into what must have been a very dry throat. He'd already downed the first pint and there was only half left of the second when he put it back on the bar.

'As I've already said, I could see he was near death's door, so I did the Christian thing.' He turned to Gregory. 'Right Christian of me, weren't it, Vicar? Just 'cause I don't go to church don't mean to say I'm not a Christian.'

Gregory smiled. 'A good deed compensates.'

There were still questions to be asked and Frances decided to start the ball rolling.

'Did you see or hear anyone before you found the boy? Any sign of anyone leaving him there for you to find, or did he get there by himself?'

Fred shifted his bulk and drained the rest of his glass and poured himself another before answering.

'Nobody.'

'And he didn't tell you his name?'

He shook his head. 'No. Just whined a bit. And 'is 'ead was floppy.'

'Nothing with him?' It was Gregory who asked.

'How do you mean?'

'Not a bag? A penny in his pocket, perhaps?'

'I told you. Nothing.' The feigned amiability of a pub landlord had gone from his voice. 'I didn't steal from 'im, if that's what you think,' he said with a warning glower.

Although Frances noticed his change of manner, Gregory carried on regardless, though concentrating on more general matters. 'No idea at all of name and address?'

The face behind the thick beard tightened as though he was holding back a bolt of anger.

Frances touched Gregory's arm. 'I think it's time we left.' She smiled at the landlord. 'Thank you for bringing the boy to us, Mr...'

'Fred. Fred Easterby.'

'Mr Easterby. Thank you again. I'll let you know how he gets on.'

'He will live, will he?'

His voice was gruff, though she sensed a begrudging kindness, the manner of a hard man trying to pretend he had no softness to his nature.

'He will live, but what happens to him after that...' She shrugged her shoulders. 'A children's home, I suppose, though he may be too old for them. Either that or an orphanage or the...' She took a deep breath. 'The workhouse perhaps. Unless someone takes him in, bed and board perhaps for some kind of work.'

'Goodnight to you.'

Their interlude over, she and Gregory left the saloon bar and made their way out through the public bar, where the smoke was thicker than ever, and a few discerning eyes watched them as they walked across the bare floorboards.

The inner door closed behind them, but before they had chance to leave, Fred Easterby came out of the public bar along with its thick and musty atmosphere.

Gregory and Frances were halfway out the door when he grabbed Gregory's arm.

'I wants you to promise me the lad don't go into the work-house,' he said, standing in front of Frances like a wall, one made of solid muscle, his restraining hand still on Gregory's upper arm.

Regardless of what she wanted to happen; Frances felt obliged to tell the truth.

'I can't really promise anything. His future, once he's well again, will be out of my hands. What happens to him will be up to the parish authorities – depending on his age and unless a relative steps forward to take him home.'

'I won't have it,' he said, his voice louder now and his finger wagging warningly in front of her face. 'If that's what's on the cards, the lad can come yur. He'll get a roof over 'is 'ead and three square meals a day. And a job. You might not think it much, but he'd be better off yur than in a workhouse, and believe me, I know what them places are like! I was born in one and lived there till I was ten.'

Mention of having grown up in the workhouse sent a shiver down Frances's spine. Fred Easterby could not possibly know what raw nerve he had touched.

'I quite understand and, as I promised you, I will keep you informed. Let's see how things go. In the meantime, I will endeavour to find out more about him – his name at least – and whether anyone is missing him.'

Fleshy jowls wobbled above the bushy beard. 'That's as may be, but don't forget. I mean what I said.'

As the night closed in around them, she and Gregory maintained a pregnant silence, both deep in thought. Obviously, they wanted things to turn out well, but so far, the boy was without a name or even a history. The police had followed up the telephone call of earlier in the day with a visit at the hospital but admitted they could shed no light on where the lad came from.

'Though there's plenty we know who'd give their sons a pasting like what he's had,' one constable had said with a disapproving shake of his head as he'd scribbled in his notebook.

'I understand that. But surely not to the point of killing the poor child, either with beatings or starving to death. There was that too.'

Frances gritted her teeth just as she had then. 'I get the impression that the boy with no name was not in a proper family. A vagrant, perhaps?' She shook her head. 'It's hard to accept that he was in any type of family.'

'Perhaps he wasn't, not in the accepted sense. He strikes me as a child who's been treated like a dog – in the very worst possible way,' Gregory remarked.

They'd gone some way when the pattering of scurrying feet came from behind them.

'Doctor.' A scrawny hand grabbed Frances's arm. She recognised the woman as being one of those playing dominoes in the saloon bar of the Goose and Gander. Her hair was grey, and the skin of her face stretched over her cheekbones. It was as if there was only skin and no flesh to pad it out and she was quite tiny, her fingers birdlike. The top of her head barely reached Frances's chin.

'That boy. Did 'e 'ave a number on his arm?'

Frances exchanged a puzzled look with Gregory. 'No. Not that I know of. What number would this be?'

'They marks some that ain't right in the head in case they runs away and can't remember who they are or where they come from.'

'Do you know the boy?'

More wisps of grey hair cascaded from beneath the battered hat the woman wore when she shook her head. 'No. I don't know 'is name, but I might know where 'e came from.'

Her name was Mrs Venables and she pointed them in the direction of the Avon and Kennett Canal and a family of water gypsies.

'Up and down all the time they are. Offloads, then comes in by bus or horse and cart to sell whatever extra they're carrying,' she said, the smacking of her loose lips as audible as a pair of clapping hands.

'That's miles away,' Frances remarked once their informant had accepted a shilling and hurried back to the pub. She wasn't sure whether to believe what they had been told, but it wouldn't hurt to find out. Not only did she want to know the boy's name, she wanted whoever had beaten him to be dealt with by law. A sudden idea came to her. 'We could get my car.'

'No.' Gregory was quite resolute. 'We'll call in at the police station. Sergeant Piper is best placed to find out more.'

'Am I understanding her right?' said Frances. 'Is she saying that he might have been a bit slow in the mind and was marked and put to work?'

Gregory shook his head. 'It doesn't bear thinking about.'

The police station was situated just before the High Street. They made a decision to go in and see if anything more was known about the boy with no name.

After rapping on the glass screen shielding the officers from the public, Sergeant Piper appeared, his bushy moustache lending much to the style of General Haig who had pointed a finger on the recruitment poster that had sent many young men to their deaths.

He stroked his moustache thoughtfully as they informed him of what the old lady had told them.

After a bit of thought and stroking, he said, 'Exactly what do you want me to do about it?'

'Find out if that's where he comes from?'

'And find out the identity of whoever beat him to within an inch of his life,' Frances added.

Sergeant Piper cleared his throat and transferred his stroking finger to his right eyebrow. 'How old is this lad?'

'I don't know for sure. He could be anything from ten to twelve. I can't even get his name out of him.' She didn't mention the likelihood of the boy bearing a number tattooed on his arm. She hadn't noticed.

The way the police sergeant blew down his nose and shook his head said it all. He wouldn't be offering any help.

'Ten or twelve years old, is it? I know lads of that age – and younger – doing a full-time job to 'elp put food on the family table. Many get fed up with it and run off to find their fortune and a softer life elsewhere. I reckon the lad ran away and don't want to go back. That could be why 'e ain't telling you his name.' He slammed shut the book he'd almost attempted to scribble in. Not worth the lead in the pencil, Frances concluded. There was nothing they could do but head for home.

Shops in the High Street were in darkness, though a full moon hovered over the war memorial which Frances still visited, because although she knew he wasn't there, Ralph's name was etched on it.

Being engaged to Ralph seemed like a lifetime ago. The war had taken both of them to the Western Front: him to fight and she to nurse as a member of the Voluntary Aid Detachment. It was after he'd died and she'd come back to England that she'd decided to follow Izzy's advice and become a doctor.

'Are you hungry?' asked Gregory.

She shook her head. 'Not really. I can't help feeling sorry for that lad. What Fred Eastbury said rings true – not so much about him ending up in the workhouse, but that he was born in one in the first place, grew up there in fact.'

Her voice became more subdued as she tried to imagine how that might have been. She herself had been born in the workhouse, but thanks to Izzy, she'd not grown up in such a feared institution. She shivered at the thought of how it could be.

When Gregory's hand landed softly on her shoulder giving it a little squeeze, she knew he was reading her thoughts. He was one of the few people privy to her personal history. 'There's nothing we can do for now and the worst thing you can do is lose sleep about something you can't change – not for now at least. You've got a busy day coming up tomorrow.' His voice was softly reassuring as he stroked her hair back from her face. 'A little food inside you, plus a glass or two of home-brewed wine, should help you sleep – or seriously knock you out!'

She could not ignore his attempt to be amusing. She managed a smile, and although she was concerned about the boy with no name, Gregory was right about her getting something to eat and drink, followed by a good night's sleep. Tomorrow was a big day. Tomorrow, with some trepidation, she was launching the family planning clinic, help for all those women worn out with pregnancies and feeding hungry mouths. Some people thought the idea against God's plan. She suspected there might even be sermons on the subject preached by men from prosperous backgrounds whose education had not even touched the lot of the working class and women's hardship. As far as they were concerned, Eve was meant to suffer. But not the Reverend Gregory Sampson.

'I wonder how many will be upset by my plans,' she pondered.

He threw back his head, the resultant laughter echoing among the brick and stone walls lining the streets they passed through. 'I can hear them now. Newfangled ideas! A woman should know her place and not upset the natural order of things!'

His laughter and the arm that hugged her close were very welcome and went some way to strengthening her resolve to make waves in the medical world. Neither of them was under any illusion that there were bound to be people who didn't agree with such things. Despite everything, either man or woman who decried what she was trying to do, Frances was ready to fight her corner. Indeed, her very survival at Norton Dene might depend on how she handled things.

5

ORCHARD COTTAGE HOSPITAL – MOTHER AND BABY CLINIC

'Here you are, love. Take a leaflet.'

Nancy Skittings, heavily pregnant and presently on leave from nursing at the Orchard Cottage Hospital, was making herself useful handing out leaflets backing up the range of services on offer. At one time, the clinic was structured purely for the treatment of mothers and babies, both pre- and postnatal. The leaflet she was passing out detailed the introduction of advice regarding family planning. Doctor Frances had warned her of the likelihood of hostility. So far, she'd not encountered any, but once the news spread outside the clinic and into the town, the situation could change.

Her feet were aching, and her belly was bulging, but she soldiered on. At least it kept her mind off her and Ned's second baby, who lay heavily on her pelvis and didn't seem that bothered about being born.

Circulating amongst these women lifted her spirits no end. She recognised a lot of them, had been there when they'd given birth or when they'd attended with babies or toddlers to have them weighed and measured, their health assessed in the early years more thoroughly than they ever had been in history.

Lots of chatting was going on, much of which centred on their children, their husbands and their lives in general. Everyone knew everyone else, and many had been attending the mother and baby clinic since its inception.

A few remarked on the contents of the leaflets she was distributing.

'Family planning? What's that when it's at 'ome?'

Her initial response was that it was something they'd be eternally grateful for, but she knew it would take some persuading.

Doctor Brakespeare – who many people were beginning to refer to as Doctor Frances – had taken a deep breath when handing her the pile of leaflets. 'Are you sure about this? I can get Sister Harrison to distribute them if you like.'

'Why not? Ned is at work and Ma is looking after Polly – and doing my housework for me. Said looking after myself means giving myself time to do things not connected with daughter, husband or housework. Hope she goes on that way for a while,' she'd added with a wicked wink.

'I warn you, you're likely to receive a mixed reception. Old habits die hard. They might take some persuading,' Frances had said quietly.

'Then I shall concentrate on how much their lives will improve if only they don't have so many children.'

'Some may not see it that way. The laws of God and all that.'

Frances had a point. The Catholic Church in particular was against any form of contraception and had even set fire to the horse-drawn caravan meant to take advice into the poorer areas of the country.

But Nancy was adamant. 'That's silly. It makes sense to only have the number of children you can afford. Especially at present. They've cut the hours at the coal mine. Ned says that some of the miners are on the waiting list to work at the quarry. But they've cut a bit too.'

Seeing her worried look, Frances had placed her hand on Nancy's shoulder. 'But he's not being laid off.'

Nancy had shaken her head. 'But it certainly makes sense not to have a house full of children. I'll stick to two, and that's that!'

Frances had eyed her ruefully. 'Do let me know if you can't cope. You know I'll do everything to help if I can.'

Nancy had nodded. 'I can cope. And I want to help.'

And so she was coping, handing out leaflets along with lively conversation, mostly relating to children.

Toddlers' heads were patted, and remarks made that it didn't seem that long ago John and Janet were babies, and now look at them, walking and talking as though they'd been doing it for years.

In return for her enquiries after children's general health, mothers and pending mothers asked her when she was due and did she already have children. She replied that the baby was overdue and, yes, she already had a little girl.

'Only two? Wait till you've got four like me,' declared a ginger-haired girl with bright blue eyes who she guessed wasn't much more than twenty-five but was already beginning to look worn out. 'I'm twenty-three and I've got four.'

And that's the reason for you looking older than you actually are, thought Nancy.

Having four children at such a youthful age wasn't that unusual. She knew families where there were six, seven, eight and even more children, some crowded into dismally small houses where the bath hung on a nail outside the back door close to a hand pump, the sole source of water for two or three houses clustered around a yard, plus the lavatory was at the end of the garden.

Fully informed of the advice given in the leaflets, she declared in no uncertain terms, 'I'm not going to have any more children after this one. Two's enough. And I intend to keep it that way. There are ways and means nowadays, you know, and this is what this clinic is all about. Whether it's a Dutch cap or your husband uses a sheath, anything's better than having children you can't clothe and feed properly. Do you or your husband use anything in bed?'

The last question resulted in arched eyebrows from some and giggles from others.

Some answered that it depended if their husband was in a rush.

'When he's got that in mind, I send him to the pub on a promise that I'll give into him when he gets back.'

'After a few pints at the pub? You're a crafty cow, Mavis Brown.'

'How about you?' Nancy asked a young woman with pink cheeks and eyes the colour of hazelnuts.

The young woman addressed shook her head vehemently. 'I don't talk about things like that. It's private.'

There were titters and whispers culminating in a comment that it was hardly private. Everybody had the same bits inside their underwear, and they all knew how babies came into being.

'And it ain't the stork who puts it under the gooseberry bush.'

'Or bakes it in the oven,' exclaimed another.

Raucous laughter followed, nods and winks traded freely, along with other sexual quips.

A woman smoking a cigarette but not known to Nancy smiled knowingly. She had a worldly air about her, was not accompanied by children but had a slight swelling to her belly. Curious as to who she was, Nancy looked for a ring on her wedding finger. There was none. 'There are ways and means, though not enough.' She glanced down at the leaflet. 'I for one am hoping to learn something useful today. I'm not a bloody brood mare. I've got my own life to live.'

Nancy agreed with her and added, 'I'm sticking at two children. That's quite enough, as far as I'm concerned. New methods of contraception have come into use of late that are far more dependable than coitus interruptus or not making love at all.'

'Coitus what?' somebody asked.

Someone offered the answer. 'Getting off the bus before the journey's end.'

Nancy's outspokenness came as a surprise to many. There were looks of disbelief on some faces, alarm and confusion on others. One or two giggled.

'The Dutch cap and the sheath have a higher success rate than getting off the bus before the end of the journey.' The fact was that she'd well and truly hit the nail on the head with the two methods they mostly used but hadn't described how they worked and what they looked like. She'd let the doctor get down to the nitty-gritty.

Conversation went back to the previous level and subjects: children and babies.

'So, you're not intending to have any more than two. What does your ole man say about that?' asked one woman. 'After all the man is 'ead of the household and says what's what, don't he?'

Women who had overheard nodded in unison; their eyes fixed on Nancy as they waited for what she had to say.

'I'm not sure what my ole man is going to say about me coming to this clinic if it's all about stopping babies,' said the ginger-haired girl.

Nancy wanted to scream at them that they owned their own

bodies and that the world was moving on. The fact was some people – and that meant men – were immovable. Many of these women had to contend with their husbands demanding his marital rights regardless of the probability of another – unwelcome – pregnancy. It most certainly wasn't just down to them.

Doctor Frances was aware that she might cause shock waves amongst what was still a traditionally minded community. Nancy wanted to show her support in any way she could.

'Well, mine is more sensible than that,' said Nancy somewhat recklessly. 'We talked things through, and he agreed that we should only have two. He worked out the sums with pen and paper and reckons on his pay he can feed and clothe two kids very well. More than that and it becomes a struggle. He reckons it's irresponsible just to pop kids out like peas from a pod. Besides which, I don't like being considered a pea pod – or a brood mare come to that.'

One or two looked a bit blank, some a bit fearful. Others chuckled at being compared to a pod full of peas or a brood mare.

'Well, I ain't no brood mare and I respects my ole man, so I'm off,' said a prissy young woman wearing a smart white blouse beneath a wool tabard-style dress. She seemed determined to leave until Mrs Lynch sitting next to her placed a meaty hand on her arm.

'How old are you, darling?'

The woman bristled, tossing her head, a stiff unyielding look to her face. 'As a matter of fact, I'm twenty-two.'

Mrs Lynch, who Nancy knew had seven children at the last count, looked her straight in the eyes. 'Darling, I'm thirty-two and ten years ago I looked like you. Look at me now. Seven kids and there would have been more except... well... we won't go into that. There's ways and means, and if there's any advice going to stop falling in the first place, then I'm all for it. Don't get me wrong, I loves me kids. But popping one out after another ages you. Take my advice, darling. Stay and listen to what's on offer.'

The woman in the neat woollen suit and white blouse stared at Mrs Lynch before thinking better of it. More contrite now, she sat back down, hesitantly picked up the leaflet and began reading it through again.

Wearing a conspiratorial smile, Mrs Lynch nodded in Nancy's direction, winked and tugged the reins holding her youngster in place. Nancy wanted to hug her. Women empathising with each other would ultimately make a big difference, as would the sharing and distributing of information.

The important thing about being a nurse as well as a mother was that she understood what Frances was trying to achieve. Like her, she'd read leaflets by Doctor Marie Stopes and even her much maligned book, *Married Love*, which had opened her eyes to quite a few things she hadn't known. To her mind, it made sense to limit one's family and thus set up the mother's and children's health. The facility was welcomed, both women and the governors of the hospital accepting that ultimately, it promised to give them a better life.

Right from the start, the mother and baby clinic had attracted many women who wanted to get through pregnancy and have a healthy baby. For some time now, posters – discreetly worded and no more than eight inches by four – had been nailed up outside the hospital and post office giving days and times. The clinic ran from ten to twelve midday on a Tuesday at first, then had expanded to Tuesday and Thursday.

Planning and preparing for this new venture hadn't been taken lightly. From the very beginning, Frances had suspected she would attract objections, charges of obscenity and upsetting family life. With all that in mind, she had thought carefully about how best to educate women in the prevention of unwanted pregnancies. Part of her had wanted to shout it out in big letters on the poster, which Gregory had pointed out was akin to grabbing hold of someone and giving them a good shake. In response to Gregory's sage advice, the more cautious side of her had decided to tread carefully.

Patiently, she'd waited to see how the mother and baby aspect of the clinic would do. At first, even that had been subject to criticism from some. A few women were oddly hostile to having anyone monitor their health, either before or following birth. With time, they'd relished being looked after, assured that both they and their baby would have the best of care. And so it was that to her great relief the clinic had been a success. Now for the next step.

To both her relief and delight, her plan appeared to have worked, though some of the women were wary of taking the leaflets, and mainly for one reason.

'My 'usband don't agree with things like that,' said one young woman, who looked to be only sixteen or seventeen years of age.

The husband was still the head of the household. Please God give us a future where men and women are created equal, Frances thought to herself and even voiced it to her nurses.

Mrs Lynch, the most outspoken and experienced of all the women there, once again put them straight. 'It's not them that gotta go through with it though is it,' she stated in her foghorn voice, her accent betraying her Dublin roots.

A younger woman, with what looked to be a nine-month-old sitting on her lap, a two-year-old at her side and her belly already swelling with another, nodded in agreement. 'You're right there. They get the pleasure. We get the pain.'

Another exclaimed, 'Speak for yerself. You didn't say no, did you? Must 'ave enjoyed it at the time.'

The risqué comment resulted in a surge of belly laughter – quite literally in the case of the expectant mothers present.

'So, when you due, love?' one of them asked Nancy as she continued to brandish leaflets amongst the gathering.

'About a month.' She'd already told one woman that she was overdue, but in an odd way she didn't want to admit it to herself so lied to the woman and herself. Giving birth could sometimes be a bit of a hit-and-miss affair. It could also be dangerous when time was running out as in her case, but she didn't want to think about it.

'Yeah. I thought you looked fit to burst. And this family planning lark. You going to do it? Know much more about it than we do, do you?'

'I'm a trained nurse and I'm very happy to choose if and when I have another baby.'

'And yur husband don't mind?'

Nancy took a deep breath. She'd foreseen this question and had an answer readily prepared. Both her look and her voice were forthright. 'It's my body, not his. I promised to love, honour and obey when we got married. I didn't promise anything else. Anyway, we've talked over how many children we want. A lot of the time it all goes back to money. We can give our children a better start in life if we can choose when we have them or whether to have any more at all.'

A bright future waited for those who had control of their fertility. It was just a case of persuading them that the future could be very different to the past. Hopefully most of her patients would come round to accepting that. For those who didn't...? Well, that was another matter.

Babies bawled and women who had read the leaflets chatted amongst themselves, each giving her opinion on whether she would find out more of what was on offer or scurry back into the same old ways, accepting whatever nature – and their husbands – decreed.

Nancy's sister, Nurse Lucy Daniels, looked up from setting out bottles of liquid paraffin, a failsafe cure for constipation, and Derbac nit combs. Fleas were an ongoing problem in crowded houses where children could be sleeping top to toe, as many as six in a bed.

As Doctor Frances had said right from the very beginning, might as well kill two birds with one stone, integrate the mother and baby clinic with family planning advice. Quite a few small children in attendance were scratching their heads. Even if they didn't yet have live fleas living off their blood, the Derbac comb would comb out the flea eggs waiting to burst into life.

Clutching a large bottle of liquid paraffin to her chest, Lucy whispered to her sister, 'How are you getting on?'

'I don't know who was the wariest at first – me or them – but one look at my big belly and ironing out a few home truths and their interest was tickled.'

Lucy chuckled. 'Doctor Frances will be pleased.'

'Is Sister Harrison around?'

'She's flitting between the wards and the clinic. Woe betide any little tyke who refuses to take a dose of paraffin. Sister Harrison can pinch a nose like nobody else can. Mouth open in no time. She's almost emptied the bottle.' She indicated the full bottles she had cradled in her arms. 'She's called for more.'

'Goodness, there's no chance of any little 'un being constipated with Sister Harrison around.'

The sisters shared a subdued chuckle.

'I take it Sister Peebles has gone cycling on the district round.'

'Another clever idea of Doctor Frances to have a district nurse do the rounds. Patients are very impressed that they don't always have to attend the hospital. Mind you, she has commented on the state of some of the houses she visits. Not fit to be lived in at all.'

'That's the way it is. It's good she gets along with Sister Harrison, though I suppose they are of the same age.'

'Too true.'

Sister Harrison and the new District Nurse, Gwen Peebles, shared the weekly duty at the hospital, although Sister Harrison had drawn the line at cycling around the town to visit patients. 'I'd prefer to walk.'

So it was that she only visited patients within walking distance of the hospital, Sister Gwen Peebles and her bicycle going that bit further.

It was Lucy's chore this morning to assist Sister Harrison when needed.

'I'll take these combs and liquid paraffin on out. Sister Harrison is waiting for these as much as the liquid paraffin,' said Lucy, holding high the nit comb and a pile of newspaper cut into squares. The children were required to bend their heads over a square of newspaper whilst the nurse combed their hair with the fine-toothed comb. Once satisfied that all the white specks – and a few mature fleas – flecked the paper, it was screwed up and thrown onto the fire, where the contents crackled and popped like a firework on bonfire night.

* * *

Pregnant mothers chatted as they waited to see the doctor. One of the children was referred for examination because his head was itching, and his hair was falling out. Frances diagnosed ringworm and sent him back to the nurses for his head to be shaved before gentian violet was applied.

Before seeing more pregnant mothers and wary-eyed children, Susan, the new receptionist, brought Frances in a cup of tea and reported that there was a patient waiting to see her.

Frances frowned. 'There's no surgery this morning. It's mother and baby clinic.' Remembering her vow to tread carefully, she bit her tongue before she could add the fatal words, family planning. Glancing at her wristwatch, she decided she did have a little time to spare. 'Unless it's one of our regulars,' she added, after taking a sip of much-welcome tea.

Blonde-haired Susan, a local just like sisters Nancy and Lucy, shook her head. 'I've never seen her before and she's coughing fit to burst.'

Frances was surprised. 'Oh dear. I suppose I should see her. Are you sure there are no records?'

'None, and anyway, I trust my own eyes. I've never seen her before.'

Susan had a strident air at the best of times. She could sort out patients with as much dexterity as a collie sorts out sheep.

'Does she have a name?'

'Mrs Devonshire. She's about fifty, a bit drab-looking but nothing a bit of lipstick and powder wouldn't sort. Funny how older women give up trying once they reach a certain age...'

'Susan!' Now it was Frances who sounded strident. 'All I want to know is why she's here and if I do agree to see her, it won't be to advise on make-up or a home perm.'

'I only said about...'

'Yes. Make-up,' Frances interrupted abruptly. 'Now let's get to brass tacks. Did you tell her that we have a clinic running?'

'I did,' said Susan, head held high and not the slightest bit contrite. 'But she had such a bad coughing fit, I had to give her a glass of water and even then, she spluttered a bit. If you ask me, she's got a problem with her lungs.'

'I didn't ask you,' Frances snapped. She gave her neat little wristwatch another querulous glance. 'Right. It sounds urgent and I don't want anyone collapsing. Tell her to come in.'

'I will.'

Of average height, Mrs Devonshire came in clutching a handbag in front of her as a sailor might a lifebuoy. She wasn't quite as drab as Susan had described, but then, thought Frances, the gay young things of today lived in the present and viewed older people as if they were never young and had once looked differently than they did today. She coughed prolifically before she sat down. Frances took in her lined face and hair that was almost white but could have been any colour in her youth.

'Mrs Devonshire. I don't think I've seen you before.'

A cough rattled the woman's chest.

'You have a nasty cough. What can I do for you?' She glanced at her wristwatch. She couldn't spare too much time.

'I can pay for your time,' Mrs Devonshire remarked, having seen Frances glance at her watch.

'That's fine,' she said, picking up her pen and aligning her writing pad, ready to take down any notes she needed to make. 'We'll come to that later. Now, before we continue, I need your full name and address for my records.' She reached for one of the index cards from a tin box on her desk.

The woman's fingers began rhythmically tapping the black crocodile material as though it might snap open if she stopped.

Another bout of coughing, a handkerchief pressed to her mouth before she explained, 'I'm boarding with Mrs Parker at Nine Elms just off the High Street. I'm only visiting, you see.'

Frances waited with pen in hand over the index card where Mrs Devonshire's details would be written. 'And your full name?'

'Mary Elizabeth Devonshire.'

'Age?'

'Forty-nine.'

She leaned forward as Frances finished writing. On looking up, her eyes met those of the woman sitting opposite. She was staring at her, not at the card on which her details were being written as most people were inclined to do. The eyes of Mrs Devonshire were unblinking.

Still with pen in hand, Frances asked, 'Will you be here in Norton Dene for very long?'

The grey eyes, fringed with dark lashes, fluttered. 'I'm not sure. You know how it is. It's all about finding work.'

'I see.'

'I've put out a few feelers. My landlady said they always want people in the big houses. I thought I might ask around.'

Frances thought of Orchard Manor. Her ladyship was always complaining about the lack of domestic servants since the end of the Great War. 'That seems a very sensible idea. So you're definitely hoping to settle here.'

'Yes.' The grey eyes, similar in shade to her own, seemed to veil over before she said, 'I did hear you haven't been here very long. Only last year, wasn't it?'

The question was unexpected and caught Frances off guard before reminding herself that it wasn't unknown for people to establish a doctor's reputation before seeking medical advice.

'Not very long. But I am well qualified. I was in London before I came here.'

Mrs Devonshire's words came thick and fast. 'Well, that's how things are. Them that live in one place for years are lucky, don't you think? There's us that are thrown to the four winds and must go looking if we're to keep our heads above water.'

Not quite understanding where this conversation was going and keen to get back to her clinic, Frances scribbled something on her blotting paper, if only to check that it hadn't run out of ink. 'I suppose so. We must go where we can be of most use –

or where there are jobs. Now, how long have you had that cough?'

Mrs Devonshire cleared her throat. 'Quite a while.'

'Right. I'll begin by examining you,' said Frances, rising from her chair. 'If you would like to take off your outer clothes...'

'Do I have to?' She looked alarmed, her eyes round and glassy as marbles and her jaw dropped.

'If I'm to advise you of what may be ailing you and prescribe the best medicine...'

As Frances clipped on her stethoscope and went round the desk to approach her, Mrs Devonshire sprang to her feet and sped for the door, so swiftly the chair she'd been sitting on fell away behind her and crashed to the floor.

'No. No. I don't want you to do that.' Her hands fluttered away from the crocodile handbag, one reaching for the door handle.

Frances, who had come across shy patients before, reassured her. 'Mrs Devonshire. Please don't be alarmed. There's no one else here. I'm a doctor. I just need to examine...'

'I'm sorry. I shouldn't have come. I made a mistake.'

A bout of coughing accompanied her dashing for the door.

'Mrs Devonshire,' Frances called out, but her would-be patient had disappeared towards the main door.

Frances spotted a surprised-looking Susan getting up from her desk.

'She ran out of here like a greyhound let loose from the trap. What's the matter with her? Your hands a bit too cold, Doctor?'

The last comment was meant to be a joke. Frances didn't see it that way.

She gave Susan a reproving look. 'No. My hands are not too cold. The woman refused to be examined.'

'After all that fuss about it being urgent that she saw you.'

'Obviously not that urgent,' Frances grumbled. 'Anyway, we

probably won't see her here again unless she gets a job locally. She's only visiting. Apparently, she's staying with Mrs Parker at Nine Elms.'

Susan had a habit of holding her head to one side when her sharp mind made a connection between one thing and another, which mostly meant she had some local gossip to pass on.

'So, what have you heard, Susan. And make this quick.' Frances took another glance at her watch. Sister Harrison would be marching in if she took much longer.

'I heard Mrs Parker at Nine Elms had a new lodger. She's been staying there for two or three days.'

'And how do you know this?'

'My Tom was doing a few odd jobs there. He said that Mrs Parker told him that she's gone wandering around town every day she's been here.' Tom was Susan's fiancé.

'I suppose she would, given that she's a stranger here and looking for a job.'

'That's what Tom was told.'

Frances frowned. 'I'm worried about her coughing. She really needs her chest examined. It was silly of her to leave as quickly as she did. Strange behaviour indeed.'

Susan fiddled with the loose-leaf folder on her desk, picking up a pen as though she was about to use it, then putting it down again once she'd made up her mind to say something.

'Mrs Parker, her who takes in lodgers where she's staying, said she was asking about you.'

'About my capabilities as a doctor, I suppose.'

Susan frowned, sat down and attended to a small pile of cards on which patient records were recorded. Using both hands, she divided them as anyone would a deck of playing cards, then once she thought them well and truly shuffled flicked them back together again. There was no point to it except to put off saying anything else until she was confident that it was well received.

'Not exactly.' Eyelids fluttered over pale blue eyes. 'She was asking what you were like, how old you were, whether you were married and had children and where you were living. She also asked where you came from before coming here – just general things.'

Although the questions seemed a bit more personal than she'd expected, Frances shrugged. It wasn't unusual for a patient to thoroughly check the credentials of the doctor they intended to visit, though in this case it seemed Mrs Devonshire had been asking questions that had no bearing on her skill as a doctor.

What Susan said next convinced her that checking her qualifications with a view to receiving treatment wasn't the likely cause of Mrs Devonshire's visit or her enquiries.

'She asked me if you were adopted.'

Frances was stunned. 'If I was adopted,' she said in disbelief. 'Why would she want to know that?'

Susan shrugged. 'She didn't say, and I didn't ask. She also asked if you knew an Isabelle Brakespeare back in London. I said that no doubt you did seeing as you were of the same name. Family in fact.'

At mention of the name Brakespeare, the house in Carwell Street sprang to mind. It had an extraordinary energy thanks to the comings and goings of both friends and strangers from all walks of life. It was not unusual for Izzy to bring home people she'd only just met: shopgirls fascinated by her air of independence, tough matriarchs of families living in crowded tenements. All sorts were welcome. However, Frances couldn't help thinking that there was another reason for Mrs Devonshire's visit. At the back of her mind, a thought surfaced that made her turn cold but also intrigued.

'I should have told you all this before I showed her in,' Susan remarked.

Frances shook herself back to the present. 'No matter. She's been and gone.'

With that, Frances left her office and headed for the mother and baby clinic and tried to put Mrs Devonshire out of her mind.

Today was a very important day for her, not just as a personal accomplishment, but for the women attending her clinic. She was here to do her best by them and that took priority over anything else.

On entering the clinic, Frances's spirits soared. She felt that all her efforts and fears about failure had been blown away. In fact, it made her feel as though she was flying when she saw women perusing the leaflets or reading them out loud to those who couldn't read or write. On spotting her enter the clinic, some women looked at her with awestruck curiosity. She liked to think she also saw hope in their eyes.

Circling around the edge of the room, Frances finally stood at the front of them, a tall figure spreading her hands but trying not to look too smug. Even though this was only the first step, it was hard not to feel proud of what she'd achieved when she looked around that room. So many appeared responsive to the leaflets Nancy had circulated. Questions were being asked, information shared.

A few words Izzy had uttered entered her mind.

'Women could take over the world if they put their minds to it.'

Indeed!

At the front, Susan had set up all the things Frances needed to put across her point. To one side of her was an easel, a bulldog clip at the top holding half a dozen large illustrations of female organs, descriptions of female contraceptive devices and step-by-step guides of how and when to insert them. There was also an illustration on how to use what the locals called 'French letters', pessaries and barrier creams. Small boxes containing the items displayed were set on a table to the side of the easel.

Ready for whatever the response might be, Frances took a deep breath and dived straight in.

'Ladies, I'm glad to see so many of you here. For those of you who haven't met me before, my name is Doctor Brakespeare. I am the one responsible for setting up this clinic, but in theory it really belongs to you, the women of this town. My aim is that we will touch on all the subjects that concern women. The main thrust is, of course, families. The mother and baby clinic has been running for some time now and many of you have taken advantage of what we have to offer: advice, information and support in the admirable task of giving birth and bringing up children.

'We all care for our families and at this clinic we will dispense advice on many things that have a direct effect on family welfare. We're not going to be talking just about children's health but also about women. I trust you will find use for everything or perhaps only a few things we have to offer.

'I am now going to talk to you about family planning – married love in general. If any of you are of a delicate disposition and feel you might be offended when I talk about contraception and how to keep your family to a manageable level, please feel free to leave now.'

Heart in her mouth, Frances regarded the sea of faces turned towards her. Not one woman whispered or turned away. Some looked a little apprehensive, but nobody got up from their chair and left the room.

'Right,' she said as Sister Harrison closed the main doors to the room that was now the family planning clinic and had once been used as an isolation ward. 'Let's start with the reproductive system of a woman's body.'

A sudden fluttering at one of the windows made Frances turn her head. A flurry of apple blossom fluttered from the tree outside. It was a pretty sight and something about it made her think of Izzy, her fiery rhetoric when she was in full flow on women's equality and women's capacity for making waves in the new century. Frances didn't believe in signs and portents as the likes of Ma Skittings, Nancy's mother-in-law, was prone to do, but on this occasion she made an exception and hoped indeed that it was Izzy applauding her efforts. She certainly hoped so.

6

ORCHARD MANOR

Within days of distributing family-planning leaflets at the hospital clinic, the trees beyond the walled garden of Orchard Manor were lime green against an azure sky.

Devlin Compton-Dixon, son of Lady Araminta Compton-Dixon, walked arm in arm with Nurse Lucy Daniels along the familiar paths he'd known all his life. He didn't lean on her too heavily and she found his arm was reassuringly warm against her side. When had she first encountered that feeling of safety he gave her? She couldn't remember, but all the same much appreciated it.

He was twelve years older than her, but she felt almost motherly towards him – or did she? Nothing else was possible. She'd kept telling herself that they were from different levels of society. He was titled, though she'd never heard him say so or insinuate in any way that there were differences between them. She quite liked that – very much in fact. They were easy going together, not really like nurse and patient at all and he liked her to call him Devlin. He often called her Lucy. When she put on her professional veneer she pouted as she'd seen the middle-aged Sister

Harrison do and declared he should call her Nurse Daniels. Then she'd laugh and he'd laugh with her.

'You're Lucy. My nurse Lucy. Yes, you're my nurse and best companion, but you must have realised by now that you're more than someone who just works here at Orchard Manor. Much more. I want us to be friends. Anything else would erect a barrier between us, the servant and master thing almost. I don't want that. I want us to be close friends and to interact with each other as though we were childhood friends.'

'You only saw me from a distance. You were the posh little boy riding past at the back of a car or on a smartly turned-out pony.'

'I remember it well. I remember you as the little girl playing with her friends in the town.' He paused as though this special vision had entered his mind's eyes. 'I no longer have my sight, yet I still see you.' He tapped the side of his head. 'You're in here. You always will be.'

She held her breath hardly daring to acknowledge the ticklish feeling beneath her heart.

They'd began their acquaintance as nurse/companion and patient which had very swiftly become what had felt more of a sister/brother relationship. Its growth into something else had crept up gradually, so slow that she'd let it happen thinking that their difference in class would curtail it becoming anything else. To even think such a thing would only lead to heartbreak. That's what she told herself and, anyway, she was only twenty-four. There was plenty of time to think about finding a Mister Right and marrying, but not yet.

In the past, since being blinded in the Great War of 1914–18, Devlin had strolled the gardens with his mother and the aid of his walking stick. Today, he leaned on Lucy's arm. She now called in twice a week to aid his recuperation. Not physical recuperation. Nothing could be done about that. His sight would never come back, but venturing outside on a regular basis had to be a good thing.

At first acquaintance, he'd been slightly prickly, but they'd been patient with each other. With time, he'd told her about the recurring nightmares when he was again in France. To begin with, his words had been rushed and his face had shone with the sweat of a disturbed man. She'd encouraged him to tell her his nightmares, helped him to face them so that in time their effect might lessen. The more often he had opened up to her, the more she'd admired his bravery, his fortitude, his striving to overcome the events that had broken his mind and body.

When first given the assignment, she'd felt some reluctance at spending time away from the hospital. Now, she couldn't imagine not seeing him twice a week and sometimes found herself missing him, the days being with him not coming round quickly enough.

Doctor Frances had discussed his mental recuperation with his mother, who had agreed that it was long overdue.

'A walk in the garden can in time become a walk around the town and, should all go well, he could get involved in the hospital committee or something similar.'

Her ladyship had agreed and although she'd once been the one who'd often found it difficult to tempt him along the garden paths, she now left the task to Lucy.

'My legs are not what they used to be. And Grimes is in semi-retirement.'

Grimes was her ladyship's long-term retainer, a white-haired man with doddery knees who extended total loyalty to the family – her ladyship in particular.

Lucy enjoyed getting out of the hospital and escorting Devlin around the garden and it became obvious that Devlin was keener to walk with her than his mother – though he'd not given that impression at first.

'Around and around the garden, like a teddy bear...' He'd said it grimly, but Lucy had taken the words and sang them to the nursery tune she remembered from her childhood.

The first time she realised she'd won him over was on a wet night when she'd come across the fields in a bit of a state whilst fleeing the unwanted attention of Brian Faulkland, a man who thought he could have any girl he wanted. Thanks to a heavy blow to the head from Ma Skittings, her sister Nancy's mother-in-law, she'd escaped and at Ma's urging ran onwards to Orchard Manor House.

On reaching there, Devlin had calmed her down and insisted on bathing her blistered heels and, after winding up his gramophone, had danced with her on the wet lawn outside his room.

The sweetness of the night had stuck in her mind. His body had been warm against hers, his breath soft against her hair, the touch of his hands.

She commented now to Devlin that it was a lovely day for wandering and they might as well make the most of it. 'Whilst the weather holds.'

Devlin inhaled air already pungent with the smell of mellow fruitfulness. 'I feel the sun on my face but can smell rain coming.' He took another deep breath, exhaling through flared nostrils. 'I can tell each season purely by smell. In fact, I can almost tell each month, though some are easier than others. And you're wearing something woollen. Wool smells different to summer cottons.'

Lucy smiled. 'Very clever.'

'I hear you smiling. It's in your voice.'

She laughed.

Her chin just about reached his shoulder and when she turned her head, her eyes met the scar on his cheek. It was only a small scar but still she thought it a great shame that his injuries hadn't stopped there. Blindness was so totally enduring, but nowadays he rarely showed self-pity as he had when she'd first made his acquaintance.

On each of those two mornings when she first reported for duty at the manor house, he'd asked her to move around the room, swishing her skirt so he could better imagine how she looked. She'd pointed out to him that she always looked the same because she always wore her uniform. Except today, of course, she wore her woollen cloak over her starched dark blue dress and crisply laundered apron.

He'd retorted that he couldn't visualise her properly until he heard her footsteps and the rustle of her clothes.

'First, I smell your distinctive smell which alters as you move. Did you know that?'

She answered that she did not. What she did know was that Devlin's blindness had heightened his other senses, which both delighted and embarrassed her.

'What's your favourite season?' he asked as they took a left around a fragrant lavender bush and headed towards the rose garden.

Lucy thought about it. 'I think autumn. The time of mellow fruitfulness.'

'Not spring? I thought you would have picked spring as your favourite, seeing as it's when flowers begin to bloom and birds to build nests.'

'I like spring too.'

'But not winter.'

'Even winter can look pretty, especially in frost or snow. Red berries against whiteness paints a very seasonal picture.'

'And, of course, there's Christmas.' He took a big breath of air and held his head that much higher and tapped his stick three times on the flagstone path before he stated – much to Lucy's surprise, 'This year I'd like you to accompany us to midnight mass at Christmas. All members of staff are invited – that includes you.'

She laughed. 'That's a long way off. A lot could have happened by then.'

His open look became one of thoughtful concern. 'Like what? You're not getting married to some local buffoon, are you?'

She swallowed a response that his calling local men buffoons was insulting. It wasn't the first time some of the old arrogance had slipped though. Thinking better of it, she said, 'Whatever gave you that idea?'

His fingers sought and found her left hand and located her ring finger. 'Ah. You're telling the truth. I do not detect an engagement ring.' He sounded pleased.

'And I'm not expecting to receive one – certainly not by Christmas.'

She bit her lip. Her response had been careless. She knew it would make him think there might be someone and he would ask more questions. What she should have said was that it was none of his business – which it wasn't.

'Who is he?' She recognised by Devlin's tone that her suspicions had proved correct. All semblance of pleasure had left his voice. She wished she could take back what she'd said. She'd unwittingly sown seeds of suspicion in his mind, which was something she hadn't meant to do.

She put all her effort into reassuring him that there was no sweetheart. 'No one that I'm likely to take seriously.'

She was telling the truth about there being no one serious. She'd been out on a few dates with Harry, a different marque to her former boyfriend Brian. Remembering her experiences with the notorious Brian Faulkland, the handsome young man fancied by just about every girl in town, she'd plumped for someone less exciting, someone who didn't drag her into a shop doorway and turn into an octopus. If she really thought about it, she had to admit that her new beau was a bit dull. Religion had a lot to do with it. His family were Wesleyans – Methodists who didn't drink, go to theatres or the pictures and resolutely attended church every Sunday. He was company and safe, plus at this moment in time, she valued her freedom.

Devlin went quiet, head down, a broody look on his face.

Was he jealous? The very thought of it surprised her. She was about to say something but movement flashing overhead made her look up.

'The swallows and swifts have arrived.'

'I can't hear them, and I certainly can't see them.' He sounded piqued by the fact that she had another life in town with young men of her own class.

However, Lucy was determined he wouldn't make her feel guilty. She carried on regardless.

'Listen. I'm sure you'll hear them.'

'You're bullying me.'

'No, I am not.'

She recognised a cantankerous mood was coming on. It was at times like this when he was capable of being hurtful that she had to remind herself that she was here purely in a professional capacity. That was how one usually coped with an awkward patient. Not that he was always so. Some days he could be most pleasant – most of the time in fact. *He's becoming fond of me*, she thought, *and there's nothing I can do to stop that.* At some point she might have to remind him that she was purely his nursing companion, the nurse who administered his medicine and took him out for a walk in the garden, read books to him, listened to music on the wireless with him and danced with him to records on his beloved gramophone. All platonic, she said to herself. But was it?

Some time back, his mother had enquired if she might like to live in. 'Only for a few days a week.'

Lucy had talked it over with Doctor Frances. 'I'm only his nursing companion.'

Frances had thought it through. 'He saw you when you were a child, long before he became blind. Isn't that right?'

Lucy had said that it was.

After more thinking, Frances had said the decision was hers and Lucy had decided against it.

'No. I need respite from duty. I'm young and need to have fun. And boyfriends,' she'd added, her cheeks flushing and dimples denting the corners of her mouth. 'No,' she'd said again and shook her head adamantly. 'No. I think not.'

Frances had told her it was a wise decision. 'Though you have improved his life and raised his spirits which, in turn, has reduced his moods and the bad dreams he was having, I don't think it fair on you to move in. You've done a good job, Lucy. His mother is very pleased with his improvement, and I can see the difference when I pay my monthly visit. You're a tonic, Nurse Lucy Daniels, better than one that comes in a bottle.'

'I'm glad I've been of some service.'

'You certainly have. But we have to accept that you have your own life to lead.' Frances had smiled. 'You're a young woman on the threshold of life. Nursing is just a part of it. Keep up the good work, Nurse Daniels. You'll go far.'

* * *

Lady Compton-Dixon was thoughtful as she watched Nurse Daniels get into the car. Today she was heading directly for the hospital. On other occasions when she wasn't needed to be on duty, she walked across the fields.

Seeing as Lucy Daniels was of the lower classes, past generations might have been horrified that she had deliberately brought these two young people together. But nowadays Araminta didn't consider herself a part of those past generations. Despite her wealthy background, she was one of those who had fought for women's rights, and she still supported the right of a woman to marry or not, to have children or not.

'I've broken the faith,' she muttered to herself. 'Though I can't say I ever adhered to that faith. Class is self-imposed. Circumstances change us. We all have an Achilles' heel that matters more to us than tradition.'

Her Achilles' heel was her son, Devlin. He'd come home from war battered and bruised; his mind as injured as his body. Before the war, he'd been something of a social butterfly, certainly a charming prospect for a debutante in search of a handsome – and wealthy – husband. If there'd been no war, he would have been married by now and hopefully with children to carry on the family name. He needed a partner in life, a female friend to rely on, to bring joy to his life and to that end she would do anything to ensure his happiness. And perhaps... It was too great a hope, but she truly hoped that Devlin would fall in love with his nurse. She suspected he was half in love with her anyway, but what about Nurse Lucy Daniels, a pretty little thing that he remembered as a child – was it too much to hope that she might fall in love with him?

The chauffeur-driven black Bentley became camouflaged by the trees lining the driveway. Once it reached the gate, it would turn left and then right towards the town.

How to orchestrate a liaison, Araminta thought. *First off, I need to be devious. A walk in the garden and dancing to a gramophone is not enough. I need to organise events where they would be thrown together.*

Dancing was an obvious choice and a ball, like the ones she used to know back in her debutante days, would supply the right atmosphere. Glowing candles, the smell of perfume and the tinkling of champagne glasses. Young people enjoying themselves. It was where she'd first danced with Devlin's father, although he'd taken her fancy before then.

Another beau who'd fancied his chances with her had been Frederick Brakespeare, married at the time but well known for chasing younger women. She'd fended off his overbearing interest, told him she would tell his daughter, who she'd met at a suffragette rally.

It had always amazed her how he could have fathered someone so exuberant and delightful as his eldest and feisty daughter, Isabelle, a woman who lived apart from her family. She had left a society ball on those occasions when her father was there.

Araminta had seen the hatred in Izzy's face and had heard a few things. A lot of families had secrets, but she sensed the Brakespeare family had more than most – and darker secrets – far darker.

Anger bred revenge and she, for one, could understand why Isabelle had never married, rarely revisited the family home and most certainly had no time for her father. And who could blame her? Frederick Brakespeare had shaped her life by destroying it. Hence Izzy had become fiercely protective of her rights, a woman who had empathy with a servant girl and a baby born in the workhouse. She had adopted Frances, which Araminta thought very commendable and a subtle act of revenge on her father and that pompous sister of hers.

Dragging her thoughts back from the past, she considered

some kind of event where Devlin and his nurse would be thrown together. A children's party? No. That wasn't the sort of party where young people might be thrown together. Better, she thought, would be to throw a party for the hospital staff. Here at the manor house. What a grand event it could be.

A doubt crept in. Would Devlin attend? What if Lucy's presence wouldn't be enough to persuade him to take part? What if—

Music drifted along from Devlin's apartments, and she heard words, muffled but familiar. She began to sing, picking at the words slowly.

'*Someone to watch over me...*'

Music. If they had a party for the hospital staff, Devlin could provide the music on his gramophone. He couldn't possibly refuse. As for Lucy Daniels, she was sure she would love to take part because it would be in aid of hospital funds; yes. It was a grand idea. Everyone at the hospital and those who contributed to its success would be invited. Even the porter who swept the floor and looked after the trees and garden. Other more influential people would also be invited – in exchange for a donation – the sons and daughters of local mine and other business owners and more besides.

Yes. She sighed with great satisfaction. A night of dancing, singing, fun and laughter, just like the old days, and who knew what might transpire?

* * *

It was the third time Harry Bascombe had taken Lucy to the little independent picture house up a back street in Norton Dene. On their other dates, he'd taken her on walks or for a ride in his pony and trap. Harry had three different jobs. By day, he was a blacksmith. On weekends, he played the piano in the bar of the Angel

Hotel, an old-fashioned place where the elite of the town dined from plates of white porcelain and made a big show of drinking champagne and burgundy from crystal goblets. On occasion, he also delivered parcels or shopping in his pony and trap, which got around the narrow streets of the town more easily than a motor vehicle.

He told her that the film showing was *It Happened One Night* starring Clark Gable and Claudette Colbert.

'I'd prefer a cowboy film really, but this looked more like a film a woman might enjoy, so I decided on that one.'

With a tug of his arm, Lucy brought him to a stop. 'Oh, you did, did you! All that shooting outlaws and Indians dead! And you a Methodist!' She thought it a funny comment and laughed as she said it.

To her surprise, Harry took it very seriously. 'We're against drink. Not cowboys and Indians.'

She tugged at his arm. 'Don't take offence. I was only joking. I quite fancy going to see Clark Gable and Claudette Colbert. It's a romantic comedy. You do know that?'

He said that he did.

'And you've nothing against romance?'

He blushed and said that he did not. 'As long as it's tasteful.'

Perhaps due to Clark Gable and Claudette Colbert starring, the queue outside the picture house wound all along the front of the building.

'Looks like we'll be lucky to get in. I think it might be best if we just go for a walk.' He took hold of her arm, took a step out of the queue but came to an abrupt halt when Lucy refused to move.

'I want to see the film. We've had enough walks this week to wear the leather on my shoes right through.'

He looked taken aback, his lips parting, which made her

wonder if he was about to burst out crying. 'You don't mind queuing?'

'No. At least we get to sit down once we're inside.'

Gradually, the queue moved forward, and the rain held off.

'I love these places,' whispered Lucy once they'd gained the foyer. 'It's got a kind of magic about it.'

Harry's chin retreated into his collar. 'I just hope nobody my mother knows sees me. She doesn't approve of sitting in the dark and things happening up on the screen. Hollywood. Film stars. She doesn't approve of film stars.' He looked furtively around.

Lucy giggled as she reassured him. 'If they're Methodists like your mother, they've got no business being in here anyway, so they're not likely to tell, are they?'

Harry didn't look too sure, his eyes flicking towards the dark-red double doors that led to the seats in the stalls, the ones to the right that wound up out of sight to eventually come out in the upper seating area – the circle, as it was called.

Harry adjusted his spectacles after tripping over a step in the darkness. Eventually, they had their seats and Lucy took off her gloves, scarf and hat before removing a bag of chocolate caramels from her pocket.

'Here,' she whispered, offering the paper bag containing her favourite sweets to Harry.

He shook his head and continued to look around nervously, like a cowboy waiting to be ambushed. Lucy smiled to herself and wondered if he would slide beneath the seat if he did spot someone he knew, someone his family knew, or, worst of all, someone his mother knew.

Harry's devotion to his mother was beginning to look obvious. So far, their dates had been subject as to whether his mother needed escorting to one of her knitting groups. In the absence of his father, who had died some years ago, Harry was the centre of her world.

The film was enjoyable, and Lucy found herself totally absorbed in the storyline and envious of Miss Colbert's glamour, her beautiful clothes, the doe eyes and the Cupid's bow lips. As for Clark Gable, well, wasn't he every woman's dream and wouldn't it be wonderful if she ever got to meet him? Fat chance. *He's never going to pay a visit to Norton Dene*, she thought whilst resisting the urge to chuckle.

It made a great change to concentrate on the film in a way she rarely had before. Unlike when she'd been to the pictures with other young men, Harry did not attempt to reach for her hand or put an arm around her shoulders or even try something far more familiar.

It came almost as a shock when the film was over, though she felt very satisfied. She'd felt moved between happiness and sadness in all the right places but didn't realise why until the film was over and some of the audience were scurrying for the exit – except Harry. Whilst some around him exited as swiftly as possible, he stood rigidly for the National Anthem and didn't move until the last notes had faded away.

Harry, she decided, was not only devoted to his mother, but he was also a stickler for protocol.

Finally, as the lights were turned up to their full brilliance, they headed out of the cinema. Spilling out into the night, Lucy declared she was thirsty.

'My throat's a touch dry. I could murder half a shandy.'

'It's getting late.'

'It's only half past nine. Come on, the Red Lion and a few other pubs I know will still be open.'

'A cup of tea would suit me better,' said Harry.

Somehow, she'd had a feeling he would say that.

'I doubt we'll find a tea shop still open.'

Harry strode on regardless without slowing when they passed a pub where the lights fell like patches of gold onto the pavement.

Regardless of the hour, he continued to look around for a café or tea shop that might still be open.

'Oh dear. It appears that everything's closed,' he eventually conceded.

'Except for the Red Lion,' Lucy pointed out. 'We passed it back there.'

'I don't go into pubs.'

'But you play the piano at the Angel. They have a bar, don't they?'

'The piano's in the dining room and for residents only. I never enter the bar.'

She was sure she detected a shiver, as though the very thought of entering an area that sold alcohol was like gaining entry to the gates of hell.

The Copper Kettle Tea Shop was in darkness. Harry pressed his face against the door. Lucy pointed out that the sign hanging on the door stated that they closed at six o'clock. She just about refrained from saying, 'I told you so.'

'I've got some wine gums. A mere trifle, I know, but I find they do moisten my mouth if chewed slowly,' Harry suddenly said.

'Is that why you refused one of my caramels? You were eating wine gums?'

'It slipped my memory that I'd bought them. And before you mention it, there's not really any wine in them. It's just sugar.'

A rustling of a paper bag brought forth the sweets.

'Ta,' said Lucy as she took one. 'My feet are killing me. I need to sit down.'

The bag of wine gums sat between them on a garden wall whilst Lucy slipped off her shoes. After she'd swallowed the first one and reached for another, Harry asked her how she'd liked the film and, if she did, what particular part of it.

Wanting to give him a bit of a shake-up, she grinned impishly. 'The bit where Clark Gable takes his shirt off.'

Harry gasped. 'I thought that particular scene quite outrageous. It was most certainly an unexpected surprise. I mean, a man of his standing, a top Hollywood actor baring his flesh like that.'

Lucy giggled. 'I think that scene was popular with most of the women in the audience. Didn't you hear them. Such a handsome man.'

Harry regarded her with disbelief. 'My dear Lucy, perhaps your interpretation is not quite correct. No, no, no. You've got it wrong. It wasn't pleasure. It was astonishment.'

Lucy wanted to laugh but decided if that was what Harry wanted to believe then that was up to him. As far as she was concerned, what she'd heard was most definitely a gasp pleasure from the audience. Harry might not approve but plenty had – especially the women.

'Clark Gable is the most gorgeous man in the world and I'm not the only one to think that. In fact,' she said mischievously, 'he looked gorgeous. I wanted to reach out and feel his skin.'

An empty shocked silence followed as Harry fought to get over his embarrassment, whilst Lucy hid her amused smile. They'd only been going out together for a short time and she sensed his determination to make an impression on her. She knew without him asking that he wanted to ask her out again and for her to say yes. Well, that might or might not happen, she thought to herself. Harry was very nice and quite good looking despite his spectacles. However, the big drawback was that he was the most strait-laced man she knew. Whether she could tolerate his behaviour in the long term was something she had to think about. He was far from being fun. Besides, there was Devlin and...

But she and Devlin were from opposite ends of the social scale. Besides which, she was only there as his nurse and companion. That was all.

In the meantime, there was Harry.

He still couldn't let the Clark Gable event die peacefully. His mouth opened and shut like a goldfish taking air before spitting out, 'His behaviour was a trifle brazen in my opinion. I cannot say the same about Claudette Colbert.'

'She didn't take her shirt off,' Lucy pointed out.

Harry drew in his chin and looked at her in outright alarm. 'She most definitely did not. In fact, she was a picture of decorum all the way through,' he exclaimed. 'My mother would have liked her – not that she ever goes to the pictures. She prefers theatre, but then only when educational.'

'She doesn't know what she's missing. It's fun.' She leaned in closer over the paper bag sitting between them. 'Was that the last of the wine gums?' She already knew the answer.

'Yes.' Harry crumpled the paper bag and shoved it into his pocket. He was a very tidy man. Some would have thrown it into the gutter or the garden behind them. But Harry was the epitome of good behaviour. He never did anything that might be considered against the grain.

'Would you like to partake in a portion of fish and chips?'

'Just chips.'

'Right,' he said, getting to his feet and offering her his arm. 'Let us sashay along to the fish and chip shop for a veritable banquet.'

Lucy placed a hand over her mouth to stifle her laughter. 'Harry Bascombe, you sometimes sound as though you've swallowed a dictionary.'

'I confess I do not know what you mean. I speak the King's English.'

'You have a tendency to use a dozen words when half a dozen will do.'

'I read a lot.'

'And play the piano.'

'I follow many interesting pursuits.'

'Is there any other pursuit I should be aware of.'

'I like acting. You know I belong to the Norton Dene amateur dramatic society?'

'I believe you mentioned it. So, you like dressing up?'

'You would too. Didn't you say you liked dancing?'

'I did. But it's my understanding that the only time they include dancing is when they put on the Christmas pantomime at the Methodist Hall.' She wanted to add that it only sold tea and biscuits at such events, never alcoholic drinks, but thought it cruel to press the point. Let the evening end on a light note.

Harry remained unaware of any criticism she might have, upbeat because she had expressed an interest in one of his treasured hobbies. 'Well, there you are then. We're well matched. We both like music and I'm sure you'd enjoy taking part in one of our productions.'

She thought of the pantomime and wondered if she might persuade them to let her tap dance although playing the lead would be nice. 'Do you think the drama society would let me take part?'

'I have some control over the production process and would be willing to ask. My opinion holds weight, so if I recommend you and you prove capable, you will be given serious consideration. Rest assured you will be given a fair chance.'

Lucy heaved a sigh of satisfaction. 'Thank you, Harry. That's very nice to know.'

Whether it was the warmth of her reply or sudden elation on his part, he tugged her arm close. For a moment, she thought he was going to give her a peck on the cheek. He didn't. It began and ended with the reassuring grip on her arm.

When it came to gentlemanly behaviour, Harry overperformed. It occurred to her that his mother might have a lot to do with it – either that or the grammar school he'd attended. Harry hadn't mixed much with the local boys – or girls for that matter. The grammar school he'd attended only catered for boys. Isolated from the opposite sex and locals had helped form the man he'd grown into.

There were half a dozen people ahead of them in the queue at the fish and chip shop. The smell of battered fish and deep-fried chips made her stomach rumble.

Fried in a deep vat of liquid lard and liberally sprinkled with salt and malt vinegar, the chips were delicious.

Conversation ceased in favour of dipping into the newspaper-wrapped food. Once it was gone, Harry took the crumpled newspaper and placed it almost methodically into a wire bin suspended from a lamppost.

As he had from the first, Harry's pace slowed as they neared the house she shared with Aunt Rose in Waterloo Terrace.

Stopping at the front gate, she entwined her arms around his neck. 'Thanks for a lovely evening.'

Rather than kiss her – that had been her plan – he caught hold of her hands and clutched them to his chest. 'It's been a pleasure, Miss Daniels.'

He looked pointedly at the front room window of the old miners' cottage. If he expected Aunt Rose to be peering out from behind the curtain, he couldn't be more wrong. Her aunt was probably in a deep sleep by now, thanks to half the contents of a flagon of cider. She refrained from enlightening him.

'I do hope we can do something similar again that will further indulge our senses and bring satisfaction to our busy minds.'

'Harry, you are incorrigible,' said a laughing Lucy.

They stood at the front gate for only minutes. Harry held onto her hands quite tightly. The message was obvious. He didn't want her to put them around his neck again. It was as though touching her and she touching him was objectionable – or downright taboo. He also continued to glance nervously at the cottage as though Aunt Rose might fly out of the door like an avenging Harpy.

Certain she'd read the message correctly, though somewhat perturbed, Lucy reassured him. 'No need to worry. Aunt Rose will be asleep by now.'

She didn't say she would be in bed because she knew she wouldn't. Aunt Rose, who poured cider down her throat as fast as others drank a cup of tea, would be snoring her head off in one of the armchairs set to either side of the fireplace.

From the very first Harry had become uneasy the nearer they got to where she lived and now he seemed desperate to leave.

'Well, sweet lady, I will bid you adieu.' He said it laughingly and was already letting her hands go and stepping backwards.

'Aren't you going to kiss me goodnight?'

He hadn't done so yet. Just those pecks on the cheek that might have been a peck by a sparrow, for all the passion they contained.

'Of course.'

Another peck on the cheek followed.

'Goodnight.'

She let him go. After all, she told herself, they hadn't been seeing each other that long. Give him a bit more time, but not for too much longer. As she'd said to her sister Nancy, 'I'm not getting any younger. I do want to be married.'

Nancy had looked at her strangely. 'Does it have to be Harry Bascombe?'

Lucy had shaken her head. 'No. But he's all there is at the moment.'

Nancy hadn't mentioned Devlin Compton-Dixon and neither had Lucy, but he was there at the back of her mind, the man she was trying not to fall in love with.

* * *

Eight in the morning at the Orchard Cottage Hospital and the breakfast trolley was doing its rounds. Lucy was on duty, ladling out bowls of porridge, and serving toast, marmalade and butter and cups of tea.

She went to every bed in turn, pausing to help a patient sit up where needed, and tying a bib around an old man's neck so he wouldn't make a mess. There was enough laundry without that.

The young lad with no name occupied the end bed and would be last to be served. He'd begun to eat a few days ago and had certainly made up for lost time. But he still hadn't given his name.

The sage-green screen was pulled around his bed. Lucy presumed he'd used the bedpan earlier and might not have finished, hence the screen still being around him.

'Hello in there.' She pulled back a single section of the screen. An empty bedpan lay on the bed. The bed too was empty. The boy was gone.

A search was raised, but the boy wasn't found.

It wasn't until midday that Sister Harrison came stomping down the ward, her face like thunder.

Lucy asked her if the boy had been found.

'No,' she snapped. 'And my cloak's gone missing.'

It transpired shortly afterwards that the gardener's dungarees had also gone.

'Just a light-fingered thief,' stated Sister Harrison. 'If I could get my hands on him...'

I'm glad I'm not him, thought Lucy, hiding her cheeky grin.

Despite her humour, Lucy found herself glancing out of ward windows, seeking the main entrance, her keen gaze searching this way and that for the missing boy.

She saw nothing, just the soughing of the trees and a horse and cart slowly exiting the drive on its way to the main road.

She sighed forlornly. The boy was gone. There was nothing more to be done.

7

District Nurse Gwen Peebles was winding a new dressing around the leg of a Mr Clarence Cook. A nasty ulcer had been left untreated for weeks before he'd been forced by a caring neighbour to get it lanced. The neighbour had spotted the district nurse and flagged her down.

The old man lived alone in a house that looked neglected from the outside and was even more so once she was inside.

Gwen was making a great effort to concentrate on the job in hand whilst trying to ignore the bugs that were scuttling in and out of the peeling wallpaper. Suddenly, the house shook. Bugs and loose plaster fell to the floor and the cockroaches scattered in all directions. The very floor quaked beneath her knees. The brim of her hat fell forward over her face and a mouse ran across the room and into a hole.

'My word,' she said, pushing the brim of her hat away from her face so she could see what she was doing.

The house was on the eastern side of town where the mean streets gave way to scrubland, which, if it had been good pasture, cattle would be chomping at eagerly. As it was, a few pigs wandered around piles of slag and abandoned mining machinery.

Gwen knew something bad had happened when Mr Cook raised his gobstopper eyes from looking at her ample breasts and loudly declared, 'That's the mine, likely the pit props gone. Men'll be injured.'

'Oh, goodness me.'

Gwen quickly pinned the new dressing around his scabrous leg and grabbed the handle of her medicine bag. Neat in her duties, she looked for the old rags, which stunk to high heaven on account of Mr Cook's leg ulcers.

'Don't worry about that.' Mr Cook wound the offending article in his hand and threw it onto the fire where it burst into flame. 'Nothing gets wasted in this 'ouse,' he said to her with a toothless grin.

It wasn't until the ad-hoc dressing had been totally consumed that Gwen realised its stink had been camouflaging the smell of the room. She wasn't sure which was worse.

'I'd better get back to the hospital. I think they might be needing me.'

Glad to leave the house, she took a deep breath of fresh air before tying the shiny tan medicine bag on the back of her bicycle. Indeed, she could very well be needed at the hospital, but the smell inside Mr Cook's house had made her nauseous. She'd had no alternative but to get out of there at the double before she threw up the contents of her stomach over the already filthy floor. Not that Mr Cook would likely notice.

The old man eyed every move she made. 'You're a fine-looking woman, Sister. Are you married?'

Her response was quite terse. 'No. I am not. And before you ask, I'm not looking for a husband. I've had one. He's gone. I don't need another.'

She hoped there was enough warning in her voice to keep him at bay.

Gwen was middle-aged and a widow with a twenty-year-old son. Her husband, like a lot of others, had been killed in the Great War. Her son was courting, and in a manner of speaking, so was she. The milkman, a former merchant seaman, had survived being torpedoed in the North Atlantic and was all for the quiet life which he didn't get at home. His wife was obsessed with contacting her mother who had passed on some years ago. To this end, she was always pursuing one medium after another, and although there had not yet been any provable connection with her mother, she was still trying. Her latest medium – quack and charlatan as far as Arthur, Gwen's milkman friend was concerned – was a man named Lancelot Knight.

'She crosses his hand with half a crown every time she meets up with him.'

Gwen felt sorry for Arthur and found him good company. Not that they got up to anything adulterous. When she wasn't on duty at the hospital, he came round with a few bottles of beer and together they'd listen to the wireless whilst he drank the beer and she knitted.

Oh well, she thought to herself. Time to move on to the next patient.

She bid Mr Cook goodbye.

'Sure you wouldn't like a drop,' he asked, waving a stone keg of cider in her direction.

'No thank you. I've more patients to see.'

She bid a hasty retreat. Not that she couldn't handle the likes of him. She'd met worse though not many who smelled as badly as he did.

Cycling through the miserable streets of grey stone houses she took great breaths of fresh air. Lungs replenished and feeling more energetic, she grabbed the handlebars of her bicycle when suddenly the faint wail of the coal mine over towards Radstock travelled west on the wind. Gwen checked her diary for the day. Two more calls and then normally she would be off duty and therefore off home – though not today. Her duty was to pedal back to the hospital in case her skills were needed.

* * *

Mary Devonshire had heard the siren and felt the repercussion of the explosion, though it wasn't so strong a tremor in the centre of town as it was in the mean house where Mr Cook lived.

Having summoned some courage and her cough being a little better, she'd made her way to the Orchard Cottage Hospital, where she'd intended reintroducing herself to Doctor Brakespeare. Perhaps she might even allow her to listen to her chest. Although a little better today, she knew it was only temporary. The cough had begun on the other side of the world and since arriving in a colder, damper climate, it was getting worse.

She got as far as the bottom of the front steps before the seriousness of the explosion hit her. The hospital was a scene of frenzied activity. Nurses were running this way and that, gathering up items that would be needed in response to barked orders.

At the centre of everything stood Doctor Frances Brakespeare commanding proceedings.

'I want to see everything readied.' Her voice was as clear as a bell. She ordered empty beds to be made ready for casualties. 'Best be prepared for any eventuality.'

Mrs Devonshire recognised this was a dire emergency and no time to approach the doctor.

Another time, she thought to herself, and slunk outside, hiding behind the gnarled branches of an apple tree.

Another time.

* * *

Inside the hospital, Doctor Frances Brakespeare stopped wondering where the mute young lad had gone and concentrated on readying the hospital for likely casualties.

She checked a few things before proceeding out onto the front steps to gaze in the direction of the mine and whisper, 'Please, God. Don't let anyone die.'

The postman arrived with the first mail of the day, which Frances took, then ordered a new student nurse, Anne Davies, to place on her desk.

'They can wait until later,' Frances added, her eyes still straining to see any movement coming their way.

The nurse wasn't gone long before she reappeared to tell Frances that her phone was ringing.

'What did they want?' she asked the nurse.

'I didn't answer it,' the nurse said, blustering on account of her nervousness. 'Telephones scare me. I don't know what to do.'

Frances rolled her eyes. 'Silly girl.' She dashed to her office and picked up the phone.

'Is that the hospital?' asked the male voice.

'Yes. Doctor Brakespeare speaking.'

'Good. This is Bert Gingell at Bankerton Mine. Some of the pit props have given out. We need a doctor here now.'

She knew Bankerton was the coal mine, one of those managed by the Graingers but owned by an absentee landlord from London.

'Can you tell me how many casualties there are?'

The man on the other end seemed loath to reply. 'We don't know. Most of them are still down there.'

She detected a shakiness to his voice, but this was no time for her to question why or fear what was happening. This was a time for being strong if she was to be of any use, to show confidence and self-control, though inside she was sick with fear.

'We'll be right there.'

Staff who had felt the hospital shake gathered round when she shouted for their attention. Their faces tense. She wondered just how many might have relatives working at the mine.

* * *

District Nurse Gwen Peebles came hurtling through the gate on her bicycle.

'Did you hear it?' she gasped as she ran up the steps of the hospital entrance, almost colliding with those on the way down and those standing behind waiting for instructions. She directed her information at Frances. 'I was bandaging old man Cook's leg when I heard the explosion. The house shook and I was outside before you could say scaredy cat!'

'There was no damage in Holcombe Street?'

'None that I could see.'

'Leave your bicycle, Nurse Peebles. My car can take four. That's you, Nurse Daniels and Student Nurse Davies.'

Stopping halfway down the steps, Frances shouted over her shoulder to where Sister Edith Harrison stood like a statue.

'Sister Harrison, seeing as you've already made a start with the beds, you stay and hold the fort.'

'I will. There are six beds prepared and more if needed.'

'Be prepared for the worst.'

For all her faults, Frances knew Sister Harrison was extremely competent and took pride in her job. She disappeared from the top steps.

Student Nurse Anne Davies, Nurse Lucy Daniels and Sister Gwen Peebles followed her to the car and scrambled inside, Gwen's rump taking up over half the room on the back seat alongside the slender Nurse Davies. It was a tight squeeze, what with medicine bags containing everything they might need. Each nurse held as much as they could on their laps, their worried eyes peering over the top of each bundle.

Frances slid in behind the steering wheel whilst a porter took charge of the starting handle. After a few strong turns, the engine spluttered into life. Room for the starting handle was found between Lucy Daniels' feet.

Just as they made the entrance, a tall figure in black robes came running through the gate.

Frances wound down the window so that she could hear what Gregory had to say.

'The manager at the mine phoned. I believe I'm needed.'

His expression was more expressive than words. If the vicar was needed, it could mean only one thing.

A chill shiver ran down Frances's back. Requesting the Reverend Gregory Sampson's presence meant someone, or more than one, would never again see the light of day.

She invited him to get in. 'It'll be a tight squeeze, but if nobody minds...'

'I'll get out and you get in the middle,' urged Lucy.

Somehow or other, the Reverend Gregory Sampson squeezed into the back seat between Anne Davies and Gwen Peebles. His long legs were doubled so that his knees were in line with his chest. In other circumstances, a reference to sardines tightly packed in a tin can would have everyone chuckling. But not today.

At deadly speed, Frances drove Molly, her little car, a present from Izzy when she'd passed her finals. The car could sometimes be cantankerous but tended to behave herself in an emergency.

The winding wheel of the mine towered like the skeleton of a giant over everything else and was easily seen from the main gate. There was no thick dust hanging in the air as Frances had encountered in the aftermath of the quarry explosion when she'd first arrived at Norton Dene. She'd already been informed that this accident had happened underground and the dust was confined down there. The atmosphere in such a confined space was easily imagined, the air thick and black, breathed in through blackened nostrils, filling and congealing in lungs fighting for oxygen.

Shaking the image from her mind, she readied her team for what was to come. Gregory had already got out of the back of the car. Prior to doing his duty, he stretched the legs that had been so cramped in the back of the car and flexed his shoulders.

The first thing that hit Frances when she got out of the car was almost total silence. Men were standing around looking worried. As yet, only a few women – wives, daughters and sisters of miners – had heard the unwelcome news. Some stood as silent as the men. Others wept softly, dabbing at their eyes. Others were stony-faced, steeling themselves for whatever the fates decreed.

In his capacity as vicar, Gregory was already mingling with the worried watchers. He smiled sadly at some, patted the shoulder of those he knew. Whatever he said to them was met with a smile or curt nod of the head. Frances knew he would say little. Empty platitudes were seldom welcome at a time like this and despite his calling, he wasn't the sort to offer them.

Eyes gazed upwards as with a jarring whine, the winding wheel began to turn. Heads turned to watch. Metal grated against metal.

Closely followed by her nurses, Frances ordered a space cleared so that her team could be there to do whatever they could.

She asked for blankets to be folded and laid out so the injured could lie comfortably whilst their injuries were examined.

Voices came from those waiting as pit ponies blackened by coal dust appeared off to the left.

Gregory appeared at her shoulder. 'If you're wondering how they got out, there's a separate drift tunnel used by them and coal carts. Only the men go down in the lift. The ponies and the trucks they pull are confined to the tracks, which suggests there's a fall between the track and the coal face.' Heavy with curbed emotion his words hung in the air.

A blockage. How many men? How many injured? How many dead?

These were the questions that ran through Frances's mind as he moved off to join the surface workers and the women who waited.

The waiting was interminable, which made her feel helpless.

At least Gregory was doing something, though that was only standing with bowed head, hands clasped together. She knew he was praying. They both had their jobs to do: her job to save lives, his to save souls. Both would be attempting to apply salve to both physical and mental wounds.

A wordless gasp of exclamation went up as the cage doors opened. It was closely followed with the gathering of men and women. More women now, surged forward.

Men began emerging from the cave-like hole. White eyes stared out of the coal-encrusted faces of those who had rushed into the mine and gone down in the lift to save their fellow miners. Each pair supported one of the injured between them, men who were so blackened that they looked to have been carved out of the coal face itself. If their eyes were open, they were red rimmed. Others remained closed, fearing to open them and let the dust scrape their eyeballs.

Frances and her team sprang into action. 'Water,' she shouted. 'I need plenty of water.'

She quickly gave instructions to her team of nurses.

'Wash their faces. Get that dust out of their eyes.'

She counted just four men. Surely there were more. She looked back towards the pithead fully expecting – hoping – to see more. There were none.

The man who had brought these out wiped the congealed mix of coal and sweat from his face.

Keeping her voice low, Frances asked him if there were more.

'These four are the lucky ones. They were at the edge of the fall.'

'There are more?' Of course there were more, but she needed confirmation.

'Eight more men. Two boys.'

Frances resisted the urge to ask him whether they were dead or alive. She must remain focused. She had to do her best with those who could be saved.

'Are you going back down to get them out?'

He looked at her somewhat disdainfully. 'There might be no point. None of us are miracle workers.'

She didn't know why, but his comment stung. She and her team were here to be of service. On reflection, she realised that he was worried. He had to have friends amongst those who had gone down in the lift on this shift. His nerves were bound to be on edge.

The sting of being snubbed was quickly banished. Pride and hurt feelings had no place in the present scenario. The antidote was to get on with the job in hand which she applied herself to do.

Eyes and wounds were washed, ointment applied, wounds bandaged. Thankfully, no bones were broken and even those whose eyes had been closed managed to sit up once the application of water had done its work.

Once they'd done all that they could, Frances eyed her team with fierce pride. The medical staff of Orchard Cottage Hospital had carried out their duties professionally and efficiently. Each of them, including the little student nurse who had been terrified to answer the phone, was reassuring as they told their patients that they would be home soon, and that their wounds were not serious.

One by one, tearful women came over to claim their men and take over from the nurses.

Feeling only slightly tired, Frances walked a few steps to the pithead. More men were underground.

The women whose men had not yet come up to the surface maintained worried looks. A baby cried. A small child stood looking as apprehensive as its mother, its hands buried in her skirt.

A sea of worried faces watched as the winding wheel creaked into movement again, this time sending the cage back down with the rescuers.

Frances checked that her team were readied once again for the next lot of injured men. *Just injured, please God*, she thought. *Let's have as many alive as possible.*

With the help of comrades and womenfolk, the four rescued men got to their feet. Gregory had a word with them and they thanked him, said they were grateful he was there, and could he ask God if all their mates got to see the light of day again.

Frances and her team of nurses kept going, tending to the most trivial things, anything to keep busy. In her opinion, keeping busy was the perfect antidote to fearing what might next come from the cage.

They were disturbed from their thoughts when a rumbling

sound, then the nickering and neighing of horses came from somewhere to their left. More pit ponies. One of them, filthy beyond description, its eyes blindfolded skittered and skipped, flaring its nostrils as if it wanted to drown in the fresh air it was breathing. Its handler did all he could to bring the creature under control. With another man's help, he unfastened it from the empty coal truck it was pulling.

Another pony followed. This one was as filthy as the first and stood trembling instead of fighting its handler.

'Is this the other entrance?' Frances asked.

A man overheard her. 'This is it.' He gave her the same information she'd been given earlier.

'The ponies and trucks come up via the drift track. The trucks are on rails. And if you're thinking the men could come out the same way, they're down deeper and there's likely a fall of rock and coal between where they are and the start of the drift track.'

She felt him staring at her and already had a feeling of what he would say next.

'You the new doctor?'

'Yes. Excuse me. I must get on.'

His eyes remained fixed on her. 'The rest will be up soon. Hope you don't faint.'

The comment was insulting, but she resisted the urge to respond or even look at him.

The turning of the winding wheel heralded the emergence of three more men with the same rescuers that had brought up the earlier survivors. These were in a worse state, gashes in faces, a boy with an arm that might be broken or merely dislocated and one man desperately trying to control the angry rasps exploding from his chest.

The boy was biting his bottom lip to cope with the pain. Frances noticed he was wearing odd boots – a brown one on the left and a black one on the right. Both were too big for his feet. She'd seen him before, recalled him saying that he was twelve years old. That was a year ago. He'd also told her that his mother had sold a pair of army boots he'd been given purely to put food on the table. She recalled that he'd worked bare foot most of the time, his feet cut and blistered thanks to the harsh environment. All that had mattered was that he help put food on the table. Large families bred poverty. It made her more determined to make her family planning clinic work.

'Young man... I hope you're brave because this is going to hurt.'

'I can take it.' Eyeing her stoically, he bit hard on his bottom lip.

'You're a brave young man. And going up in the world. I see you've now got some decent shoe leather,' she added with a smile remembering him from the time before when his mother had sold his boots.

'I got one from one bloke and one from another.'

'So long as your feet are protected.'

She asked him all the usual questions, most of which she'd asked when she'd seen him before; how old he was, where did he live and when was he going back to school. She suddenly remembered that his name was Tommy.

Telling her he was only at school part time didn't come as a great surprise. Children were being taken out of school because poorer families needed a few extra shillings if they were to keep a roof over their heads. She counselled him that he really should stay at school full time and asked him about his favourite subjects.

Taking advantage of his concentration on the answers, she nodded at Sister Peebles, who had been watching proceedings, waiting for a signal from Frances. In a flash, she pressed her hands down onto the boy's shoulders whilst Frances did a quick jerk of his arm. A loud click and the ball joint was back in its socket.

'Bloody 'ell!' he shouted. 'Bloody 'ell!'

'Not broken. Just dislocated. Rest it for a few days. And I mean rest it,' Frances warned.

'But I can't lie around doing nothing,' he protested.

'Go to school. That should keep you occupied and is not as physically demanding as working in a coal mine.'

Judging by his grimace, he wasn't too keen on her suggestion.

The gashes on another man's face were cleaned and dressed. His wife hung over his shoulder, clinging to him whilst telling him she had a mutton stew on the gas with heaps of onions, carrots and potatoes. 'And doughboys,' she added.

'Suet dumplings,' Lucy whispered to Frances, assuming the local terminology wasn't known to her. She was right. It wasn't.

The man with breathing problems was the only one who needed to be admitted to the cottage hospital.

'I'll have to take him in the car,' Frances said to her nursing team. 'I'll come back for you three later.'

She looked over to where Gregory was looking the most serious she'd ever seen him, his eyes fixed on the rescuers going down one more time. Judging by his stance and solemn expression, she guessed he'd been told that this time there would be no injured men coming up. Those still down there were buried under tons of coal.

A thin wailing rose from the women still waiting, those whose husbands had not been among those rescued.

'I'm finished here,' she softly said to Gregory.

He sighed before replying. 'Your work here is over. I believe mine and God's work is only just beginning.'

* * *

Lengths of black cloth were suspended from the war memorial in the centre of town. Curtains were drawn and death cards edged in black fastened to windowpanes. Despite the sunshine, the town had a sombre air. The mining disaster had left four women without husbands and many children without fathers.

It was a week after the disaster that the town shut down, allowing almost the entire population to throng the square and the high street, everyone dressed in black, keen to pay their respects.

Frances joined them, leaving just Sister Peebles and Student Nurse Anne Davies behind at the hospital.

She found herself standing next to Sister Harrison as they filed into St Michael's, where the Reverend Gregory Sampson was conducting the service for those deceased who were members of the Church of England. The Methodists and Baptists were having their own services.

The mining company had paid for the funerals and the Miners Widows and Orphans fund had distributed from the insurance fund that the miners had paid into. It wasn't much and was boosted by a collection from the townspeople and an extra sum donated by Lady Compton-Dixon.

Once the service was over and only the relatives remained at the graveside, Frances made her way to the town square, where the war memorial was still swathed in its black shroud.

She stood in front of the memorial with her head bowed, though felt slightly guilty that it was not the recently killed that occupied her mind. *The past*, she thought, *is never far away*. With the warmth of the sun on her back, she recalled the field she'd lain in with Ralph, the fiancé who was lost to her forever, one of the six chosen, one of which was selected to lie in Westminster

Abbey, the tomb of the Unknown Warrior, a place to mourn. Only his wasn't the body that lay there. His had been identified by Gregory, reburied as ordered in a grave marked, 'Known Only Unto God'.

'The more we live, the more we see death.'

It was Sister Harrison. Frances had to agree with her.

* * *

Back in the town, watching from a vantage point between the post office and the greengrocer's, a lone figure stayed in the shadows, tears streaming down her face. She felt for those who had died, but she also felt for herself.

It had only been a matter of weeks since she'd left the work-house with the information she'd been seeking. From there she'd asked a shady character who called himself a private detective to track down any friends of Miss Isabelle Frances Brakespeare. He'd come up with a Miss Deborah Goldman.

She hadn't responded to the letter she'd sent her, so she'd gone round to her house. That was where she was told where her daughter was. That was also where she was told not to breathe a word that it was her, Deborah Goldman, who had told her.

At this moment in time, she fully appreciated the wonderful woman who had adopted and brought up Frances Brakespeare. Her heart quaked with pride at this woman who had tended the injured men at the pit – and injured they surely would be.

'God bless her,' she whispered to herself and added a prayer for all those who'd been killed or injured.

8

Lucy stopped rubbing embrocation over Devlin's bare back and, in a way, she was glad she could stop. She'd felt his muscles knotting beneath her fingers, the smoothness of his skin, the fact that he was purring and saying how good it was. As a result, she'd felt the heat rush to her cheeks.

'There you're all done. Does it feel good?'

'Better than it smells.'

'Oh come on. It's not that bad,' she said laughingly as she screwed the lid back onto the jar.

Devlin persisted. 'It smells like horse liniment.'

'That's not true,' she said defensively. 'It smells of wild herbs and I know for a fact that it's mostly elderflower and beeswax. Ma Skittings believes that bees are God's little healers. She swears by everything they produce.'

'I don't believe it. I think she got it from some stables where it's used on the legs of broken-down old nags.'

'You could be right. Ma Skittings also treats animals,' she said, half believing it to be true.

'Is there anything she doesn't do?'

Lucy felt a sudden sob at the back of her throat. Ma Skittings had been busy last week laying out the men who'd been killed in the pit explosion.

'Did you go to the funerals?'

'Yes.'

'My mother went. She also donated some money for the widows.'

'That was very good of her.'

Lucy placed the jar back into the cupboard of the ornate credenza, which Devlin had informed her was French and that the blue, gold and hand-painted decorations were identical to that of Sèvres porcelain. She folded up the towel she'd used to dry her hands and placed it next to the bowl on the washstand.

When she'd first come here to tend to the injured war hero, she'd been in awe of who he was and who his mother was. Back then, she'd been something of a mouse, not daring to stand up to him and let him have his way. Those days were gone, and she'd found her courage. Nowadays she exchanged words with him with the same skill as a swordsman parrying a blow.

He reached for his shirt. At one time, he'd had Grimes to help him dress. Now he managed himself, though had tried to get Lucy to do it.

'I like the way your fingers work,' he'd said to her.

'You can do it yourself,' she'd responded quite sharply, relieved he couldn't see her flushed face, though he must have heard her sudden busyness in an effort to regain her self-control.

Surprise bordering on petulance had registered on his face when she'd refused.

'I'm not your servant,' she'd said to him. 'I'm here to administer to you, but only in a medical capacity, and besides, you're quite capable of doing simple things for yourself.'

Grimes had always been there for him, but that, thought

Lucy, had led to him being dependent on someone else, and not doing what he was quite capable of was a form of self-pity. Doing things for himself would contribute to greater confidence. That's what she told herself and had also relayed the same advice to her ladyship. Her ladyship had stared out of the window whilst considering what Lucy had said but eventually agreed that she was right. Her son, despite his injuries, had to be more self-sufficient.

Lucy understood how she felt. There had been so many times when she badly wanted to stand close to him, to do up his shirt buttons, to shave him, to cut his hair, to smooth his forehead when bad memories threatened.

Besides the massage, the only time she allowed such closeness was when they danced to a gramophone record, her hands clasped in his, their bodies only inches from each other. Both the massage and the dancing had curative qualities and in the case of the latter a respite – almost a reward for everything he'd achieved, and he'd achieved quite a lot since she'd come.

His blind eyes turned in her direction. 'My mother has a gruff exterior but would never shirk what she regards as her responsibilities. Neither will I.' He paused and faced her. At times, she could almost believe that he saw her. 'You've been a great help to me, Nurse Daniels. One day I will take over the Orchard estates. At one time, I thought I was incapable of doing that. But you've changed all that.'

She felt herself blushing. 'Oh really.' She said it in an offhanded fashion as though it didn't really matter. But it did matter. It mattered a great deal. 'It's only small things. Step by step.'

'Big steps to me. I'd almost forgotten how to button up my shirt. How silly is that?'

Lucy continued to tidy up as she said, 'Very silly.'

'Though, I have to say, the feel of your hands on my back beats anything Grimes ever did. You do know that, don't you?'

Recalling the feel of his flesh beneath her fingers, she closed her eyes and only barely refrained from sighing. Instead, she said, 'I'm a nurse. I've been trained in such matters.'

She busied herself folding up the towel he had lain on.

'There. All done. I'll go and throw this water away.'

She picked up the bowl which was decorated with a desert scene of camels and palm trees against a sunset background.

'I'll come back to finish tidying up.'

Even before she'd fully closed the door behind her, he was winding up the gramophone and placing a record on the turntable. A lilting voice singing about love and hope followed her into the bathroom, where she poured the water down the sink.

'Don't fall in love with him,' she whispered to her reflection in the bathroom mirror. 'You're just his nurse, not his equal.'

There was regret and a little hope in the eyes that looked back at her. For a moment, she held that gaze, then shook her head, convinced that it could never be. They were from two different worlds. 'And never the twain shall meet,' she told herself.

Whilst wiping out the bowl, she tried to settle her emotions, scrubbing vigorously at the camels and palm tree pattern on it as if she could erase them along with what she was feeling inside.

She recalled her first meeting with Devlin, his off-handedness, that she now knew had been a defensive shield against her, the world and the memories that lived on in his mind. He had improved greatly since her arrival.

'I'd like you to massage me every day,' he said on hearing her footsteps and the crack of her starched cotton apron as she re-entered the room. By this time, he'd pulled his braces back up over his shoulders and was reaching for his tie, his fingers walking their way to where she'd placed them together with his jacket.

'I can't do that,' she said, putting the bowl back on the wash-stand. 'Certainly not every day. The agreement with her ladyship was for two days a week. The hospital cannot possibly release me every day.'

'I can arrange for you to be paid extra.'

'May I remind you that I'm a nurse and am needed at the hospital. You can't keep me all to yourself.' *Though I wish I could be*, she thought to herself. *How sorely I wish I could be.*

'We could pay you more than the hospital.'

'Devlin Compton-Dixon, you are simply incorrigible.' Outwardly, she treated it as a joke. Inwardly, she craved to be with him every day, to be something more than just his nurse or even just a friend.

She went into the adjoining bedroom to busy herself changing the pillowcases and gathering up other laundry to take downstairs. Her heart was racing, her emotions even more tangled and confused.

Still struggling with his tie, he came in behind her.

'I'd like to go out more. But I can't go alone.'

'Grimes or your mother would go with you.' She said it quickly. In her heart, she wanted to be his daily company – but that was impossible.

He was leaning against the door jamb behind her, his tie still hanging loose, arms crossed now. 'I want to choose my company. I like the sound of your voice.'

'Better than Grimes's?' she said with some amusement.

'A growly bear as opposed to a linnet.'

She laughed. 'Is that what I am? A linnet?'

'Well, you're certainly not a growly bear who smells of hair grease.'

She suppressed a chuckle because, like Devlin, she had noticed that Grimes plastered his thinning hair with perfumed hair grease.

'You smell of fresh air as though, like a linnet or a skylark, you soar high into the sky, and bathe yourself in the clear blue yonder before coming back to earth.'

She laughed. 'How very poetic you are.'

'I blame you. You bring out the poet in me. If we went out more, I think I might be the next Byron or Shelley.'

'You aim high, sir!' She said it with humour in her voice, which accompanied what she said next. 'And is your mother a linnet too? Does she smell of fresh air and flying through the sky?'

'No. She smells of gardenias. Her favourite perfume. She's worn it all her life. How do you feel about my smell?'

The question took her by surprise and certainly needed some thinking about. She patted her hot cheeks and was grateful he couldn't see the consternation on her face.

'I'm not sure.'

'Come closer.'

'Enough of this nonsense!' She was unsure whether she sensed a tone of intimacy or just gentle demand.

'I need you to come closer.' He said it more firmly this time.

Her knees trembled at the thought of it. This could be the moment when she had to draw back or cross the line that existed between them.

She hoped she would say the right thing – whatever the right thing happened to be.

As it was, he took her by surprise. 'I need you to do this. Or I can call for Grimes.' The ends of his tie dangled from his hands. 'Bloody tie. Can you do this?'

The moment of consternation hadn't entirely vanished, but it had dissipated.

Willing her hands not to tremble as their fingers touched, she settled the tie around his neck and began getting it in reasonable order.

His breath was warm and moist upon her hair as she steeled her fingers to complete the process.

'Why do men wear ties?' she said somewhat lamely. It was all she could think of to say. Saying something helped camouflage her nerves. Now where had they come from? She feebly searched for something else to say that would lend a guardedness to the moment. 'You smell of shaving soap, warm wool and expensive cotton.'

'What?'

'In answer to your question about how you smell to me. Good smells all of them. You don't remind me of a linnet.'

He laughed. 'I should hope not.' His laughter faded. 'Neither am I an eagle, though at one time I might have thought I was. Eagles are sharp-sighted. I'm far from that. So, in consequence of my physical shortcomings, I think a penguin might be my bird persona. Flightless and a bit awkward on my feet. What do you think?'

'No. Not a penguin. More like a...' She fought for a more reassuring symbol of how he was now. 'A swan. Mute but elegant and somehow...' She paused again. 'Mysterious. A creature of hidden depths.'

As she patted the tie flat against his chest, she felt the faint beat of his heart, the warmth of his flesh. She was also aware of his sudden stillness and the increase in his breathing falling soft upon her hair.

He didn't say any more but left her there.

She needed to compose herself. A few deep breaths failed to

totally calm her racing heart. One more, and she felt back in control.

Gathering up the laundry in her arms, she passed back through his sitting room and saw him gazing out of the window onto the parkland beyond, his stance almost identical to the very first time she'd seen him.

'I would like you to increase your time here. I want you to walk with me. I want a massage at least once a week.'

'As I've already said—'

'Perhaps twice. And walks now that summer's coming. Perhaps Doctor Brakespeare could find me something to do at the hospital – even if it's sitting outside under a tree and listening to the birds. Anything to get me back out into the world with people I trust.'

Her heart felt close to breaking, though she couldn't let him know that. Adopting a manner borrowed from Sister Harrison, she said she would think about it.

'I promise,' she added, forcing her voice not to reflect the tears that threatened.

'I'll keep you to that promise.' He paused and asked a question he sometimes asked. 'You will be back, won't you? You're not going to run for home and never come back again?'

'Of course not.'

On the surface, he was much better than he had been, but occasionally his hidden vulnerability came through. Like now.

Much as she hated to admit it, she needed the small moments when she was away from him – even if it was only taking the laundry to be washed. It gave her time to recover and put her thoughts into some kind of order.

Her route to the laundry room took her past the kitchen, storerooms and cellars to where a washerwoman from town prodded the contents of the boiler down beneath the bubbling surface of grey soapy water.

Lucy added to the existing pile awaiting the laundress's attention.

'Some more for you, Mrs Fiske.'

'Just what we want,' the laundry woman said gruffly. 'As if we ain't got enough. Ain't that right, Mary? Mary 'ere is my new help. Couldn't come early enough she couldn't. Boil, bubble, soap and trouble... like a song, ain't it.'

Mrs Fiske cackled like a witch in a pantomime. Not that she looked like one. She was too fat ever to imagine riding a broomstick, though her face was as round as a pumpkin and almost the same colour. Folk said she'd worked in munitions during the war, making mustard gas in Avonmouth.

The woman she'd addressed as Mary wore a white apron over a long blue dress. Her face was partially hidden by a scarf which covered her head and drooped like a worn-out peaked cap halfway down her brow.

Lucy nodded as she greeted the new arrival. 'Good morning, Mary.'

There was something familiar about the woman's profile; not that she could see much of it amongst all that steam. She tried tilting her head to see better. Mary moved deeper into the steam-filled room, as though unwilling that her face be seen.

Mrs Fiske swayed from side to side like a drunken sailor as she accompanied Lucy back through the kitchen. Once there, she helped herself to a slice of sesame seed cake that was a few days old but still edible. Cook often placed leftovers on the sideboard for staff to help themselves.

'How long has your new helper been here?' Lucy asked her.

'A few days and not before time. I've been without 'elp for a week or so since Gertie got married again. Fancy gettin' married at 'er age. Best to stay a widow or spinster once you 'it fifty. Ain't as if you're going to start a family, is it.'

She laughed at her own joke.

'I take it Mary isn't a local?' asked Lucy.

'She ain't, but that don't worry me a jot. I needed a bit of 'elp. It's me legs, you see. I got 'orrible veins. 'Orrible they are.'

Lucy already knew that Mrs Fiske's rolling gait was due to her bad legs and her wobbly flesh, her weight added to each time she passed through the kitchen.

'You should come to the hospital, and we can see what we can do to make things easier.'

'I will if they gets really bad,' said the very plump laundress as she helped herself to another slice of cake, which she popped into her mouth all at once.

Lucy rolled her eyes. The more Mrs Fiske ate, the weightier she'd become and the worse her legs were likely to get. Still, there was no point lecturing the fat laundress to change her ways if she was happy in herself.

She made an effort to change the subject, to ask details of the new employee. 'I take it Mary doesn't live in.'

'Of course not. Not many servants do nowadays. Not 'ere at Orchard Manor anyways. She comes in from town.'

Mrs Fiske's piggy eyes scrutinised the sideboard for something else that had tickled her taste buds.

'She lives in town. At a lodging 'ouse,' she said in an absent-minded fashion, her attention fluttering between the remains of a pork pie and the slivers of meat left on a ham bone.

The name was familiar. 'Would that be Nine Elms? Run by a Mrs Parker?'

Mrs Fiske nodded as she reached for a lone portion of apple pie.

'That's the one.'

'What's Mary's surname?'

Mrs Fiske eyed her a bit warily whilst chomping a mouthful of pork pie. 'You want to know a lot.'

'I'm thinking I might have met her before.'

'Devonshire. Yes. That's it. Mary Devonshire.'

Her curiosity roused, Lucy left the kitchen and Mrs Fiske's consistent quest for food.

To her surprise, Devlin was waiting for her in the hallway wearing a sports jacket and carrying a shooting stick.

'It's fine out. I'd like you to walk with me.'

Lucy laughed. 'I thought we were going to dance for the rest of the day.'

'I need some fresh air. I want to hear the birds. I want to smell the flowers. I want to...' He stopped and in a determined manner cupped her elbow. 'I want to be with you.'

Torn between duty and delight, Lucy checked the floor-length clock in the corner of the room. She so wanted to, but she couldn't ignore her duty to the Orchard Cottage Hospital and Doctor Frances Brakespeare.

'I can't walk with you for long. I'm on duty at one.'

'You can go in the car. It'll give the chauffeur something to do.'

'I'll put on my cloak so I'm ready to get going afterwards.'

Afterwards, she would come down to earth. Afterwards, she would be back in the life that was her experience and not his. In the meantime, she would enjoy these precious moments that were becoming even more precious the longer this relationship went on.

9

A wicker basket of laundry beneath her right arm and a peg bag dangling over her left elbow, Mary Devonshire headed for the washing line. Although clouds scudded over the sky, the day was dry, and a light wind was blowing. Just a few hours and it should all be dry, although ironing could wait until the next morning when it would be properly aired.

Mary ignored the cloudy sky. She really wanted to get this washing hung up before taking her half-day off.

'Any plans for this afternoon,' asked Mrs Fiske, her plum-coloured face shrouded in steam, tresses of damp hair plastered to her brow. Her upper arms wobbled as she pummelled a fresh lot of washing down into the hot soapy water with the wooden dolly, a four-foot-long device with prongs at the end.

'A walk into town.'

'Walking, are you?'

'Jack Pound said he'd give me a lift. He finishes at noon today.'

Even through the hot steam, Mary saw the cheery look on Mrs Fiske's face. Jack was one of the gardeners and this afternoon was taking excess vegetables and fruit into town to the grocer's shop.

By tomorrow morning, cabbages, carrots, potatoes and fruit would be displayed in boxes, ready for the townspeople to purchase, the proceeds going into Jack's own pocket.

'That'll be nice. You being a widow and him being a widower. I did 'ear he's looking out for a new wife.'

She said it cheerfully enough.

Mary's response was terse. 'He's giving me a lift. That's all. I've no intention of ever marrying again. Not ever! Never!'

Fists clenched with temper, she stomped off to squeeze more laundry through the mangle and fill the wicker basket. Why was it some people read things into something simple? she thought. Women could live without men and vice versa. That was her opinion anyway.

Behind her, undeterred and not believing what Mary had said, Mrs Fiske chuckled and made comment with the kitchen maid who had brought in a mid-morning pot of tea.

'Jack Pound's giving Mary a lift into town. Romance could be in the air, so I say. What say you, Eunice?' She said it loudly so that outside at the mangle, Mary could hear clearly.

'Is that right, Mrs Devonshire?' asked the young girl in all innocence as she handed Mary her cup of tea.

'He's giving me a lift. That's all,' Mary snapped, returning from outside, her face flushed and her hands red from feeding wet laundry through the iron-framed mangle.

Eunice flinched at Mary's sharpness. 'Sorry. Have a nice afternoon anyways.'

Disgruntled, Mary didn't respond. Romance with Jack Pound was the last thing on her mind. She had other fish to fry that had nothing to do with him, or her future, more to do with her past. Getting into town quickly would give her more time to carry out the obsessive plan that occupied her mind, her sleep and every waking hour. Something she dreamed of.

Something that lit up like a light bulb whenever she thought about it.

Untouched, her tea was stone cold by the time a smiling Jack Pound popped his head round the door and swept his cap from his head of iron-grey hair.

'I'm outside waiting for you, Mrs Devonshire. When you're ready.'

'I'll be with you shortly, Mr Pound. I just need to get my hat and coat.'

Behind her, she felt Mrs Fiske and Eunice exchanging silly looks and equally silly grins but paid them no heed. Having collected her hat and coat, she nipped along the passage to the back door rather than go back through the laundry room and perhaps face more unfounded asides and chuckles.

Sitting in the driving seat of his pony and trap, Jack tipped his hat at her, then got down and offered her his hand. 'If you can spring up there beside me,' he said in his affable but slightly shy way.

'I'm not sure I can,' she said, perhaps a bit too brusquely.

He looked disappointed. 'Well...' he said slowly. 'If you can't manage the climb, you can sit in the back, if you don't mind sitting on a bag of potatoes.'

'I don't mind at all,' Mary said quickly on noticing that the back flap was down, and the rear of the trap was far more accessible than the seat beside the driver. 'I can stretch my legs.'

She made it sound as though stretching her legs was the prime consideration for sitting in the back. The truth was she knew of Jack's interest in her, though had given him no reason to be hopeful. Men had let her down in the past, taken advantage and left her broken and alone. She wanted none of that ever again.

As they jogged along, the pony's hooves beating a gentle

tapping on the gravel road leading from the house and clopping more firmly on the asphalt road into town, Jack tried to make conversation. He spoke mostly about the trees, the fields and the weather. He talked to her about what he was planting at this time of year and the increase in yield for next year.

'I'm not boring you, am I?' he said when she didn't respond.

'No. No. Listening to you is very restful. I have to say, I know nothing much about gardening or agriculture.' She looked up at the sky. 'I think it's going to rain.'

'It might later, but not just yet. If I'm wrong and the skies do open, there's a piece of tarpaulin back there you can pull up over yer head.'

'Oh. Yes. I see it.'

She hoped he was right, and it wouldn't rain just yet. The truth was that she'd been only half listening. It was hard not to dwell on the anger that had come into being long ago but still lingered, though now it had changed somewhat since coming to Norton Dene. Apprehension cramped her stomach and two small words kept bouncing around her mind. What if? What if? Small words but big in consequence. Sometimes she daydreamed about how things might have been if she'd not done this or that. Still, what was done was done. There was no going back. No changing anything.

Jack pulled the pony to a halt outside the greengrocer's and almost opposite the war memorial. Once the pony's muzzle was in its nosebag, he came round to help her down from the back of the cart.

'Are you all right from here?' he asked her.

She quickly snatched her hand from his. 'I'll be fine. Nine Elms isn't far.'

She felt his eyes searching her face, trying to make her out and perhaps looking for some sign that she had enjoyed his company. A kind word, that was all he was waiting for.

'Thank you very much, Jack.'

'Any time,' he said to her. 'I'm always coming backwards and forwards if you 'ave need of a lift.'

Unwilling to continue the interchange, she dashed off, holding onto her hat as a light drizzle drifted on the breeze.

On her way to her destination, her footsteps slowed, then stopped beside a child of about a year or more sitting in a pushchair outside the post office – a little girl wearing a pink cardigan.

Mary couldn't help smiling, couldn't help her fingers reaching out to touch the pink cheeks.

The child returned her smile and, giggling, waved her podgy hands excitedly.

'Do you want me to pick you up?' Mary asked, her voice soft and her face wreathed in smiles.

The little girl chuckled, her rosebud mouth exposing two front teeth, pure and white as pearls. Her expression was open and full of trust, the little hands waving in expectation.

Mary knew that she had guessed correctly. The child, left alone in its pushchair, wanted company, wanted to be picked up. Willing to comply, Mary bent so low, her face was only inches from that of the child.

She drank in the details of this child, the round pretty face, the large eyes and that little smiling mouth. 'Oh, how pretty you are,' she whispered. 'Just like my baby was. But she's gone now. She left my life a long time ago.' Her eyes watered and a single tear ran down her cheek.

The little arms waved some more. The baby grizzled when Mary turned away, afraid she might do as she had done before, pick up the baby or push the pram away. Both would be lethal and would get her into trouble.

'Yes. I can see you want me to pick you up,' she whispered, her voice even softer than before.

Mary glanced at the post office door. The mother had to be inside buying stamps or envelopes or sundry items like *Woman's Realm* or a knitting pattern. She knew from her few visits there some days ago that it was stocked with more than stationery, pens and ink. There were also newspapers, magazines and a few pocket novels and knitting patterns.

'Fancy leaving you out here,' she said softly, her heart racing, one half of her mind telling her not to do anything stupid, the other encouraging her to think that she could take care of this baby far better than her natural mother.

The battle inside raged. Somewhere deep in her mind, a voice told her she deserved to have this baby. There was also a second voice telling her it was wrong. The little girl belonged to someone else.

The baby dribbled.

'Oh dear. If I leave that, your chin will get sore. Wait a minute...'

She got out a newly laundered handkerchief and wiped the child's face.

'There. That's better, isn't it? And the rain's stopped. Isn't that marvellous. It's almost nice enough to go for a walk. You'd like that, wouldn't you? Yes,' she said answering her own question, her foot on the brake, fingers curled over the pushchair's handlebars but hesitant. She knew only too well what it was like to have a baby taken away, to never see it again, forever to have a hole in her heart.

'What are you doing?'

An alarmed Nancy Skittings almost fell down the single step

of the post office as she dashed out, her eyes round with horror. She pushed Mary aside and took hold of the handlebars.

'I was just...' Mary stuttered over her words, her feet beginning to move again in the direction she'd planned to go. The baby had stopped her. The baby was what she'd really wanted, not this baby, but the one that was stuck in her mind, pinching her thoughts, paining her nerves.

'Keep away from my baby.' Nancy's voice was strident but laced with fear. Her belly betrayed that she was pregnant with another child.

It's not fair, screamed a voice inside Mary's head. 'It's not fair,' she whispered.

Nancy did not appear to hear her but watched the retreat of a woman who'd looked to be about to kidnap Polly. Nancy's sister, Lucy, had loitered in the post office a little bit longer searching for a birthday card for her sister without her knowing.

Forehead furrowed with concern, she came out of the post office to stand beside her sister. 'What's the matter?'

Still looking unsettled, Nancy nodded in the direction of the retreating figure. 'That woman was about to take Polly.' Her voice trembled as she said it.

It was almost as though her suspicion had been overheard because the woman glanced over her shoulder.

Lucy saw her face and gasped. 'That's Mrs Devonshire. She works at the manor house. Mrs Fiske the laundress says she's quiet, gets on with the job and never says a bad word about anyone. Susan said she came to the surgery to see Doctor Brakespeare coughing her lungs up but ran out when Doctor suggested she unbutton her bodice so she could examine her chest.'

Nancy expressed her surprise. 'She went to see Doctor Frances?'

'Yes. I'm sure it's her. She insisted on seeing her even though the clinic was in full swing. You were handing out leaflets. Didn't you see her?'

'No. I don't recall seeing her. As you've just said, I was handing out leaflets.'

The two of them watched the slight figure until she disappeared.

'What the bloody hell was she up to?' said a worried-looking Nancy.

'With regard to Polly or going to see Doctor Frances?'

Nancy shrugged, her eyes narrowed and still focused on the end of the High Street where Mary Devonshire had disappeared. 'Either. Maybe she's got a screw loose.'

'Maybe she has. Are you going to tell the police?'

Nancy thought about it. The woman she now knew to be Mrs Devonshire had been smiling and talking sweetly to her daughter. Was she mistaken, or had she seen a tear rolling down her cheek?

In two minds, she analysed what she had seen and then shook her head. 'The thing is she looked so sad. I wonder if she once lost a child and my Polly reminded her of her own child.'

'I don't know much about her background except that she's a widow and is staying at Nine Elms and working at Orchard Manor. Mrs Fiske might know more.'

Exasperated and more than a bit ruffled by the experience, Nancy tucked the blanket more securely around her daughter and stroked her pretty cheeks before handing her a biscuit. 'There you are, darling,' she said, her face shining with motherly love. 'Now let's go home for our afternoon nap.'

Lucy offered to walk with her. 'Would you like me to push the pram?'

'No. I can manage.'

Lucy noted her sister's belly pushing against the handlebars and couldn't help but make comment. 'This one's taking some time to be born. It must be a boy.'

'What makes you say that?'

'Men and boys are never in a hurry to get round to anything, whereas women... well... they can't wait to get things done. Plus, of course, they're capable of doing more than one thing at a time.'

Nancy laughed. 'Come to think of it, that pretty well sums up my Ned. Though I will say he works hard to put food on the table and a roof over our heads, so I won't complain. But you're right, one thing at a time. That's all a man can manage.'

'Go on,' said Lucy and laughed with her. 'And what did Ma Skittings say?'

'That I should have a dose of her honey and liquid paraffin to keep me open and ready for when the baby comes.'

With the advent of laughter, their mood lifted once they'd decided that the woman had merely been overattentive, bowled over by the sight of a pretty little girl who thought everyone in the whole wide world was her friend.

'I think I'm in love,' Lucy suddenly exclaimed.

Nancy was immediately interested. 'Who with?'

'Life. I'm in love with life.'

Lucy felt her sister's eyes studying her, turned her head and met them face on.

'What did you think I meant?'

A tickle of a smile tilted the ends of Nancy's lips.

'Her ladyship's son. Or am I reading something where in fact there is nothing?'

'There's nothing,' Lucy said determinedly. 'Nothing at all. It's my job to administer to him and that's all it is. Although...' She felt her face turning red, kept her eyes lowered. 'He has asked me if I can come in three days a week. I think he'd like me to live in, but...' She shook her head. 'I can't do that. I can't let Doctor Brakespeare down. The hospital has to come first.'

Her tone was uncommonly formidable and that in itself led Nancy to believe that her sister was not telling the truth. Either that or she wasn't quite sure of the truth and couldn't yet even admit it to herself.

* * *

Out of the sight and sound of Lucy Daniels and Nancy Skittings, Mary Devonshire's footsteps increased, not so much with the urgency of getting to where she wanted to go but because she'd been about to do something she'd done once before, something which had got her into trouble. Shame washed over her at the thought of repeating such an awful thing. Her only excuse was that it was a long time ago and she hadn't been herself back then. There was no need to ask herself why she'd done it and why she'd almost done it for a second time. It wasn't as if she'd intended the child any harm. She loved children and would have loved to have had a big family, but it wasn't to be. So no children born in holy wedlock – just one born and taken away at birth and she herself exiled to the other side of the world. The very thought of it saddened her.

The feather in her hat began to wilt and hang over her face thanks to the unrelenting drizzle that had resumed the moment she'd moved away from the post office.

Thinking of what had happened brought tears to her eyes. What a beautiful child and so happy to have someone talk to her, to respond with a cherubic chuckle.

The attractive young woman who had surprised her was obviously the child's mother and by the looks of it was expecting another child any time soon.

One child in the pushchair and one about to be born. Mary heaved a great sigh at the unfairness of life. If only she had been so lucky, but she hadn't.

Pushing recent events to the back of her mind she turned into Quarry Lane and was soon outside the Orchard Cottage Hospital.

A nurse who looked to be in her thirties smiled at her as she entered.

'Family planning is that way,' she said in a helpful and efficient manner.

Mary made no response and followed where she pointed until she came to where she thought she should be. She refrained from entering the sparkling clean room where several women were sitting on metal chairs facing the front. Instead, she loitered half hidden by the door, listening to what these women were saying.

She wrinkled her nose. Whether the women knew it or not, they smelled of poverty. Some of the children were relatively clean. Others had matted hair or bald patches showing the tell-tale signs of ringworm, scabs on mouths, warts on ears and fingers. Mothers with clean children kept them as close as they could rather than risk infection from those whose mothers weren't so fussy – or simply lacked the means or the energy to do anything.

'I don't want any more,' said one of them, shaking her head in a resolute and no-nonsense fashion.

'How many you got then?'

'Too bloody many.' The loud exclamation brought looks of understanding from some of the women there, puzzlement from the younger women.

One conversation quickly melted into another. The women were on a subject they all understood.

'I got six,' declared another, who had few teeth and a wart to one side of her nose. 'My old man works all the hours God sends, but there's never enough to feed them all. Not properly. Potatoes most nights, bread and dripping, pinky fruit when the greengrocer's got any. Falls on deaf ears, it does. You know what men can be like. They wants their oats no matter it's likely to bring another babe into the world.'

'I told mine to sleep out in the garden shed, but you know how blokes are. Expect it as their right. Never mind the right to starve and work yer fingers to the bone...'

The young woman who'd been handing out leaflets came close. Mary Devonshire pressed herself closer to the wall and avoided being noticed. The babble of conversation going on around her filled her ears and her head. All this talk of marriage, sexual intimacy and babies. The urge to warn them that they were trapped by their sins. The husbands and children were the result of their giving into temptation. They had only themselves to blame.

Her gaze returned to the young woman handing out leaflets. She was heavily pregnant and that's when it struck her that she was the mother of the baby left outside the post office! Her legs felt as though they had turned to jelly. She did not wish to be recognised. Did not wish to be challenged. All she wanted to do was see the doctor again, listen to what she had to say without getting too close and without anyone asking her questions she did not care to answer.

Unrecognised by Nancy, Mary Devonshire found herself a nook close to the door into the clinic. Nobody really noticed her, a middle-aged woman clinging to her handbag as though it was a life raft and might prevent her from drowning. Not that it mattered much nowadays, but things hadn't always been that way. She'd been a pretty girl when she'd been younger, but hard toil and disappointment in life had left their toll – the wages of sin her father had told her. *'Full of sin, you are, a daughter of Eve who tempted man in the first place.'* That's what her father had said before she'd left for London where she'd gone into service at the Brakespeare household. Neither parent had told her exactly what sin they were referring to, only that she was to keep herself pure. She'd had no idea about the sexual act and how babies came into being. Not until the worst had happened and she was all alone. She'd never heard or seen her parents ever again.

The rumble of conversation ceased when Doctor Frances Brakespeare arrived and headed to the front of the room. Mary Devonshire was taken aback at how many faces had turned in Doctor Brakespeare's direction. Smiling faces for the most part, some of which regarded the doctor with something bordering on adoration.

Mary's eyes followed the doctor to the place at the far end of the room where she turned to address the women sitting there.

She had no podium or lectern from where she could deliver her message. Her height and imposing presence were enough for the audience to stop chattering and look forward with bated breath – and only the occasional sniff, cough or sneeze.

She's a handsome woman, thought Mary. *Not pretty as a picture, but handsome and serene.*

A whore. Daughter of a whore, said the voice in her head.

Sometimes her parents' voices were hard to silence. Today she found it strangely easy.

Doctor Frances Brakespeare began to speak, her voice clear and worthy of being listened to. 'Welcome, ladies. I won't add gentlemen because there are none here. More's the pity. As is commonly said, it takes two to tango. They too could learn something from our sessions.'

A soft chuckle ran through the audience.

'I know that each and every one of you love your children, but the expense of feeding and clothing them does put a strain on the household finances. There is another factor to consider. The fewer children you have, the less tired you are, which means you can give them more of your time. Be in no doubt, ladies, that your care and attention to your children in the early years strongly boosts their confidence when they start school. Ultimately, your input in those early years may very well stay with them for the rest of their lives...'

Mary felt as though her heart would burst. The words uttered were wise. Nobody who had children could fail to notice that. She looked around the room and was pleased to see that the women were listening.

Someone asked, 'What about our men? How do we cope with their needs?'

A subdued tittering travelled from one woman to another, along with nods of agreement.

'There are ways.' Frances held up a sheath. 'This is one. I know you'll get grumbles from your husbands, but I would suggest that either he agrees, or he'll get nothing.'

Tittering turned into laughter. A few women whose husbands could not be told anything had grave – almost fearful – expressions.

Mary Devonshire, fearing the voice of her father or mother, or both, thundering again in her ears pressed closer to the door surround, as if by doing so she might make herself smaller.

Frances went on to show and explain the uses of condoms, diaphragms and a cervical cap, all made from vulcanised rubber.

'Thanks to Mr Charles Goodyear, all these items came onto the market in the last century. The more popular these devices become, the more they're likely to be improved. Who knows, one day it might come down to merely taking a pill to prevent pregnancy, though such a miracle is yet only a dream. But then, who knows what the future may hold? He went on to make car tyres.'

Titters of amusement ran through the gathering at the very thought that such a thing might one day come into being.

* * *

Frances smiled as she looked around her at the familiar faces. She knew some of them had monitored their pregnancies, their miscarriages, their tears of helplessness on being told they were pregnant for the fourth, fifth or even more times. Helping women plan their families and make a better future was fast becoming a passion for her, another battle for women to fight – the right to have a say in their fertility.

Her voice rose in line with her passion for her subject, and even though she couldn't see the zeal shining in her eyes, she knew it was there. Inside, she brimmed with the same fervour as those women who had fought for the vote. In her mind, she could see Izzy smiling whilst exclaiming that this was the next step on the road to equality.

Buoyed with a feeling that she'd achieved her goal, her gaze swept around the room. A slight movement to the side of the entrance drew her attention. It was only a glimpse, but she recognised Mrs Devonshire, the woman who had come to the surgery with a severe cough but refused to be examined. She told herself the woman was simply bashful. Some women were reluctant to have a doctor – any doctor, male or female – examine their near naked bodies.

'Now,' she exclaimed, her smile and shining eyes falling on her audience, 'I will leave you to talk further with my nursing team. If you need me for anything extra, you know where to reach me. And if anyone wants to talk about any of this in private, I am available, as are my nurses.'

A buzz of renewed conversation surrounded her from the

women who'd listened to her talk. Their enthusiasm fuelled her own exuberance, although she was slightly distracted as she looked for Mrs Devonshire. Why was she here? she wondered. Her problem couldn't be anything to do with family planning. She looked to be beyond childbearing age.

With Sister Harrison in charge of the team and the items of contraception sitting on the table, many of the assembled women left their seats and surged in her direction. Some touched the items tentatively as though they might burst into flame if their curious fingers stayed too long. Others were more outspoken, grabbing the items, waving them about and making ribald jokes about how the condom reminded them of a cucumber, the diaphragm and cap resembling egg cups, though one giggling woman suggested the spring of the former might come in useful to mend a broken mantel clock!

One woman put into words what was uppermost in the women's minds. 'I had heard of such things, but it's the first time I've seen them up close.' She rubbed her swollen belly. 'Wish I'd had at least one of these a while back. The little 'un will be welcome once it's born, but that's it for me. No more.'

She turned out to be one of those who wished to be advised in private. She leaned in close to Frances and whispered, 'Will I be able to have one of those fitted?'

'Yes. We can talk about it and work out which one will suit you best.'

'And you won't let my husband know,' she whispered. She'd been one of the most raucous in the audience, but meeker and milder beneath the surface.

'Goodness me, no. It's your body.'

As the crowd began to dissipate, Frances moved amongst them, her height enabling her to see over most of their heads to the door where Mrs Devonshire had been leaning. On the way, she was asked questions. Will I still have my monthlies? Will it hurt to have one of these caps or diaphragms? Frances explained the use of a pessary which would make insertion easier.

Most of them had heard and used sheaths, but only in the early days of their marriage.

'It's 'im. Reckons he can't feel anything.'

'You've seen the alternatives on offer. Come and talk to me privately when you're ready.'

One or two women, their opinions bequeathed by their husbands perhaps or because of religious convictions, proclaimed that they would never resort to such contraptions.

'Abstention! Self-control. That's what I believe in.'

Frances responded that the choice was theirs.

By the time she had made her way through to the exit, a quarter of the women there had asked to speak to her in private.

Once a few feet from the door, she looked for Mrs Devonshire, but she was gone. There was only a throng of women chattering, laughing and discussing what they were cooking for dinner that night.

Women's lives, she thought. *If Ralph had returned from the war, it would have been mine too.*

But Ralph hadn't returned and although she'd tentatively agreed to marry the Reverend Gregory Sampson, there was a part of her wanting to hold on to her freedom – or spinsterhood as the more disparaging might say.

As for Mrs Devonshire, well Norton Dene was only a small town. No doubt they would meet again. Frances only hoped that the poor woman lasted that long. The severity of her cough was worrying and needed investigating. But like the women at the clinic, she couldn't force her. She just had to wait and see.

10

The alcove in the small room the boy had found smelled of soapsuds and fresh laundry and nobody bothered him there. He felt safer and cosier than he had for a long time. Because of the boilers next door, the room was extremely warm and so was the nurse's cloak that covered him. Sister Harrison's cloak was not the only thing he'd taken from the hospital. He'd also taken the dungarees from the garden shed and food from the kitchen. The hunk of bread and cheese he'd taken from the hospital was almost gone and he was beginning to feel hungry. Thirst was not a problem because he'd found water to drink from a tap outside, the spout hovering over a series of watering cans used by the gardener. He brought one full watering can inside so he wouldn't have to go outside too often in case he was seen. Night was the best, necessary when he wanted to relieve himself.

He'd been here undiscovered in this cosy little hidey-hole for three days now, though he'd heard voices next door – women's voices. He'd also felt the increased heat when they'd lit the boilers that heated the water for the laundry. He knew they were boiling laundry, had heard the creaking of the mangle outside and footsteps heading towards the washing lines he'd seen on his first day here, sheets flapping in the wind like the wings of huge monsters.

Once the last crumb of bread was gone, his stomach began to rumble. That he could cope with; after all, he was used to being hungry, used to being beaten too when he was too tired to work, so tired that, unseen, in the depths of the night, he'd fallen off the boat.

Nobody had heard the splash and he guessed that once they'd discovered him missing had presumed he'd drowned. He hoped that was the case and that they truly believed that he was dead. It was the best thing they could think as far as he was concerned. The worst thing would be for them to come looking for him, drag him back onto the narrow boat, set him back to work and probably beat him for having fallen overboard in the first place. And he'd starve. They never gave him enough food to eat. Even the mangy dog they kept on board got better food than he did. Sometimes he'd stolen its bone or even the scraps they'd thrown into his dish.

He had no intention of going back, none. That was why he'd refused to speak to anyone; to the pub landlord who had found him or to the people at the hospital. He'd played dumb, refused to give his name and even to eat – at first, that was.

He'd relaxed a little when nobody came for him, and the nurses and that nice doctor had stopped asking where he'd come from and what his name was. They were just pleased when he'd begun to eat – small portions at first, but once his empty stomach was able, he'd begun to eat more and more. They weren't to know that he was building his strength for what he intended doing next. He couldn't stay. Not in a hospital. He needed somewhere warm and safe where he might even earn a living, even if it was clearing manure from a cow barn. Slowly but surely, he'd firmed up the rather flimsy plans he'd first made. His aim was to run away in the middle of the night and, to that end, he'd saved some of the food to sustain him on his travels, hiding some beneath his pillow when the nurses weren't looking – except they had been looking.

Sister Harrison, who was older than the other nurses and not nearly so pretty as Nurse Daniels, had discovered his hoard. She'd looked down at him with beady eyes. In response, he'd pulled the bedclothes over his head, huddling deep and waiting for her to drag him out of bed and take the food he'd stored beneath his pillow. It had surprised him when she didn't do that. She'd shaken her head sadly and left his stash beneath his pillow, which brought him great relief. Not that it would last for long, of course. He wasn't stupid. He knew it would only sustain him for the first few days and so he'd made plans for when the food ran out. His idea was that he'd steal leftovers from bins, from a pigsty or an unoccupied kitchen in some lonely farmhouse. The other option was to dig potatoes, parsnips and carrots from a field and eat them raw if he had to. Or to hunt hares and rabbits or hide in the reeds on a river or canal bank and wait for a passing duck or moorhen. Although he wasn't keen on the idea, he might even do as the gypsies did, capture and cook a hedgehog, placing it in a clay casing and cooking it deep within the glowing embers of a spent fire. He knew how it was done. If all else failed, he would steal eggs from a hen house or even take a whole chicken from its nest, strangle it there and then to stop it making a noise and dash off to pluck its feathers and draw its innards.

He had it all planned – or thought he did. In the meantime, he was cosy and warm – though beginning to feel hungry.

The small room in which he hid had only one window and the alcove he slept in received no light at all, so it wasn't always easy to tell day from night. A slight variation in light happening in

the outer room between him and the backyard never quite
reached into the alcove.

On the morning when his planned escape fell into disarray,
his eyes flickered open later than usual. The night before he'd
forced himself to stay awake, enthralled by the sound of the night.
Owls called to each other from one barn to another. A rabbit
screamed in terror as the jaws of a fox clamped around its throat.
From the rafters above him came the sound of roosting pigeons
accompanied by the scurrying of rats. He was used to all these
sounds from his journeying in the narrowboat along the calm,
shallow waters of the canal. Revelling in all these beloved sounds
had contributed to keeping him awake and consequently him still
feeling tired this morning. No matter what the reason for his lack
of alertness, he had not heard Mrs Fiske tramping into the outer
room searching for rat poison.

'Blinking creatures,' she was muttering to herself. 'I'll teach
you to steal from me...'

Her voice trailed away when she spotted the bundle in the
alcove, saw it move and thought the worst.

'Stay right where you are,' she growled. 'I'm going to cave yur
bleedin' head in.'

She grabbed a shovel used to clear out the fires beneath the
boilers, raised it over her head and charged into the alcove. She
was about to bring the shovel down onto what she assumed was
the vermin who had stolen half a pie she'd left in the laundry
room overnight, then froze.

A pair of round blue eyes peered from over the collar of a coat
of some sort.

'Well, I'll be blowed. We got a stowaway.' Mrs Fiske's grandfa-
ther had been a stoker on a banana boat and told her all about
the stowaways found on board. Young men wanting to see the
world, or at least get away from the grim deprivation the working

poor had to put up with. She brought the shovel slowly back down to hang at her side. 'And who might you be, me lad?'

The boy said nothing, the eyes stayed wide and frightened as he peered at her, his hands clutching the dark piece of clothing at chin level.

'You got a name, boy?'

Nothing.

'What you doing yur?'

Nothing.

'Are you dumb? Not got a tongue in yur 'ead?'

Mrs Fiske was not a harsh person. She also understood why the boy's eyes looked so round and set in deep hollows. She'd seen plenty enough in her lifetime. Seen enough hardship in the town of Norton Dene and many others. A hard done by young boy, she thought to herself.

'I ain't going to hurt you,' she said, setting the shovel to one side, where it rattled to the ground. 'Anyone who knows me will tell you I'm a kind-hearted soul. Wouldn't say boo to a goose.'

She waited to see what his reaction might be. He looked unsure. There was one more thing she could say that was sure to work.

'Are you hungry?'

'I don't want to go back.'

Even to his own ears, his voice sounded cracked, as though it hadn't been used in quite a while. Which it hadn't. Talking, cheeking back and speaking out of turn had never been encouraged where he'd been before. The slightest mistake or wrong word had resulted in instant punishment.

His world had been a silent and lonely one, except for harsh words, the barking of the dog and the chug, chug of the single-cylinder engine propelling them along the waterways of England.

Mrs Fiske placed her beefy knuckles on her ample hips and asked, 'Back where, lad?'

The old fear he'd arrived with at the hospital came back in spades. He looked beyond her to the other room and the yard outside and thought about making a run for it.

It might not be possible. She looked strong enough to grab him, shake him like a dog and take him to the police, who in turn might send him back to the narrowboat. He was determined not to go back to the boat. To that end, he vowed he would not tell her where he'd come from.

Despite all her faults, and she freely admitted she had many – almost took pride in them, in fact – Mrs Fiske had a soft heart where youngsters were concerned.

'Lad, whatever yur name is, I've seen more meat on a sparrow's leg than I see on you. Are you sure you don't want to tell me yur name?'

He didn't blink, just stared, wondering what she was going to say or do next. Feel his collar and take him to the police station? *No*, he thought to himself. *I'm not going to let that happen.*

'Well, names don't count for much.' She waved one hand dismissively. 'That's neither here nor there. Now, what shall we do next that will make you more friendly?' She placed a finger against her cheek as she considered what would be for the best. 'I know,' she said and patted her belly. 'It's breakfast time and I 'appen to know that there's bacon, eggs and sausages left over. Mrs Webber always cooks too much.' She laughed. 'She knows us lot downstairs will soon finish it up. It's hot work in that laundry, you know. Are you hungry? Yes! I bet you are. Well, come on. Let's get cracking.'

Her chubby hands waved him out of the deepest part of the alcove, but the boy was hesitant.

'I'm not going to eat you. I'm offering you food. As much as you want.'

Finally convinced, the boy pushed aside the nurse's cloak and slowly got to his feet. His eyes remained fixed on Mrs Fiske, wary in case she made a sudden lunge in his direction, caught him by the scruff and hauled him off to answer for his actions.

Mrs Fiske noticed his uncertainty and the way he looked beyond her. She stood aside, back against the wall so that the light from the outer area was more obvious than it had been.

'There,' she said, gesturing towards the exit into the backyard. 'Nobody's stopping you from going if that's what you want.

'Come on.' She crooked her index finger and invited him to follow her.

His footsteps were hesitant, his thin form overshadowed by her wide body. She walked out ahead of him, her gait resembling that of a drunken sailor.

She gave him little attention once they were outside, though fully prepared for him to take off. Not that she'd attempt to stop him, but she had seen his skinny form and had reservations about him running anywhere. The lad needed a good feed and that was a fact.

The boy was in two minds. He didn't know for sure that they would send him back to where he didn't want to go. *I'll kill myself if they do*, he thought to himself. More than one thing stopped him from running away. His legs were weak, his stomach empty and the fat woman's description of fresh eggs, bacon and sausages was too good to resist. His stomach rumbled with longing. Besides that, there was nowhere he really had to go. He had no one, no home and no way of making a few pennies to at least buy a loaf of bread.

Mrs Fiske eyed him speculatively. Starving and homeless. What would she have done if her son had been in that situation.

As it was, he'd had a good life, been loved and looked like having a decent future and would have done if the war hadn't come along.

Her plump face creased into a jolly smile. 'Come along, boy. No need to be scared.'

She knew he was still behind her when they entered the laundry room, though wouldn't turn round to look – just in case he scarpered.

It was his taste buds that stopped his feet from straying. The smell of food mingled with the sudsy atmosphere of sheets being laundered, clothes drying, all manner of cotton, linen and Turkish towels being folded into wicker baskets.

A middle-aged woman of lesser proportion than the one who'd found him stood plating up food from dishes placed on a long pine side table. Serving tongs in one hand, plate in the other, she turned round and looked directly at him.

For a moment, he thought he might be told off, but she didn't do that. She sniffed and wrinkled her nose before saying, 'One extra for breakfast is it, Mrs Fiske?'

'Yes, Mary. As you can see for yerself, he could do with feeding up before we put him to work.'

A look of panic appeared on the boy's face at mention of putting him to work and he began taking backward steps from where he'd come.

A kindly though heavy hand landed on his shoulder and stopped him before he'd gone three paces. 'There's no need to be scared, lad. This is Orchard Manor and it's a good place to work and very fair as regards money and conditions. You'll get bed and board, lad, plus three meals a day – plus a bit extra if you get hungry in between meals, which is only right. A growing boy should pack it in. That's the only way he'll grow up big and strong. Just like my Reginald. He grew up to be big and strong.'

The boy looked at her wide-eyed. 'You won't send me back?'

'Back where?'

His scraggy neck fluctuated when he swallowed, more like fear than anything else, thought Mrs Fiske.

'I don't want to go back.'

'If you're working here, you're working here and won't be sent off to anywhere else. Now then, you can tell us yur name in a minute, but first let's get some food inside you before you fade away and are only skin and bone. Bacon? Sausages? Eggs?'

He nodded to all of them. His plate contained more food than he had ever eaten in one day, never mind one meal.

Mary Devonshire exchanged a questioning look with Mrs Fiske as she passed the lad a hunk of fresh bread.

'There's butter and honey there on the side,' said Mrs Fiske, whose own plate was overflowing with leftover bounty from the Compton-Dixon breakfast table.

'I'll pour the tea,' said Mary. She looked at the boy, then at Mrs Fiske. 'I think two sugars are in order, don't you, Mrs Fiske?'

'Three, Mary. If this lad's going to work here, he needs some building up. How old are you, lad?'

The boy gulped back the contents of his mouth. 'Twelve.'

Mary pulled in her chin. 'You're a bit small for twelve. Are you sure that's what you are?' She knew from experience that some children had no idea of the day they were born, let alone the year. Especially kids from orphanages or the workhouse, and in her opinion, this lad looked like one of them, small for his age, badly treated and undernourished.

His nod was nervous, and his eyes were like bats' wings flitting all over the place.

Mrs Fiske and Mary Devonshire exchanged pitying looks.

As he filled his belly, he pushed aside how it had been in the dark mists of his past.

He'd been nine when he'd been taken from the workhouse and given as an 'apprentice' to Greville Matthews and his wife who had no children of their own and had pleaded a case of needing someone to help them take loads all around the canal systems. They also hinted that in time the 'apprentice' would inherit their boat.

'We'll treat 'im as our own,' he'd heard them tell the three workhouse governors who'd assessed their application and gave their decision. All had seemed well but turned out to be far from well and he'd been far from being an apprentice. He'd been taken on as cheap labour. Both husband and wife were greedy, selfish and had a cruel streak, dishing out corporal punishment for the slightest infringement of their rules, sometimes for no reason at all. After such occurrences, they'd thrown him outside with the dog whilst they remained inside, eating mutton stew and drinking beer.

'And your name, me 'andsome lad. What's yer name?'

Mrs Fiske's question jerked him back from memories he wished to forget.

'Billy,' he said softly.

'Billy what?' asked Mary Devonshire.

'Billy Noakes.'

'There,' said Mary. 'That weren't so hard, was it. Now, how about getting some more eggs and bacon inside you. Or there's kippers. Have you ever had kippers before?'

Billy had to admit that he had not.

He tried a small one dripping with butter and washed it down with more tea and a slice of buttered toast.

The very act of running away was now totally beyond him, his stomach being so full that he suspected his legs wouldn't carry him to the back door, let alone further afield.

After they'd piled the empty breakfast plates onto the sideboard for the kitchen maid to collect, the two women had a little conflab about what to do next. Having finally come to a decision, they dug at the bubbling laundry tubs before confronting Billy, both towering over him with kindly looks on their faces and not looking inclined to beat him with a boiler stick or a laundry dolly.

'Well, Billy Noakes. This is what we'll do. Neither of us lives in. We both live in town, but seeing as you've got nowhere to live and no money, it makes sense for you to stay yur. We've decided we'll set you up a proper bed in the outhouse. It's warm and you'll be well fed in return for helping us get the washing boiled, keep the boiler going, tend the gas boiler and chop kindling for the old-fashioned one that's lit by a fire from beneath it.'

'All in,' said Mary. 'And you'll get paid.'

'Once I've had a word with the housekeeper.' Mrs Fiske threw Mary a warning look. Hiring and firing for domestic staff had to be agreed with the housekeeper, Mrs McCarthy. She was sure she could persuade her. 'If we can't find enough for you to do, the gardener's been after a lad to help him for a long while and he'll be glad of the help,' she added brightly.

Billy's jaw dropped. A few minutes earlier, he had still been in two minds whether to scarper, terrified of being sent back to Greville Matthews and his loathsome wife. Thanks to them, he distrusted many people, especially when they mentioned work and being looked after. After all this time, it seemed he'd landed in heaven and Mrs Fiske, despite her girth, and the other lady she called Mary, were two angels dead set on having him stay.

'Help yerself to more tea, lad,' said Mrs Fiske, who even Mary thought was not half as ferocious as she'd first thought.

Whilst Billy poured tea, added milk and two sugars, the two women sat close together and discussed the jobs he could do.

'Stoking the boilers.'

'Sorting the laundry.'

'Carrying the baskets out to the washing line. My poor old legs are nearing the end of their usefulness,' said Mrs Fiske, whilst briskly rubbing her bulging thighs, which hung ever so slightly over the sides of the chair.

'And seeing as Tabby went and got herself in the family way,' Mary added.

Mrs Fiske shook her head. 'Poor girl. What a daft tuppence she was to go and do that.'

The two women fell to silence. Each harboured similar thoughts as to what life might be like for the sixteen-year-old girl in future. No husband, no home and a babe in arms to slow her progress through life.

'I feel for her,' said Mary, the corners of her mouth downturned.

Mrs Fiske tutted. 'Silly of her, but there, that's how it is when you're young and your head's full of romance. Still, at least her family ain't thrown her out – thanks to her ladyship, she won't end up in the workhouse. Nobody wants to end up there, that's for sure.'

Mary winced at the remark. Not all young girls were feather-brained. Some were ignorant of the birds and the bees. She'd certainly been one of them. It was a subject she had no wish to talk about. Any other subject was better than that. She made a determined effort to return to the subject of Billy and his duties.

She leaned in closer to Mrs Fiske. 'What about Mrs McCarthy? What if she says no?'

'Don't you worry about her,' said Mrs Fiske, who was on her feet now, pummelling the boiling whites down into the washtub. 'Anyways, it's her ladyship who has the last word on who works here and who don't.'

'Are you sure about that? What is she likely to say when she finds out that we've given him a job? I mean, it's not up to us to give out jobs, is it?'

'Don't you worry. It's her ladyship that gets the final say and, mark my words, she don't miss a trick and when it comes to helping the needy, she's all for it.'

Mary had not exactly met her ladyship, but the other night when waiting at table had drawn the conclusion that she did not have the airs and graces of some women of her rank, plus she'd heard stories in town that she was a great philanthropist, was involved in many charities and was much respected in the town.

'All will be well,' said Mrs Fiske, patting Mary's thigh.

Mary hoped it would be.

Mrs Fiske insisted on him having a bath in one of the tubs of hot water once the laundry was out of there and blowing dry on the washing line.

'I won't look,' said Mary with a dimpled smile as she laid out a worn but clean towel plus some suitable clothes they'd managed to find.

Reassured, the boy took off all his clothes and tentatively dipped himself into the hot water. He gasped when only his legs and lower torso were in. This was the moment when Mary darted forward and snatched the dungarees meaning to return them to their rightful owner. His lower body was submerged in the water, but his waist up was on view. That was when she froze and sucked in her breath. His back was criss-crossed with lines of purplish and paler weals. She surmised he'd been beaten and that over a long period. The poor boy.

Running to join Mrs Fiske out at the washing line, she told her what she had seen.

'The boy's been beaten. Not recently. It's possible that the hospital applied salve. I'm sure that's where he's been.'

Mrs Fiske regarded her with a dropped jaw. 'How do you know he's been at the hospital.'

'That's a nurse's cloak he was sleeping under.'

'You think he was up at the cottage hospital?'

Mary was all of a fluster. 'Hang on a minute. Let me think. I know,' she said, her face brightening as an idea took hold. 'There's a name inside that cloak. I saw it. I'm sure I did.'

'A name. Go on. Tell me the name. I knows all of them at the hospital and Nurse Lucy comes up here to see to Mr Devlin. Is it her cloak the little tyke pinched?'

'Sister Edith Harrison,' she said without hesitation. 'That's the name I read.'

'So he came here from the hospital.' She nodded affably. 'What with the nurse's cloak and them oversized dungarees, I reckon he did a runner from there. They should be told.'

Mary agreed with her. 'I'll let the hospital know.'

'No need to go there. You can tell Nurse Daniels. She'll know whether he was there.' Her cheeks dimpled. 'She'll probably know if Sister Harrison's champing at the bit on finding her cloak gone missing. She can be a right tartar the sister can!'

'That poor boy,' said Mary, recalling the marks and shaking her head. 'The people he worked for must have done that. Apprenticeship indeed! Why didn't the workhouse check their backgrounds before handing him over? It's not right,' she said, continuing to shake her head. 'It just isn't right.'

Mrs Fiske sighed, her fat fists pinned to her sides as she shook her head and remarked that the people the boy had worked for should have been horse-whipped themselves.

Mary agreed with her. 'I'll make up a proper bed for him out in the outhouse.'

'Right,' said Mrs Fiske. 'There's blankets over in that cupboard and an old eiderdown.'

All the items in the storage cupboard were too worn for using up at the main house for the Compton-Dixon family, but both women agreed they would be a darn sight better to what the lad was used to.

Loaded up with bedding, Mary made her way to the outhouse whilst Mrs Fiske kept Billy occupied with loading a tin bath with wet washing ready to be taken outside and put through the mangle, a large contraption with two big rollers and an ornate metal frame. The contraption stood over a drain where the water squeezed out by the rollers from the laundry ran straight into the drain.

Before making up the bed, Mary lifted the navy-blue cloak Billy had been sleeping under. The material was of superior quality with a chain fastening. Although she trusted her memory, she double-checked the name tag: Sister Edith Harrison. Her memory proved correct. She determined to return the cloak to its rightful owner, which meant taking it to the hospital where she would have yet another glimpse of the lady doctor who most people spoke highly of.

Before going back to the laundry room, she prepared a response to the suggestion she knew Mrs Fiske would make. Yes, it did make sense to hand the cloak to Nurse Daniels when she was here attending Mr Devlin. But she wasn't due until tomorrow, and besides, seeing as Mary lived in town, it made sense that she should take it.

With the cloak over her arm, she passed Billy Noakes in the passageway. The zinc bath was perched on a set of wheels so he could more easily get it to the mangle out back. Wet laundry was notoriously heavy. The set of wheels had once been part of a cart made by Mr Devlin some time before he'd gone off to war. Mrs Fiske had told her he'd been a clever lad back then, always making useful things, many of which had eased the burdens of the household staff.

Back in the laundry, Mary spoke to Mrs Fiske.

'I'll take it back to the hospital. Sister Harrison is bound to be missing it.'

'No need. As I've already said, you can give it to Lucy Daniels when she comes in to tend to Mr Devlin. I'll give it to her...'

'No.' Mary held onto it. 'I'll take it to the hospital. I live in town, and I don't mind the walk.'

'Up to you.' Suds on the gas-powered boiler began to bubble over, dripping down the sides in soapy clouds. Mrs Fiske bent to turn down the gas. 'Sister Harrison ain't known for being generous, but she might tip you a farthing for bringing it back.'

Mary didn't care about getting a tip or even a thank you. The cloak offered another chance to see Doctor Frances Brakespeare and it was a chance she couldn't possibly forego.

She took the cloak home with her that night. The following morning, she would return it to the hospital, perhaps to the doctor herself.

* * *

Nancy lay back in an armchair, her swollen feet resting on a footstool and her hands resting protectively on her swollen belly.

Her sister, Lucy, knelt beside the footstool and began kneading Nancy's feet, her fingers flexing her toes, her knuckles pressing into her insoles.

Nancy sighed. 'That's lovely, Lucy. I don't know how big my feet are going to be if this baby doesn't come soon. Like two boats on the river, they'll be.'

'It's not the size of your feet I'm thinking of. It's the size of your belly.' Lucy gave her sister's lump a sharp prod. 'Come out, why don't you?'

Nancy laughed. 'He's choosing his time, that's for sure.'

'You've got to be at least two weeks overdue, but never mind, he'll come when the time suits him.'

The sisters exchanged reassuring smiles. It was good that they were both nurses, each understood that babies didn't always arrive spot on nine months. They also both knew that if the new baby didn't come soon, then drastic measures might have to be taken.

'I don't want a caesarean,' Nancy said, suddenly mirroring the conclusion in her sister's mind. 'I want to have my baby at home like I did Polly.'

Lucy patted her hand so vehemently that Nancy wanted to tell her to stop in case it fell off.

'I'll be here for you, Nancy. I'm your sister and don't you forget it.'

She shook her head. 'You're working, Lucy. I don't want to take you away from work.'

'Now don't you worry. If the worse comes to the worst, I'll look after Polly.'

'I don't know about that.'

'Well, you can't inconvenience Ned. He's working too and, besides, men are useless where babies are concerned.'

Nancy chuckled. 'I can't argue with you there. And as for Aunt Rose...'

They both waved the very thought of their unreliable aunt away. Rose drank and at times was barely in charge of herself.

'Right,' exclaimed a resolute Lucy, slapping her hands on her thighs. 'You rest whilst I take Polly out for a walk. No ifs, ands or buts.'

Glad of some respite – being pregnant and plagued by a two-year-old was draining – Nancy agreed.

'Bliss,' she said with a heartfelt sigh, leaned her head back in the chair and closed her eyes. She was all alone and easily fell asleep.

* * *

Within just half an hour, the door was pushed open. Not that Nancy noticed.

Ma Skittings, Nancy's mother-in-law, was surprisingly light on her feet for a large woman. Nancy had once confided in her sister that she was like the fairy godmother in Cinderella, appearing when least expected.

Nancy's visitor smiled down at her daughter-in-law's face, then at her bulging belly. Having been present at hundreds of births in her time, Ma Skittings believed this one was downright lazy. She'd offered Nancy some of her many brews to bring on a birth, so far to no avail.

'I'm trusting to modern medicine, Ma. I'm a professional nurse, remember?'

It wasn't in Ma's nature to argue. Live and let live was her motto. She'd told Nancy not to worry. It was her choice, but she was there if needed.

'A little lemonade,' Ma whispered. 'You'll be thirsty when you wake up.'

She fetched a small tumbler from the dresser and poured some of the lemonade she'd brought with her into it, set it on the stool that doubled as a side table next to the armchair Nancy was sleeping in.

Once that was complete, she crept back out again, certain that her new grandchild would be born before midnight. She was also certain it would be a boy.

Pleased with herself and looking forward to a celebration, Ma Skittings headed for home.

Halfway along the High Street, a woman approached her she knew only by sight.

'Excuse me.'

The woman held a handkerchief to her lower face. Ma immediately wondered why.

'Do you want me, me love?'

The woman's nod was immediately followed by a coughing fit.

'You sound as though you need a drink, me girl.'

'It's this cough,' said the woman, coming out from behind the handkerchief. 'I heard that you're a healer and thought you might be able to help me get rid of this cough.'

Ma's eyes narrowed. She saw the yellowish rim to the woman's eyes, the hollows beneath her cheeks. 'Give me that handkerchief.'

The woman handed it over without comment, though seemed to surprise herself that she did.

Ma looked at the handkerchief, unfolded it, then refolded it.

'My name's Mrs Skittings. What's yours?'

'Mrs Devonshire. Mrs Mary Devonshire.'

Ma nodded slowly and kept her expression neutral as another series of coughs erupted.

She handed back the handkerchief.

'Have you seen a doctor?'

'No.'

Ma Skittings had a gut instinct that she was lying. Whatever her reason, she decided not to press the point.

'I can give you a cough mixture.'

'Do you have some with you?'

'I'm not a wandering pedlar touting my wares.' She jerked her head in the direction in which she was going. 'Walk with me.'

Mrs Devonshire noted the greetings Ma Skittings received from local people and mentioned it.

'I've lived yur all me life,' said Ma, her strong accent coming into play, bright eyes sparkling from within a nut-brown face, the colour partly due to being outdoors such a lot and partly to walnut juice applied for protection.

Apple Tree Cottage was approached down a cobbled lane that wound parallel to The Shambles where animals used to be slaughtered. The cobbles were dotted with pale pink apple blossom. The sound of bees filled the air as they buzzed from blossom to blossom collecting honey for storage in one of three hives standing beneath a canopy of fruit trees.

Old thatch, dark with age and looking close to the end of its days, formed the roof of a cottage that dated from earlier than the town itself. The door was not locked but was stiff in its frame. A kick from Ma Skittings and it shuddered, then bent inwards.

Shelf after shelf groaned with glass bottles of all shapes and sizes. There were also tins which at one time had contained general household things like biscuits, tea or tobacco.

Ma Skittings told Mary to sit down whilst she readied a small bottle with a glass stopper, filling it from a larger bottle. The liquid within was the colour of honey. When she held it up to the light, it became golden, though was not totally clear but had tiny grains of something darker floating around within it.

Once the liquid settled to her satisfaction, Ma Skittings offered it over.

'Here you are.'

'What do I owe you?' Mrs Devonshire reached for her reticule and the purse it contained.

Ma Skittings stayed her hand. 'It's a free sample.'

'That's very kind of you.'

'It's your first time, but hopefully not yur last. Take a sip now, just to see if you like it.'

Mary Devonshire took a small sip until, deciding she liked the taste, she took another. The liquid felt warm and soothing as it slid down her throat and went some way to preventing a threatening cough.

'That feels very good,' she said. 'Thank you.'

Ma Skittings opened the door for her.

Mary thanked her again and said she was sure the tincture would cure her cough.

Ma waved her exuberant thanks away. 'It was nothing.'

As she trotted off up the path and out onto the cobblestones of the alley, Mary told herself that natural medicine was the way to go. No matter the doctor in London who'd said her lungs were in a bad way. No matter either Doctor Frances Brakespeare who had wanted to examine her. She hadn't been ready for that. This whole journey she had taken was about Frances Brakespeare. She wanted sunshine when she finally told her life story and they embraced and cried on each other's shoulders – at least that was the vision in her head.

She was sure she'd gained a little more time thanks to Ma Skittings, who was known to all and sundry as a natural healer who put more faith in her bees than she did in modern medicine.

Back in Apple Tree Cottage, Ma Skittings watched silently as Mrs Devonshire exited the garden gate and turned right to follow the lane back towards the High Street.

There was no joy on her face, no expression determining a job well done. She felt only sadness. The tincture she'd given the woman would bring some relief from the coughing. Whether she would last long enough to come back for more was doubtful.

'God bless and keep her,' she murmured, then went back to her favourite armchair to drink a cup of tea whilst she awaited the birth of her newest grandchild.

11

The day was pleasant, catkins rustling on trees and the first discernible scent of May blossom on the spiny hedgerows. Because of this Lucy went for a longer walk than planned. The stile gate led to the track that wound through a harvested field where Orchard Manor House beckoned through the trees. Not being a day for visiting Devlin, she was unwilling and unable to enter the grounds through the main gate. So why had she walked in this direction? She could have gone elsewhere, into the centre of town or down Quarry Lane, diverting onto a track bordered by boughs heavy with elderflower and the buzzing of bees. The bees were in the throes of gathering an abundant harvest this year.

'Listen to the bees, Polly. Your grandmother will be very pleased that they're still gathering pollen to make honey.'

Nancy's mother-in-law, Ma Skittings, kept bees. Besides making honey for spreading on toast, she also made medicinal honey, some of which had helped heal the injuries Ned Skittings had suffered during a quarry accident when the prescribed medicine had been temporarily unavailable.

Her feet continued to head along the path that led to the rear entrance of Orchard Manor House as if drawn to it. Caring was in her blood. She cared for her family, she cared for her patients, one of whom lived in Orchard Manor imprisoned in darkness but gradually, very gradually, adjusting to the world he was forced to inhabit. Her thoughts had centred on him a lot of late.

Devlin Compton-Dixon had been badly injured during the war and for a long while had lived in isolation, refusing to see or write to old friends. She could understand his mother wanting him to have company. He'd lived in a suite of rooms on the ground floor, attended mostly by Grimes, the ancient butler, who read to him when required until nodding off and leaving Devlin to his own devices.

It had been Devlin's mother, Lady Araminta Compton-Dixon, who had come up with the idea to have a nurse to come in. Any nurse at the hospital could have been given the job, but it was Nurse Lucy Daniels who was chosen.

'He has enough elderly retainers, plus an elderly mother fussing around him. I believe a young nurse would lighten his days.'

And so it was that Nurse Lucy Daniels now called in on a regular basis. So far everything had gone well. A relationship had struck up between the blinded veteran of the Great War and the young nurse, who he'd had sight of when she was a child playing in the streets and him passing by in the back seat of the family limousine. Although a tenuous connection, it seemed to have been enough to boost Devlin's self-esteem and go some way to him finding some joy in the world despite his physical short-comings.

Had any of this been foreseen? It was, thought Lucy, quite likely. The more often she attended Devlin at Orchard Manor house, the more she suspected that her ladyship had been purposeful in choosing her to tend her son. Thinking herself unseen, her ladyship had watched them from her window. The music from his gramophone had drifted on the damp night air and she must have heard it. Lucy had been aware they were being watched as she and Devlin danced barefoot on the lawn. The thought of that dancing, the sensuality of the wet grass beneath her feet and his arms around her brought the colour to her face and a tingling down her spine.

She'd been running through this very same field in shoes that were not made for running. Consequently her feet had been blistered. She'd held her breath as he'd bathed them for her, drying them in the thick folds of a towel. Looking at the top of his head whilst he was doing that, she'd ached to touch him, had dared reach out her hand to run her fingers through his hair and had only just stopped herself. The moment had been unbearably intimate but breathlessly short, but the ache persisted. She'd so wanted it to happen again and felt – indeed hoped – that the moment would recur.

Was it possible that Lady Araminta Compton-Dixon had thrown them together for a reason? That she had no qualms about bringing together her son and a lowly girl from the town? Lucy dared to hope.

Nancy was still waiting to give birth on the following day and Lucy had just enough time to take Polly out in the pushchair again.

'It'll give you a break.'

Nancy didn't argue and Polly waved her little hands with glee as she was strapped into the pushchair.

Stopping to take a rest from pushing over the hard-packed mud and scattered stones of the uneven path, Lucy leaned forward over the chubby-cheeked little girl. 'Into the garden,' she whispered in the secretive manner that made Polly chuckle with glee. 'If nobody's around, you can get out and run on the grass. Would you like that?'

Polly chuckled and beat her little hands on the sides of the pushchair.

Lucy's own excitement was palpable. There wasn't much chance of seeing Devlin – she couldn't imagine him ever coming into this part of the garden – but she was closer to him and that, in a funny kind of way, made her content.

The part of the garden she entered was surrounded by a high wall of red brick. She understood this walled garden dated from Elizabethan times and at its heart was an apple tree, its gnarled elderly branches propped up with wooden supports.

The gate snagged on a tangle of ivy clinging to the back of the gate as she pushed it open. Inside was like stepping back in time and away from everyday life. Cocooned within the ivy-covered brickwork, a mix of vegetables grew in strict battalions and the smell of woodsmoke rose from refuse and sticks burning on a bonfire. So did the heavy perfume of summer roses from the private garden on the other side of the ancient wall.

Although the urge to enter the private garden was strong, Lucy veered off to the right and through another door into the area of lawn and vegetables where servants took their ease with a cigarette or a cup of tea when the weather was fine. This was where deliveries were made via a gravelled drive leading to the rear gate. It was also the place where laundry cracked and ballooned on six separate washing lines.

A woman came out of the door that led along a passageway past storerooms carrying a large wicker basket piled high with laundry recently boiled and bashed into cleanliness. From her shoulder hung a linen bag which Lucy guessed contained wooden clothes pegs with which to affix the washing to the line.

A sudden burst of sweet-smelling breeze sent a billowing

sheet across her face, for an instant obscuring her line of vision. Without any breeze to give it life, the sheet fell back into place and there was the woman about to peg out her ladyship's household linen. One lot of laundry was going out to replace another lot that was due to come in.

She recognised Mrs Devonshire, the woman who had been so interested in Nancy's daughter Polly. Thinking she might have a moment's discourse, Lucy raised her hand. The 'hello' she called out was lost in a windy gust which sent another sheet stretching like the sail of a boat across her face. 'Mrs Devonshire,' Lucy shouted out, one hand on the pushchair, one cupped around her mouth.

For a moment, the figure froze, stared, then without pegging out the washing disappeared back inside the house.

Yet Lucy knew the woman had seen her, but why the sudden rushing away, leaving the laundry behind piled up in its basket? Would it be worthwhile following her inside?

Her mind was made up when a few spots of rain fell from a solitary cloud that had dared to infiltrate an azure sky. In time, the woman would have to come back out to take the washing in.

Instead of Mrs Devonshire, however, another figure came out of the back door, this one spidery thin and obviously a young boy, a cap on his head and dressed in waistcoat, trousers that ended at his shins, and a shirt of as nondescript a colour as the rest of his clothes.

He kept his back to her and Lucy had no reason to guess who he was. Most of the servants from below stairs were not known to her. When she called at the house to see Devlin, it was Grimes who took her to his suite of rooms.

It was almost time for Polly to munch her way through a Farley's rusk or perhaps have it mulched with milk and a spoonful of sugar or honey. She was already beginning to grizzle and no amount of picked flowers was going to make any difference.

Either way, it was time to get back. Nancy would be waiting for them, and if experience was anything to go by, they'd share a pot of tea before Lucy made her way to the afternoon shift at the hospital.

Besides, Lucy was beginning to worry that the baby seemed loath to be born. She couldn't blame it, the way the world was going. Strikes, accidents, lack of jobs and people working six days a week – seven sometimes – just to keep a roof over their heads and a meal on the table.

'All right, Polly. Give me a minute turning this contraption around.'

With a bit of bumping and manoeuvring, Lucy achieved her aim, and the pram was facing the direction she wished to go. Once she'd removed the tufts of grass that were preventing the wheels turning, she made haste to get back to Nancy's place.

The sparse fall of rain began to increase – just as it had on the night she had danced with Devlin on the wet grass.

'Get such foolishness out of your head,' she muttered to herself, bending her head into the wind so it wouldn't sting her face quite so much. She pulled the hood on the pushchair up so it covered Polly's head.

On gaining the road and more even surfaces than the field she'd come through, she began to run. Water was running like a river along the gutters and splashing up from pavements that were so slick with water they gleamed like glass.

'Home at last,' she muttered as Nancy's place came into sight. 'Dry us off and then a nice cup of tea,' she said out loud. 'And a Farley's rusk for you, sweetheart,' she said to Polly. 'Nancy,' she shouted as she pushed open the door, the sides of the pushchair banging against the rough plastered walls of the old cottage.

'You'll never guess what. That Mrs Devonshire is washing her ladyship's laundry. I saw her there, but she pretended not to know me. I wonder why that is.'

Polly was settled with something to eat and eased out of her pushchair before Lucy went into the living room.

'Now for the kettle. Fancy a cup of tea, Nance,' she called out.

The response she received was unintelligible.

'Sorry, Nance, I didn't hear what you said...'

A loud scream was all the answer she needed.

The conversation went no further. Lucy took stock of the situation. Nancy was lying half in and half out of the armchair. There was an urgency in her eyes and her breathing was coming in short, sharp gasps. Her abdomen was heaving, rolling from side to side as the baby moved position preparing to enter the birth canal and make its entrance into the world.

'It's coming,' Nancy cried, her hair stuck to her forehead with beads of sweat.

Lucy's first thought was to get a message to Ma Skittings to get over here and take Polly back with her.

'There's no time,' said Nancy as if reading her thoughts. 'It's coming fast.'

Lucy agreed with her. There wasn't even time to get her upstairs to bed.

'Right. Let's get organised. Polly, come here, darling.'

The little girl, wide-eyed and unsure of what was going on, did as she was told.

Lucy gave the little tot a wet flannel and set her at the side of the chair. 'Mummy's not feeling well, darling. Can you mop her forehead with that flannel? Yes, that's it, darling. Keep mopping your mummy's brow.'

Once she'd put the kettle on, gathered old towels and a few bits of flannelette cut down from full-size sheets beyond their best to infant size, she reminded her sister to take a concentrated breath, counting between that and the next one.

It was sometimes said that people of a medical background could end up the worst patients. In Nancy's case, that just wasn't true. Experience from attending other women's births had prepared her well. She was determined to get through this, so much so that she even managed a smile.

'Thank goodness you're here,' she said to her sister, then gasped for breath.

'It's here,' said Lucy, who was knelt between her sister's wide-open legs. The baby came so fast that she had only seconds to catch it in her hands, otherwise it would most certainly have hit the floor.

'What is it? What is it?' cried Nancy, the pain and exertion almost forgotten in her excitement to know the gender of her newborn.

Her sister Lucy put her out of her suspense. 'It's a boy. A healthy little boy.'

She was just cutting the umbilical cord when she became aware of a pair of big blue eyes gazing down at the baby, a pair of pink Cupid's bow lips parted in wonder.

'Baby,' said Polly, pointing hesitantly at the wrinkled little stranger who had entered their world.

Nancy beamed down at her as best she could from her position, drenched in sweat and breathing heavily, though feeling as though she wanted to dance. 'Yes, darling. Your little brother.'

Polly's chubby little face lit up. Lucy had barely had time to get her out of her pushchair or arrange for her not to be present. But she was here, a bit unsteady on her little feet, but taking it all in.

'He's a little gem,' said Lucy. 'Not a cry of protest since leaving the warmth of the womb and finding himself in a colder place.'

'He'll find it warm enough. He's welcomed and will be loved.'

'Yes,' said Lucy, smiling as she wrapped the child up in one of the pieces of flannelette, then winding it round with a second piece. 'There's no doubt about that.'

She turned aside to address Polly, thinking it a good idea to include her from the start in an effort to avoid sibling resentment.

'It's a baby,' she whispered to the little girl. 'A little boy. Would you like to tell your mummy it's a little boy?'

Polly's face lit up. A small gasp came from between those rosebud lips.

'Yesp. Mummy!'

Polly appeared beside one chair arm at the same time as Lucy, baby held in her arms, came alongside the other.

'Baby,' she said to her mother, who was looking drained but happy.

'A baby boy,' Lucy mouthed to the little girl. 'Go on. Tell your mummy.'

The little girl looked perplexed for a moment as she sought to form the words that would confirm she had a new baby brother.

'Ben,' she said softly.

Lucy placed the baby into her sister's arms. 'Ben? Is that what you're going to call him?'

Nancy laughed. 'Ben is the name of the butcher's boy. Polly thinks he's wonderful and when he knew that I was expecting, he told Polly that all baby boys should be called Ben. He'd repeated the name to her over and over every time we went into the shop. I think it's stuck.'

'So will you call him Ben?'

'I suppose it's as good a name as any, though Ned has to agree.'

'Ben, Ben, Ben,' said Polly, swinging her arms and jumping up and down, her gaze fixed on the new baby, who was now suckling at his mother's breast and yet had not uttered a single cry.

Lucy looked from mother and baby to the little girl who was standing awestruck, fascinated by the little stranger who had popped out of her mother.

'So, what do you think of your little brother, Polly? Do you like him?'

Polly seemed to think about it for a moment before she nodded.

Lucy looked at the mantel clock. 'I'm on duty this afternoon.'

'You go on. I can manage.'

Nancy pulled herself upright in the chair whilst Lucy finished the clearing up of bloodstained sheets and towels, wiping the remains of the birth fluids from the floor.

'What about Polly? You can't manage both.'

Nancy laughed. 'I wouldn't be the first woman in this town to juggle a newborn and a toddler immediately following childbirth.'

Lucy had to agree that she was right. Many women just 'got on with it'.

'I'll call in at Ma Skittings on the way to work and get her to pop in.'

'I knew it,' said a loud voice, and as if by magic there she was. Ma Skittings had arrived on cue. 'I had a feeling that today's the day.' Like the whirlwind that she was, she took the soiled items from Lucy and tickled her little granddaughter under the chin. 'And it's a boy, I bet,' she further stated as she peered at the newcomer who lay contentedly, asleep now having taken his full of mother's milk. 'A little brother for you, Polly.'

Lucy confirmed that it was and asked her how she knew.

'She was carrying high. It's always a boy when it's carried high.'

Lucy wasn't sure it was true, but when Ma Skittings declared that something was so, it was best not to contradict.

'Then if you can manage without me, duty calls.'

'We can manage,' Ma Skittings replied. 'I've brought more babies into the world than you've had hot dinners.'

Lucy knew it was true and took no insult from it. Nancy and her children were in safe hands. For her, the Orchard Cottage Hospital beckoned.

12

————

Evening. A pleasant time of day, a day which had begun very early that morning when Frances had been called out to a difficult birth which had turned out to be twins. It was Nurse Bennett who had been called to the birth and on examining the woman's abdomen had declared it was twins. She might have not called the doctor if it hadn't been a breeched birth. Two little girls had resulted from the birth. The mother, Mrs Maude Digby, had been ecstatic. Waiting downstairs for it all to be over, the father had looked shell-shocked, even more so when he'd been allowed into the bedroom where his wife had given birth.

'I didn't know it was twins.'

'Neither did anyone else,' Frances had replied as the nurse swaddled the babies and tucked one into each arm of the mother.

Mrs Digby had not attended the mother and baby clinic. She was one of those influenced by her mother's generation, who insisted on letting nature take its course, that doctors and midwives only cost money. That it was best kept in the family – if they could spare the time that is. On this occasion, poor Mrs

Digby had been in labour for two days. Her mother-in-law had insisted everything would be fine. Her mother had intervened and insisted the doctor was called. Only once her mother had offered to foot the bill did Mr Digby relent and send for help.

One twin had been wedged up in the corner at the top of the womb. The other twin, the one closest to the birth canal, had been lying across, preventing either of them being born. Nurse Bennett had suggested she might have to go to the hospital for a caesarean section. Mrs Digby had looked scared. Mr Digby had baulked at the idea and opted the doctor being called.

On arrival, Frances too had advised him that a caesarean section would be the best course to follow.

Mr Digby had puffed out his cheeks and shook his head vehemently. 'I'm not allowing my wife to be cut about like a joint of pork on a butcher's block. No doubt I'll be paying off the bill for the rest of the year. You're a doctor. Surely you can do something now that you're out here. That's what I'm paying you for.'

Turning a baby in the womb was always a difficult procedure, more difficult when it was twins. Frances wouldn't have attempted it at all if she hadn't been convinced that Mr Digby would not allow his wife to have surgery. Getting angry and refusing would do no good if both the mother's and babies' lives were to be saved. Fearful and biting down her nerves, Frances had agreed to turn the first baby – and as quickly as possible. If she took too long, the baby tucked up in the corner of the womb could become stressed, the heart rate increase, and the baby die.

Whilst he was downstairs, both Frances and Nurse Bennett had massaged Mrs Digby's belly, pushing the first baby's buttocks from the side to the middle. They'd worked silently, both very concerned that the poor woman had been in labour for two days. It wasn't usual to attempt manipulation at such a late state when the contractions were strong and ready to push the baby head first down the birth canal.

'It's moving.'

It was slight, but Frances had detected a shift.

She had instructed Nurse Bennett to keep applying pressure whilst she washed her hands with carbolic soap in an antiseptic solution. She had no option but to physically insert her hand into the birth canal.

With Nurse Bennett pushing from the outside and her manipulating from the inside, something had happened. The baby had turned. Its head engaged with the birth canal at the same time as a huge contraction pressed it downwards and in one big burst the first baby was born.

More slowly, and without the same drama, the second baby – smaller than the first – was born.

There'd been no time for doctor and nurse to share worried looks that this little one had not been held up too long. Nurse Bennett was concentrating on the first born, checking it over and only too happy to hear its lusty cry.

The second baby did not cry, but it did mew and made a sucking motion as though feeling hungry after all that exertion. And it was moving, waving its arms around and taking big gulps of air.

Doctor and nurse had smiled at each other.

'You have two beautiful little girls, Mrs Digby.'

'You've been lucky this time,' Frances had told her. 'But next time you might consider attending our pre-natal clinic.'

Whilst Nurse Bennett had stayed to finish the cleaning up, Mr Digby had accompanied Frances as far as the bedroom door.

'Just one thing,' he'd said before she left, 'I don't mind my wife attending the mother and baby clinic, but I totally forbid her having anything to do with this... this... family planning malarkey!'

Frances had barely kept her temper. She'd wanted to say that surely the decision was up to his wife who'd just given birth to twins. 'Sir, your wife has been through quite an ordeal, for which neither she nor I were prepared. I would have preferred to have known she was having twins prior to their being born. I would have been better prepared for this if your wife had attended the clinic. That's what it's there for, to monitor progress of mother and unborn babies. We can learn such a lot from examinations carried out prenatal.'

'She's fine,' her husband had exclaimed in a loud enough voice to disturb the newborns. 'All she's done is give birth.'

Frances had bristled. 'Twice, not once,' she'd said icily. 'Bringing one into the world is hard enough. Bringing two is harder and doubles the risks involved. I suggest it would be a good idea to take precautions during sexual intercourse until she's properly recovered. We can offer advice on that score...'

'Are you deaf? I've already told you. We won't be 'aving any of that.'

'Perhaps your wife should have a say on the subject. After all, it's her body.'

Mr Digby's face had stiffened with barely contained anger. 'Time you were going doctor.'

His voice was cold as he opened the bedroom door and pointed down the narrow staircase.

'You'll find the money on the kitchen table,' he'd shouted after her.

Glancing around the kitchen as she picked up her fee, Frances had noted its low ceiling and cold floor underfoot. Daisy-patterned yellow curtains made a stab at brightening the sombre room. It was an uphill task. There was a larder, a table, a deep kitchen sink and a draining board. Both the latter were piled with dirty dishes. Despite his wife's lying in with twins, the man of the house had not polluted his hands with what he regarded as women's work.

It was raining when Frances had left, the tyres of her little car splashing in and out of the puddles.

Back at the hospital her first task was to inform the district nurse, Gwen Peebles, of the birth.

'If you could put them on your roster.'

Nurse Peebles had said that she would. 'Sorry you had to step in, but Mrs Turner's baby was being stubborn. Still, all went well in the end. I've recorded events as you've asked and placed them on Susan's desk.'

Frances had thanked her. Her predecessor, Doctor Walker, had had a seat-of-his-pants kind of attitude to keeping records. According to Nurse Lucy Daniels, when asked about records for such-and-such patient, he'd tapped his forehead and said, 'I don't need to write it down. It's all in here.'

Well, it wouldn't be now, thought Frances. Doctor Walker's forgetfulness had been one of the reasons he'd been replaced. Since then, his condition had deteriorated. A keen motorcyclist, often seen charging through the town on his trusty BSA, he'd had an accident the day before and was currently lying in the men's ward with a suspected broken arm and contusions, the result of a collision with a blackberry bush and a brick wall. He was one of the patients Frances would see on her rounds today.

Although it wasn't visiting time, his wife was sitting at the side of his bed.

'This is very inconvenient,' she'd said, her cotton gloved hands resting on her patent handbag. 'When can I take him home?'

'I haven't examined him yet.'

'Can you get on with it, please? We've got a bridge party on Saturday and need a four.'

As it turned out, Doctor Walker was just battered and bruised. The moment she'd agreed to him going home, Mrs Walker had Susan, the receptionist, phoning Mr MacDonald, the funeral director. His long black hearse also doubled as ambulance and taxi. The town wasn't big enough for separate services.

Frances had informed Mrs Walker that on this occasion she would allow him to go home. 'Is the motorcycle damaged?'

'A new dent, but that won't stop him. He'll be back on it in no time.' She had leaned in closer. 'It gets him out from under my feet,' she'd whispered.

There were other patients to see so Frances didn't accompany them to the door.

A giggling Susan consequently told her that Doctor Walker had panicked a bit on seeing the hearse draw up. 'Mrs Walker had to almost push him into the seat.' The front seat of the hearse was a bench affair with enough room for three people. Susan had covered her mouth to stifle her giggles. 'He must have thought his time had come.'

Frances had laughed before pronouncing, 'It will do, if he keeps riding that motorcycle.'

* * *

'It's been a long day,' Frances said to Gregory after they'd had supper. She unfastened the T-bar of her shoes, kicked them off and folded her legs beneath her on the overstuffed sofa, one of two in the vicarage parlour.

Once that was done, she sighed, sighed and sighed again as she wiggled her toes.

'Bliss.'

A smiling Reverend Gregory Sampson poured into her glass from a fresh bottle of wine. This one was honey-coloured. One sip confirmed that it was sweet, an apt 'pudding' wine following the bread-and-butter pudding Gregory's housekeeper, Mrs Cross, had made for him.

Frances held the glass up to the light, where the golden liquid fought for dominance with the faceted pattern of Waterford cut glass. 'I love the colour of this wine. I would suggest that you've excelled yourself.'

'Not one of mine,' he said, the envious lilt to his voice allied to a smile on his face.

'Let me guess,' said Frances. 'I did hear a rumour that Ma Skittings makes wine as well as healing elixirs.'

'Much as I hate to admit it, you are spot on. Mrs Skittings has a knack for distillation – of both medicine and wine – all dependent on her very busy bees.'

For a while, they sat thinking their own thoughts, looking into the firelight, where coals that had been red were turning white, ash tumbling from the grate onto the hearth.

Setting down his glass, Gregory got up to give the fire a poke.

'There's something I wanted to discuss with you,' he said as he sat back down.

'That sounds ominous.'

'You think so?'

'You're also wearing your serious face, the one you wear when you're delivering a sermon.'

He rolled the glass between both hands before setting it down on a side table just a little too firmly, enough anyway to cause it to wobble.

'Ah,' she said, her eyes seeking his. 'I'm right. You've got something serious to say and it isn't about us.'

Gregory was one of those people who forever wore a look of

wry amusement. Sunday sermons were indeed the only time he went anyway near looking serious. He applied a light touch to his ministry of the Church of England, a manner which went a great way to putting people at ease. Gregory had the capacity to become their friend. Being their religious guide seemed to happen almost without them knowing. He cared for people and was good at putting them at their ease.

This serious look was unexpected. It didn't worry her but did make her curious.

She followed his lead and set down her unfinished glass of wine.

'Have I done something to offend the Church?'

His expression wasn't so much fallen as divided between two allegiances – she guessed one of those was the Church.

Her smile faded. Worse still, a cold dread weighed down her stomach. She thought she knew what the problem might be – but it had to come from him.

'Go on. Tell me what I've done.'

He looked as though he was searching for the right words. Having found them, he nodded and took hold of her hand.

'This isn't from me. It's from the bishop. He received a complaint.'

Frances's eyebrows rose quizzically. 'That sounds serious.'

'Someone complained about the birth control classes you've been holding. This person pointed out that humans were told in the Garden of Eden to go forth and multiply. According to this person – and unfortunately also to my bishop – the Church does not condone the use of contraception.'

Frances jerked her hand out of his and eyed him as she might an enemy, certainly not a friend. 'Do you know who complained?'

'I'm not sure.'

She'd expected opposition right from the start and had

thought herself prepared for it. Now it was here, she was finding it more difficult to deal with than she'd expected.

'This is the twentieth century. We're not Catholics. I could understand this attitude if we were, but we're not. We're Protestants. Aren't we?'

She looked at his face for some sign of agreement.

'I'm sorry, Frances. Not all members of the synod take that attitude. In time – and not too long, I think – the progressives will win through with more enlightened views, but until then...'

'On account of one little letter? I presume it was a letter.'

He nodded. 'I'm afraid so. And before you ask, I don't know who it was who picked up their pen and wielded it like a spear. The bishop wouldn't tell me, except... He hinted that it was not a member of my congregation; not my church.'

Frances stiffened, her hands now clasped tightly around her knees, an angry glare fixed on the fire. 'Men! They take the pleasure regardless of the ravages on a woman's body of having too many children and fretting on how they might feed them. One would have thought the Church would show more compassion.' Jerking her head away from the fire, her fiery glare met his look of apology – an apology he could not give or change.

'It's not my personal opinion, Frances. It's the Church – or at least some members of the Church.'

'Your bishop!'

'He's my superior. It riled a few, but not everyone.'

'Her ladyship supports me. I will not close my clinic. If the Church doesn't approve, then that's up to them. I'm doing this for women. I'm giving them the knowledge to make up their own minds and no longer be told that it's their duty to succumb to the needs of their husbands and produce children ad infinitum.'

'Frances. Please, please calm down.' Gregory made downward motions with his hands. 'Someone has complained. Someone who lives here in town. I would suggest they have some kind of axe to grind, but why...' He shrugged.

Frances took a deep breath as the unpalatable truth took hold. A resident of Norton Dene had complained. Someone who'd attended the family planning event? But who? All the women there had known they were to learn something about contraception and were prepared to learn. Nobody had walked out, except for... Mary Devonshire. She'd been there one minute and gone the next. Was she the letter writer? Beyond childbearing age, she'd no need of the help on offer. So, had she been there only to observe and make trouble?

Gregory's voice broke through. 'This isn't me complaining, Frances. I'm just the messenger. I had no part in the missive from the bishop.'

The evening ruined, Frances slid her feet into her shoes with undue haste, refastened the T-bar and prepared to leave. 'Thank you for a very pleasant evening. It certainly wouldn't have been if you'd not kept your declaration to the last.' Her voice was bitter, annoyed and disappointed.

'I'll walk you home.'

'No need,' she said brusquely, smoothing her skirt as she got to her feet.

'Indulge me. I like walking you home through the moonlight.'

'There isn't a moon tonight.'

'Through the darkness then.'

'Do as you please.'

The night was cool and very dark and the path narrow. Frances walked slightly in front of Gregory so that he couldn't hold her hand or wrap a protective arm around her. Because of the fact that she was in front and him following behind, there was not the usual thrill that usually coursed through her when there was little distance between them.

'Shall I come in and light the oil lamp for you?'

The oil lamp sitting on the circular pine dining table was a contrary artefact, even worse at times than Molly, her little car, which had become better behaved since moving to Norton Dene.

'If you like.'

He followed her in. The shallow bed of the range threw a rosy glow over the roughly plastered walls. Once Gregory had lit the oil lamp, the glow changed from rose to amber as the two sources combined.

He paused by the open door, filling the gap as solidly as any door could. 'I'm sure everything will be fine. Just give it a bit of time.'

Arms outstretched, he took several steps towards her. She stood stiffly as his fingers touched her shoulders and felt the tension there.

'I'm tired,' she said, an obvious brush-off. 'I've got an early start tomorrow.'

She couldn't help feeling a little bereft as he dropped his hands, but her indignation was effectively dampening her emotions.

The door shut softly behind him, leaving her alone in the glow of the coals and the oil lamp, feeling annoyed and strangely adrift. She would not give up advising the women whose lives were dictated by ovulation and the continual production of children. They deserved better and, regardless of opposition, she would be the one to help them take control of their lives.

* * *

Mrs Dagmar Bascombe had a jolly face. Her cheeks were pink and round as ripe apples. Out and about, she held her head high, though it did little to increase her height. Height, she'd regaled her son, didn't make anyone superior to herself. It was piety that set her above other people.

'And you, my darling Harry, will follow my example. That's the way I've brought you up. You must follow my lead, as should many other people I could mention. Just because they attend chapel on Sunday doesn't mean they're as pious as they should be. Some of them are riven with sin; do you hear me, my son?'

Harry always agreed with everything she said, which made her very proud of him. Her husband had always said that she'd kept him tied to her apron strings, not let him think for himself as a man would think. Not that it mattered much now. Her husband, Abraham, had disappeared with a Sunday School teacher some time back. Teacher indeed! The woman had been a harlot and Abraham, a sinner. As for the issue of their union – three children! It could be more by now. Disgusting! They were like rabbits. They had no self-control. Eve tempting Adam all over again. As for that abomination happening at the Orchard Cottage Hospital, giving people advice on how to stop having children when the only true Christian way was to abstain. She'd voiced her viewpoint to Mr Brockworth, her own Methodist minister. To her great surprise, his response had been less than supportive.

'Medicine is marching forward at a great pace, Mrs Bascombe, and in my opinion its progress is with the blessing of the Almighty.'

He'd hurried away before she'd had chance to bestow her belief that such devices being peddled at the clinic was condoned by the devil, not by the Almighty. He always tended to march off before she'd given him the benefit of her devout beliefs. One sentence and he was gone.

The impudence of the man! Turning his back on a woman who had trod a godly path in life. Well, he wasn't the only church in town. She'd gone over his head and written to the bishop. It was with great satisfaction that he'd written back and thanked her for bringing the matter to his attention.

He might not have the righteous wrath to protest that these people were profane, and what's more, encouraging others to be profane, but she knew there were a few who felt as she did. *I know*, she thought, laying aside her father's old Bible. *I'll set up a group of like-minded people and decide together how best to drive the devil out of our town.*

13

It was hard for Frances not to feel apprehensive when the letter from London had arrived. Judging by the postmark, it had been posted only the day before and brought in by the postman to hospital reception. She'd gritted her jaw at the prospect of reading it before ripping the envelope open and unfolding the missive it contained.

Dear Doctor Francis,

'Dear God. They could at least spell my name correctly,' Frances had exclaimed angrily. She threw back her head, closed her eyes and muttered, 'Give me strength.' Her upbringing in a household dominated by women, and Izzy in particular, had made her strong. Recent events that had strewn obstacles and setbacks in her way had made her even stronger. She still hadn't got over Gregory telling her about a letter opposing her family planning clinic having been sent to the bishop. Hopefully the whole matter would be forgotten. She certainly hoped it would be and so did Gregory.

Even before she'd opened the letter, Frances knew that Mrs Beatrice Trinder, Izzy's sister, was at the bottom of this. It was hard to believe that someone could be so vindictive as to set a legal process in motion designed to take away the name bequeathed to her by the woman who had rescued her from the workhouse. It wasn't even as if there were any Brakespeares around to object – besides Beatrice, who was now Mrs Trinder.

And what was the reason? After great thought, Frances had decided that she must be doing it in a bid to undermine her self-esteem. What had she or Izzy done to deserve this? Yes, Izzy had not followed an ordinary life of marrying, keeping house and having children – except for her adoptive daughter, herself, Frances.

Her first response had been for her trembling hands to tear the letter into a hundred pieces. She just about refrained from doing so. If she was to continue to fight this unfair challenge, she needed to see what they had to say.

Acting on our client's instruction, we are willing to accept agreement from you that you will henceforward desist from using the Brakespeare name to which you have no legal right. Should you not agree to do so, my client will have no other option than to apply for a court injunction. Please be aware that such court action is likely to disclose details of your private life, your history and of those closest to you. It will also cost you a not insignificant sum should you lose the case.

We await your reply,

In a final act of contempt, Frances had crushed the letter in her hands, her anger fit to burst in a flurry of expletives she did not normally use. But this! Beatrice Trinder, with her tight, pointed features which had reminded her of witches in fairy tales, was vindictive and selfish when she'd swept into the house following Izzy's death. Why did it offend her so that Izzy had bestowed her family name on the baby she'd rescued from the workhouse? What difference did it make to her?

She'd voiced all these reservations the night before when, just for once, she had provided an evening meal of fresh bread, cheese, ham and bright yellow butter. Gregory had supplied the wine.

'I really must get round to seeing a solicitor,' she'd said to Gregory. He'd shook his head and told her that seeking legal advice was long overdue. The fact was that the Orchard Cottage Hospital was her priority, the only baby she would ever have – although she didn't tell him that.

'I will get round to it, but this town comes first. I provide an important service.' She'd sighed emphatically. 'I only wish I could make that stupid woman understand that.'

'You could pray for her.'

Frances had shot him a dagger-like glare. 'As you know very well, Gregory, I am not particularly religious, but it isn't for that reason that I'm not likely to pray for her. The fact is, I truly believe that she is beyond redemption.'

He'd laughed at that, and she was glad to hear it because it meant they had made up for the slight tiff they'd had when he'd mentioned the phone call from the bishop.

The letter stayed on the mantelpiece in the coach house whilst the contents letter remained etched on her brain and would no doubt remain with her for the rest of the busy day. There were patients to see in the surgery and arrangements to be made for the next mother and baby clinic. After that, she needed to do her morning tour of the wards, which were far busier than they used to be. People had begun accepting a female doctor more readily. At first there'd been scepticism, but that was when she'd arrived and been a stranger in town. People were now addressing her as Doctor Frances if they met her in the street, coming along to surgery more readily with their illnesses.

From the busy wards to her surgery, a calmer place where she could concentrate on the patients she had to see, each of them shepherded into her by the very capable Susan.

Aspirin was the most prescribed medicine, a cure-all for coughs and sneezes or for alleviating the pain of an elderly person with arthritis.

The last patient dealt with, she began to relax and think of other things. The future beckoned with even more new ideas and improvements to both the hospital and medicine.

Suddenly, there was a ruckus on the other side of the surgery door, which was flung open so violently that it bounced off the wall and remained swinging.

A man came barging in, Susan trailing in his wake, a look of alarm on her face.

Frances got to her feet. 'What is this?'

'This,' he said, 'is about you peddling this nonsense about private stuff between a man and his wife.'

'Do take a seat,' she said to him, sinking slowly back into her chair with as much of a smile she could muster.

'No thanks. I'll say what I've got to say stood up. It won't take long.'

He had the kind of face that could look soft as a pudding one minute and hard as an anvil the next. Like two glittering chips of coal, his eyes fixed on her as though daring her to make the slightest move.

'You,' he shouted, the tip of his finger barely two inches from her face. He stank of cider.

'Can I have your name, please – for future reference?'

'Fred Mercer. Now get this,' he said, his meaty hands slamming down on her desk. 'All this filth you're teaching our women's got to stop. What goes on between man and wife is no business of yours.' He frowned suddenly as a thought gripped him. 'What do you want my name for?'

She'd scribbled it down.

'For the police. I will not have people barging in here, assaulting my receptionist and myself.' It was only a small defensive measure, but she hoped it would work.

'I ain't done anything.' He looked totally surprised.

'Your wife is Brenda Mercer, I believe, and she's given birth to four children. None of them lived long.'

'No, they didn't. And I still wants children so you can 'ave this back for a start.'

He threw a box of pessaries onto the desk which had been given to Mrs Mercer when Frances had fitted her Dutch cap. Both were recommended to be used together. Obviously, Mrs Mercer had admitted to the pessaries but not the Dutch cap.

'The Lord God dictates whether we 'ave babies or not. That's the way it is.'

'Mr Mercer, outwardly your wife seems healthy enough, but during a routine appointment when she complained of being breathless and lacking strength, I detected a slight heart murmur. It might be something or it could be nothing. Either way, I must mention it.'

He baulked as the news sunk in, but only momentarily. 'She's my wife and I put the bread on the table. I'll provide for my family without the need of any of that filthy stuff,' he shouted.

'If you've any regard for her health, you might look at things a little differently. Might I suggest—'

'No,' he shouted, shaking his finger in her face for the second time. 'You don't suggest anything.'

'Your wife might not...' She was going to say that because of her heart condition, Brenda Mercer might not survive another pregnancy, but his masculine pride deafened him to reality.

'My wife will do as I say. I married her. She belongs to me.'

From out of nowhere, Izzy's old fighting spirit made Frances jump to her feet, eyes blazing. 'Your wife does not *belong* to you. No human being can own another. It's called slavery if that does occur. So, you, Mr Mercer, are breaking a law that was passed at the beginning of the last century. Slavery was abolished back then, though to hear the likes of you and some other men, the law doesn't apply to women. Well, let's get this clear, Mr Mercer,' she said in a low and firm voice. 'Women own their bodies. Not you!'

Now it was her who pointed the finger, stabbing it at him so forcefully that he had no option but to take a step back.

Although he looked taken aback by her vehemence, the unmove-able trait of masculine pride was still there in his eyes. Like many men, he could not envisage a future where women were equal to men. His was the sort who would always view women as the weaker sex, the ones paid less than a man for doing the same work, the ones who gave up their freedom to run a house, give birth to children and raise them as best they could whilst giving way on a man's right to spend half his wages down at the pub. It made her blood boil to think of it.

Witnessing all this, Susan stood with her mouth open. Suddenly, Sister Harrison appeared behind her and barrelled her way in to stand firmly beside Frances.

'Mr Mercer. I suggest you leave.'

There was a commanding element to Sister Harrison's deliv-ery. No matter that she wasn't that tall – certainly quite a bit shorter than Frances – she had the air of someone who commanded respect, and when it came to the final call, a matron was as formidable as a sergeant major – in Edith Harrison's case, perhaps a bit more so.

Faced by three women, Frances could see that Fred Mercer was barely controlling the urge to lash out. She knew he was capable of it and recalled seeing his wife with a bruise on her face. She had no doubt the poor woman was subjected to violence from this man who crowed that his job was to put food on the table and a roof over their head and so what if he spent a quarter of his wages in the pub. A man had a right to ease his thirst after a tough day down the mine.

Sister Harrison's domineering air and that uniform stretched tightly across her broad chest stood between him and the door. She was like a terrier that had cornered a rat and her bite could be just as lethal. 'That way,' she stated in a commanding voice, pointing at the exit.

There was tension in the air. Fred Mercer was a big bruiser of a man who most likely dominated his workmates the same as he did his family. He was that sort of man. He had to be top dog and capable of standing up to anyone. Except now he was faced with a woman who could stand up to the best of them.

Frances covered a stray smile with her hand. *United we stand, divided we fall*, she thought to herself.

The senior sister had certainly risen high in her estimation. But she was the doctor here and she too needed to show some true grit, to square up to him, even though his fist could knock her down if he so wished.

'I believe it's time you left, Mr Mercer.' Her voice did not waver. Even to her own ears, it sounded full of purpose.

Sister Harrison stepped aside to give him room to pass.

Fred Mercer glared at both Frances and Sister Harrison but didn't seem to have noticed Susan, who was framed in the doorway.

'You just wait,' he said, eyes blazing, face red from both strong cider and anger. 'I ain't finished with you yet, but mark my words, you won't be seeing my missus yur again!'

With that, he was gone, venting his anger halfway out, punching the door jamb with his clenched fist.

Sister Harrison gave no sign of being rattled.

'Gosh,' said Susan, her face tight and her bottom lip quivering. 'I thought he was going to punch you, Doctor. Or you Sister Harrison.'

Frances frowned. 'Is it correct that they have no living children?'

Sister Harrison confirmed that it was so.

'All weakened and taken within weeks or months of being born.'

Frances frowned. 'That's tragic. I take it my predecessor had an opinion on the reasons why they weakened and died?'

Rarely had Frances seen Sister Harrison looking as uncomfortable as she did now.

'It strikes me you have an opinion on the matter, Sister Harrison.'

Sensuous lips, oddly suiting the senior sister's strong features, pursed as though unwilling to spit out her considered opinion.

'I don't want to sound disloyal to Doctor Walker.'

'I need to know.'

Sister Harrison cleared her throat. 'Doctor Walker was of the old school. He firmly believed that a wife had a duty to cater for her husband's needs no matter what.'

Frances turned slowly to face Sister Harrison, her expression one of disbelief, not because of anything that had been disclosed, but because of what she feared might come next. 'The babies were born sickly, or they steadily deteriorated?'

'Both. She's not too well either. The last baby died before you came here. There's been two miscarriages since.'

Sister Harrison's eyelids flickered, and an uncharacteristic pallor made Frances think she was about to faint. Whatever she was about to say it seemed not to sit easy on her strong features.

'Do you want to sit down?'

Sister Harrison shook her head. 'I saw those babies. I knew what was wrong, but Doctor Walker... I suggested his wife should be advised not to have relations with her husband. Doctor Walker wouldn't hear of it. He said that we had no right to come between man and wife. Mrs Mercer asked us why her children were so sickly and died in infancy. She asked if it was something to do with her husband.'

Frances's gaze stayed fixed on the hospital's senior sister. 'Go on. What did Doctor Walker say?'

Sister Harrison clasped her hands together, her fingers knotted of one hand with those of the other. 'He assured her that her husband was quite healthy and that she must continue to "do her duty" by him.'

Frances felt as though her flesh was no longer attached to bones. There was anger but also a nauseous feeling even though Sister Harrison hadn't put what she suspected into words. 'But you saw those babies. I need you to explain. If you would, please.'

'They didn't do well. No matter what the nourishment, they failed to thrive.'

'And likely any future babies would also die,' whispered Frances, her thoughts warped with horror. 'That's why she came here and went away with an item of contraception. She'd worked it out and we failed her.'

'No. You didn't fail her and neither did I. But I knew,' Sister Harrison said, her jaw clenched, and her hands held so taut her knuckles showed white through her translucent skin. 'Doctor Walker was not an unkind man, but he was a staunch churchgoer and believed that a man owned his wife.'

Frances shook her head. Her predecessor, Doctor Walker, had seemed like a good enough sort on the few occasions she'd met him. As for owning his wife, well she'd met Mrs Walker and she'd seemed a very balanced individual who knew her own mind. But this...

Sister Harrison made her excuse to leave. 'I've to do my rounds before Sister Burton comes on duty.'

'Sister Harrison.'

The senior sister stopped at the door and waited.

It seemed to Frances as though her mouth was too dry to speak of the horror expressed. If she'd got it right. 'Just to confirm. Those babies were syphilitic?'

A sad look came to the strong face, and she nodded curtly. 'Yes. All of them.'

Poor Mrs Mercer. She wasn't only childless, but her husband's wayward morals had caused him to contract a disease that had led to a plethora of dead babies. There would be no more, thanks to the fitting of the small rubber device in the neck of her womb. The poor woman obviously had enough heartache in her life without having to cope with losing one baby after another.

14

'You really should contact a solicitor about this and get them to write back to Mrs Trinder's solicitors.'

Gregory he was standing over Frances as she flipped through files containing the ongoing roster for the week and the notes she'd pinned with them detailing the improvements she thought in order.

The coach house felt stuffy. Perhaps it was the proximity of Gregory, or the heat generated by the latest letter from Beatrice's solicitors.

'I can't. I'm too busy.' She carried on with what she was doing rather than look up at him.

'I love you when you're flustered.'

'I'm not flustered.'

'Well, I think you are.'

The files were taken from her hands one by one. He also took her pen.

Frances buried her head in her hands. 'I really can't spare the time to go up to London.'

He pulled her hands away from her face, kissed the tip of her nose and said, 'Guess what. Solicitors are found in other parts of the country besides London. We even have them here in Norton Dene.'

There was reassurance in the way he gazed into her eyes, the palms of his hands gentle on her face.

'The fact is...' she began.

'You don't want your neighbours knowing your business.'

One corner of her mouth turned upwards acknowledging that he was right.

'Can you imagine the fuss it would generate? *Have you heard? Doctor Brakespeare must change her name because she's no right to it.*' She brought her clenched fists down on the table, sending the papers flying and the crockery rattling.

Gregory took hold of her hands. She felt a tingle of rather pleasant apprehension when his eyes bored into hers. 'You could take my name.'

Her breath caught in her throat. Marriage was a subject they'd discussed, but she'd asked him to give her time until she was established in both her job and the town she'd chosen to practise in.

It was instinctive to pull her hands away, a sign she was not quite ready for the future he was suggesting.

'I can't,' she said whilst putting notes back into their relevant folders. 'I must establish myself in my own right first. I have this urge...' Her teeth were on edge and her lips sucked inwards. She raised her eyes and looked into his. 'I have to prove myself.'

He gave her a quirky little frown. She guessed what he would say next.

'You don't have to prove yourself to me. I think you're wonderful.'

She laughed in a light-hearted way and shook her head. 'You're biased.'

There was gentleness in his eyes. 'I fully admit it. Now, how about you? Do you think I'm wonderful? Do you foresee a shared future, or have you changed your mind?'

She looked down at her hands. They were white and soft, the kind of hands any respectable woman would be proud of. But sometimes, just occasionally, she saw those hands differently, smeared with dried blood, fingernails black and broken. Occasionally she also saw a smiling Ralph on those special days when they'd escaped to a corn field. Artillery had exploded in the distance. They'd made love with eager abandon, grabbing the moment whilst they still could before the guns came closer and the smell of ripe corn was replaced by that of cordite and blood.

'Frances?'

She heard his voice, but for a moment did not respond. In her mind, she wondered what it would have been like if she too had died in that dreadful war. Izzy would have mourned her passing. Her sister, Beatrice Trinder, would not. Good riddance to bad rubbish as far as she was concerned.

But what about qualifying as a doctor? What about Norton Dene?

Wanting to lift her mood, Gregory eyed her pensively. He judged that a change of subject was in order.

'I hear new blood is coming to Norton Dene. A London company is taking over the leases of the coal mines, some quarries too.'

'Brigadier Grainger is getting a bit old, I suppose.'

'Indeed. Lady Araminta was telling me that there will be a position for her son in the offices.'

'That would do him the world of good,' Frances responded.

'I thought so too.'

Frances turned thoughtful. This town was her home and its inhabitants were becoming precious to her. This nonsense with the awful Beatrice Trinder had to be faced. She wanted to hold her head high here.

'Back to my little problem. Can you recommend a solicitor in Norton Dene?'

'Yes,' Gregory said without appearing to give it much thought. 'Gunther Seeburger.'

Frances frowned. 'I've noticed one or two solicitors' signs around town, but not him.'

'If you don't fancy using him, you could try Turnpocket and Whiteshaffer.'

Her jaw dropped before she burst into laughter. 'They sound positively Dickensian!'

'That's no excuse for condemning them out of hand,' he said, his own amusement lighting up his face and crinkling the corners of his eyes. His expression turned serious. 'They're good, but I've a preference for Gunther Seeberger. He keeps a low profile and is tucked away in The Shambles.'

She frowned and chewed the name over in her mind. 'Gunther Seeburger. That's a German name. No wonder he hides himself away.'

'He's lived here for years and his father before him, but you're right. He's kept a low profile in recent times.' He shrugged. 'You know how it is. Some people hold a grudge forever, even when they themselves never took part in hostilities. Gunther lost a son there – on our side.'

'Poor man.'

'You'll find him chipper enough. Would you like me to make an appointment and go with you?'

She shook her head. 'No need. I'll go later in the week. Friday perhaps.'

She needed time to think about it and decided a little distraction was in order. Work provided that. Work always provided that.

She flicked her fingers at the pile of paperwork. Each one held a record of the women who'd taken advantage of the free issue of contraception on offer. One woman had confided to her that she and her husband never seen each other without clothes. Others admitted that the light was always turned off before they got into bed, by which time they were wearing their night attire and covered from head to toe.

Frances wondered how it was some of them ever got pregnant. But behind all that, she thought of the likes of Mrs Mercer, one baby after another dying from a disease inherited from her husband.

Poor woman, she thought. Forced to bed with her husband whether she wanted to or not, and ill advised by Doctor Walker, who really should have paid more attention to what was going on and had a care for the welfare of the mother and sick babies.

The outside door of the offices of Gunther Seeburger had been daubed in white paint with one single word: HUN. Frances knew that the solicitor recommended to her by Gregory was of German extraction but had been born and lived in England. He'd also told her that Gunther had lived in many other places before landing in the small town of Norton Dene. He'd begun seeking a safe haven where his name would not be picked on in the first few years following the Great War. The name, it seemed, was everything regardless of how long he'd lived in this country and even in Norton Dene he was still being victimised. The thought that anyone could be so churlish both sickened and angered her. It also decided her that he was the man who would act for her against Izzy's vitriolic sister.

Most of the buildings in the Shambles dated from the

sixteenth century. Bumpy plasterwork lined the interior walls. The stairs up to his office creaked like the bones of excessively arthritic joints. The door gave out a mouselike squeal as she pushed it open.

The diminutive figure of Gunther Seeburger was dwarfed by the large ebony desk he sat behind. His facial features paled into insignificance by a pair of large brown eyes and his incisive look made her feel as though he knew everything about her before she'd opened her mouth.

'My name is Doctor Frances Brakespeare – or at least it has been up until now,' she said, unable to keep the bitterness from her voice.

'Yes.'

He didn't say, pleased to meet you, or yes, I know who you are. She took it from this that he was not a man to waste words.

His eyes fixed on her, a visual prompt that he wished her to continue.

'I'll begin at the beginning.'

He waited silently whilst she decided where the beginning actually was.

She outlined her background, her place of birth and Izzy coming into her life. Then she cast her mind back to the first time Beatrice Trinder had sought to make life difficult – attempting to snatch back the car Izzy had bought her. The car had been bought for her by Izzy when she'd passed her medical exams. She'd bridled at Beatrice's vindictiveness. On reflection, no car could be as important as losing one's name, one's identity conferred on her by a loving woman.

When she'd finished, Mr Seeberger leaned back in his chair, head thrown back and eyes closed.

'Brakespeare. Almost Shakespeare, but not quite.' He smiled benignly. 'She is married?'

'Yes.'

'So no longer holds the name.'

'That's right. She's now Mrs Beatrice Trinder.'

'Hmm.'

His double chin became triple as he looked down at his hands, eyelids lowered over those dark, discerning eyes.

It concerned her that he'd written nothing down, though, oddly, she didn't think that counted for much. She wondered if she should have gone to London after all. This man, Gunther Seeberger was just a small-town solicitor and, judging by the bareness of the lumpy office walls and the small square window looking out over the Shambles, barely made a living. In the offices of London solicitors, the walls were usually hidden by mahogany bookshelves where gold lettering reflected from the spines of leather-bound books hinting that the man behind the desk – it was usually a man – had actually read some of them.

His eyes flashed open. 'Mrs Trinder's solicitors must be rubbing their hands together. I would guess they have asked her to reconsider. It is, after all, of paltry importance. You do not live in London. You do not move in high society. Therefore, I have to ask myself what is driving her to do this. Is it purely sibling rivalry, an old score being settled? Or is there something more?'

Frances gave the only answer that made any sense. 'Isabelle and Beatrice never got on.'

Bushy eyebrows lowered along with his thoughtful brow. 'One has to ask oneself why that should be, but the reasons are myriad. It has always struck me, Doctor, how different in character siblings can be. Not just in looks but in attitude. I have not met either of these family members, but from experience would diagnose jealousy as the main factor driving this matter.'

Frances frowned as she thought about it before saying, 'Izzy was like a Roman candle, bright and capable of lighting up the direst surroundings. Beatrice...' She shook her head.

'Was more akin to a damp squib?'

'I can't say, because I didn't really know her.' She smiled. 'Izzy once described her as being a bit like a doll cut out from cardboard. Not durable. Not real, I think she said.'

'Hmm.'

Mr Seeberger returned to his thoughtful mode, his small hands clasped in front of him, eyes half closed.

Impatient for progress, Frances pushed him to find out what he would do next. 'Will you write to the solicitors?'

'If that is what you wish. You want me to tell them you will not comply with their request.'

'Yes.'

When he nodded, she was reminded of a small dog, not exactly cuddly to look at but inoffensive. It occurred to her that even small dogs had sharp teeth.

'I would warn that if Mrs Trinder is that determined, the matter could go to court. Do you have a birth certificate?'

'Yes. It lists my mother as Mary Baker, a domestic servant. There's no name for me. Just Baker.'

'And I take it the father is entered as unknown?'

She nodded. 'Yes.'

'So, your benefactress entered the name Brakespeare on the adoption certificate.'

'Yes.'

He looked down at his hands again and said, 'Oh what a tangled web we weave...'

Frances pointed out that this wasn't about anyone being deceived. 'Or at least not from my part.'

'Yet truth a beacon shining bright untangles webs in darkest night. And that, dear lady, with all due homage to Sir Walter Scott and his marvellous poem, "Marmion", is what I think we need to find out.'

His tongue slid the length of his lower lip. It seemed to Frances that he was relishing the fight, though a fight was the last thing she wanted.

'It all seems so petty,' she finally said.

His eyes glittered. 'I suspect that something very serious is driving this woman, something from the past that she cannot easily get over. Something known to her but not to you.'

'Do you think the matter will go to court?'

There was something devious about the slow way his smile spread from one side of his face to another. 'And thereby hangs the tale. Has it occurred to her, I wonder, that this matter could make the national newspapers?'

'Goodness. It hadn't occurred to me.'

'A woman, a member of the medical profession, being robbed of her name. The story could sell many newspapers.'

Frances sighed. 'I really do not want us going to court or the story being published. My name is important to me. My reputation is hung on that name, a name my patients have come to trust. I want to serve this community without some sleight of the past impeding my progress. I want this to go away.'

There was admiration in his deep brown eyes as he nodded and smiled approvingly. 'I will write to the other party's representatives. Let us see where we go from there.'

15

Mary Devonshire fingered the navy-blue cloak that young Billy had used to cover himself when first discovered sleeping rough in the outhouse. By rights, she should have returned it by now. She'd told Mrs Fiske that she would return it straight away and when asked had lied and said she had. The truth was, she was nervous. Her cough had not gone away but wracked her ribs to the point that they felt as though they were shattering in pieces. The time was coming when she would have to confess and confront both her past and the present.

Nobody knew that she had not taken the cloak back. Neither she could tell them the reason why. She had a far more important task to perform. Nothing to do with Sister Edith Harrison but everything to do with Doctor Frances Brakespeare. There was a truth to declare and no straightforward way to go about it.

Learning that family planning advice was being given out at the clinic had given her a kind of reassurance that she had not been a wicked woman as some had said she was. Back in her time of sin, she had felt wicked. She'd been told so. The view had been – and still was to some extent – that women were expected to endure whatever men said they should put up with. It was their lot to suffer. A priest had told her that when she'd gone to confession and dared to ask why women should suffer the pain and fear of childbirth. He'd blamed Eve. It was her that had tempted Adam and so it was that women still had to suffer the pain of childbirth, were still handed in marriage from father to husband because they were the weaker vessel and needed to be guided by a man. Was it so that women still tempted men? She didn't stay long enough to ask him but had run crying through the nave and out of the door.

A shudder ran through her as she sat on the single bed where she slept alone all night long. Sometimes during the night, she would wake from a recurring dream. In the dream, rough hands were groping her body and a harsh voice was rasping in her ear that she'd been asking for it, that he'd seen it in her eyes, in the way her hips swayed, in the rampant curls encircling her face in such an impish, mischievous way.

Her heart raced following these dreams. She'd awake soaked in sweat; her nightdress stuck to her body. The pills to still her rapidly beating heart and the tincture that helped her cough were always close at hand and she'd take what she was supposed to take. Not that they were working so well nowadays. She knew instinctively that death was a shadow waiting in the corner, watching her panic, not from fear of death but fear of dying without putting her affairs in order.

The doctor she'd seen had told her that she needed to calm down and take life easy. But how could she? How could she when there was unfinished business she had to deal with before it was too late?

She'd had that dream again last night, which was why she was sitting on the side of the bed staring at the world beyond the window recognising that today she had to do what had to be done. She would take the cloak to the hospital, return it to its owner and then... She took a deep breath. Today was the day to make confession again, though not to a priest. Today she would lay bare everything that had happened in her youth and let it spill into the present and possibly have repercussions for the future. The truth had to come out. She would indeed go to the hospital, though had considered knocking at the door of the coach house but that would mean going there in the evening. She wasn't sure she wanted to do that. Doctor Brakespeare might not wish to be disturbed. She deserved a rest after a day at the hospital, and anyway, it was possible she wouldn't let her in, might even tell her to make an appointment at her surgery.

How stupid she'd been to run away when Frances had suggested she examine her lungs. She hadn't wanted her to do that. In one way, it had seemed too intimate. In another, she really hadn't wanted Doctor Brakespeare to know how ill she was – not yet anyway; not until she'd told her the reason she'd tracked her down.

Yes. The hospital. Returning the cloak was as good a reason as any to go there. Hopefully today was not the day for the mother and baby clinic or for family planning. The latter upset her more than seeing the mothers with their darling babies. How could anyone not want a baby? The circumstances had to be right of course, but basically babies were meant to be cherished.

She blinked back tears. Doctor Frances Brakespeare had good intentions advising women on family planning, though some members of the Church did not approve. Neither did some of the townsfolk. She resolved to enlighten her, to tell her she might be happier if she desisted from giving such advice. There was a movement in the town to stop her. Mary herself had been asked to join it by a Mrs Bascombe, whom she'd met at the Methodist chapel. She'd replied that she would reserve judgement and that she needed to learn more about it. But deep down she had reservations and so did many others. The doctor needed to be warned. She would tell her about Mrs Bascombe who had confided to her with immense pleasure that Mr Brockworth, their own minister, had ignored her so she'd appealed to the Bishop of Bath and Wells to do something about it. Mary would warn Frances to be careful.

* * *

Nurse Lucy Daniels had popped in to see her sister and the new baby, only intending for the visit to be five minutes not thirty-five. It turned out to be long enough to take in a cup of tea and a slice of home-made fruit cake.

'Lovely cake,' said Lucy after taking a bite. 'So, is he sleeping through yet?'

Nancy pulled in her chin and laughed. 'You are joking, aren't you? Early days! Very early days! He's waking up three times for a feed.' She cupped both breasts. 'Good job I've got plenty to give him. I sometimes wake up in the middle of the night thinking I've turned into a Jersey cow.'

They laughed together before Nancy asked her sister for the latest gossip about town and what was going on at the hospital.

'Well,' said Lucy, who had finished her slice of cake and was already considering whether she should have a second piece. 'Did you hear that a Mr Mercer came in shouting and swearing and threatening to punch someone if his wife ever brought home anything to do with family planning?'

'Oh dear,' said Nancy, biting her bottom lip. 'I thought there would be repercussions but didn't expect anything quite this early. Was he very angry?'

'Livid. Shouting at Doctor Frances, though she did hold her

ground. Poor little Susan was shaking in her shoes. He was ordered to leave by Sister Harrison.'

Nancy's grimace edged on a smile. 'I would go too if Sister Edith Harrison showed me the door! She doesn't take no for an answer.'

Lucy smiled. 'Funny, but I never used to like Sister Harrison very much, but nowadays she seems to be softer than she used to be.'

'I haven't been on the wards for a while, so I can't say yeah or nay,' said Nancy. She smiled. 'Still, it's bound to make for an easier atmosphere.'

'That reminds me to have a word with her. Do you recall me telling you about that young lad that was found by a pub landlord half-starved and covered in scars?'

'I do.'

'He was found in the laundry outhouse at Orchard Manor snoozing under a cloak. A nurse's cloak. With a name tag inside.'

Nancy noticed the sparkle in her sister's eyes. 'You don't mean... not Sister Harrison?'

'You've got it. It seems the young lad pinched her cloak as well as a pair of dungarees from the gardener's shed and he'd hoarded food in the bedside cupboard.'

Nancy laughed as she reached for her newborn whose mouth was already open, like a small bird waiting for a breakfast of worms. She bared her breast to expose her pert nipple. The baby's pink lips closed over it.

'It seems I'm missing all the fun. I take it Sister Harrison now has her cloak back.'

'No.' Lucy shook her head as she pinched the last crumbs between finger and thumb and popped them into her mouth. She frowned. 'That's the funny thing. Mrs Devonshire, that strange woman who came into the hospital a couple of times, was supposed to bring it back. For some reason, it hasn't happened, and Sister Harrison is getting a bit annoyed about it. If that woman doesn't bring it back soon, Sister Harrison will be round to where she lives demanding she hand it over immediately. Either that or traipsing up to the manor and asking her where it is.' She grinned. 'I wouldn't like to face her.'

A kiss for her sister, one for Polly and one for the new arrival, and Lucy took her leave. There were a few things she needed to do at the hospital before the car arrived from the manor house. She smiled as she imagined Devlin pretending not to be impatient, desperately trying not to pace up and down as he awaited her arrival.

* * *

'Are you still seeing that... person?' Devlin said to her, barely giving Lucy chance to remove her cloak.

'That's none of your business,' she said loftily.

'What did you say his name was?' Devlin asked, his fingers folded over the handle of the gramophone.

'Harry. Harry Bascombe.'

'Is it serious?'

Unseen by Devlin, Lucy smiled to herself and made conjecture as to the man he was seeing in his mind. A rival. A handsome devil of sweet words and soft caresses. As if, she thought to herself!! Harry was safe. That's what she told herself. She could go out with him and know that he would not take advantage. A goodnight kiss was short and sweet, a mere peck on the cheek. If she should dare to kiss him in a strong and purposeful manner, he would blush profusely and make tracks for home. Dear Harry. He might have been a different man if his mother hadn't been so dominant.

Devlin prepared himself for his weekly massage, unbuttoning his shirt, his torso laid bare.

Lucy left him to find his own way onto the base of the authentic massage table that his mother had acquired from a specialist supplier in London.

When first giving him a massage, the oils she'd used had smelled like horse liniment – in fact, she suspected that was exactly what it was. The local chemist just wasn't geared up for what he described as 'anything fancy'. Luckily, Ma Skittings was able to concoct oils and creams that were not only suited for the task but smelled nice as well.

'Your muscles are not so tense as they once were. I understand you requested some weights be supplied you. Have they arrived?'

'They have indeed. I started lifting them a few days ago.'

'That's good,' she said as she kneaded his back and tried not to let undue emotion enter her voice. Undue emotion meant any feeling the likes of her shouldn't be showing towards the likes of him. That's why she continued her association with Harry Bascombe. It kept her grounded. She mustn't care so much for Devlin, but the truth was that she did and it was getting more and more difficult to keep her feelings in check.

A sudden knocking at the door heralded the arrival of Devlin's mother. In the past, she'd entered without bothering to knock. Nowadays, at least on the days when she knew Lucy was in attendance, she always knocked.

She swept into the room in a flurry of pale green silk, a string of pearls at least eighteen inches long hanging from her neck. Grimes followed behind her, holding what looked like a notebook and pen.

'My dear Devlin. I need some ideas for the garden party. Should we just stick to food and drink, or should we provide some kind of entertainment?'

'You mean like a fairground,' he countered, turning his head in the direction of his mother's voice.

'I was considering that.'

'Don't. The May fete is quite enough for anyone. Besides, isn't this event purely for the staff at the hospital, not the whole town?'

Her ladyship gave a little grunt of what might have been agreement, though it wasn't always easy to tell. She directed Grimes to sit at the table with his pen and notebook. 'Have you told the staff about the garden party?'

'I have indeed. A notice has gone up in the reception area. That young woman Susan has dealt with it.'

'Are you ordering them or inviting them?'

'Inviting of course.'

She sounded quite taken aback.

Devlin smiled at the fact that his mother didn't know when she was being lofty. Lady of the Manor she would always be. He couldn't help but add reassurance.

'I'm sure they'll be delighted.'

'Make notes, Grimes. Let's list what are definite requirements and also those we might wish to consider.'

Grimes, old retainer for ever, did as he was told whilst her ladyship paced up and down.

'Do not let me interrupt you, Nurse Daniels. I truly believe that my son's massage does him the world of good.'

'It's for me to say that, Mother,' grunted Devlin, head turned sideways and resting on his crossed arms.

'But surely I'm correct?'

'Surely you are.'

Lady Compton-Dixon did not confine herself to concentrating on the staff garden party as she trod up and down the room. She studied Lucy, so shapely in her uniform, and thought how attractive she was. Any debutante presented at this summer's ball could not be as graceful or beautiful as Nurse Lucy Daniels. She watched as her nimble fingers pulled and prodded at her son's back. She thought she heard him purr and couldn't blame him for doing so. What a lovely couple they made.

'Lucy. Do you have any idea what the staff at the hospital might like best?'

Lucy continued working on Devlin's back. She felt a bit self-conscious having other people in the room whilst she was carrying out her treatment. After all, Devlin's back was exposed and she was here touching, feeling and becoming more and more engaged with his knotted muscles, his beautiful skin, and the nodules of his backbone. Nobody could know just how engaged.

'Laughter would be good. Laughter makes people – all people – relax.' She paused as another thought came to her. 'Music. Music in the background but also music to dance to.' She turned her head towards her ladyship. 'If you don't mind people dancing on the beautifully manicured lawns.'

Her ladyship paused as though a sudden recollection had come to her. 'I think that's a very good idea. Yes. Music, that which doth soothe the savage breast.'

'And beer,' added Devlin, raising his head from its place on his folded arms. 'And other alcoholic drinks. Anything that's drinkable,' he laughed. 'And the weather. You need to order the weather to behave itself.'

For a moment, her ladyship seemed to be considering something else that she wasn't sure about putting into words. The idea was not new. She'd been thinking about it for some days – getting people together – two people in particular.

Finally, it came out. 'On reflection, perhaps I'm too old to be organising this. It should be you two young people. What I suggest is that I order what needs to be ordered, and you two oversee the setting out of everything on the day. Yes. I think that will work very well.'

'If that's what you really want, and Devlin is agreeable...' Lucy began.

'Good. It'll be an early start, so I would suggest that you sleep over the night before.'

With that, Lady Araminta Compton-Dixon commanded Grimes to follow her out of the room. The door shut firmly behind them.

'Did I hear what I thought I heard?' said Devlin.

'It seems we've been requisitioned to organise a garden party.'

Devlin laughed. 'That's what I thought. And you've been ordered to stay overnight to ensure that everything goes according to plan.'

'Our plans or your mother's?'

It was easy to laugh, to take it lightly, but Lucy couldn't help thinking that her ladyship had ulterior motives. But what were those motives? Lucy knew what she wanted them to be – that she was trying to throw her, Lucy, together with her son. Just because it seemed that way didn't mean to say that it was true. She had to be sure and only then could she act accordingly.

'I don't know about you, but I'm looking forward to it,' said Devlin, his head once again resting on his folded arms.

'Yes,' Lucy said softly. 'I think I am too.'

If she'd cared to glance at the face turned sideways on his arms, Lucy would have seen the look that could never quite transfer to his eyes. He was thinking about his mother's plan to have him work at the offices of the new lessee of the Compton-Dixon mineral reserves.

He found himself outlining the plan to Lucy. 'I sometimes think I feel my mother's hands pushing me back out into the big wide world.'

'She only wants the best for you. And anyway...' She paused, unsure whether she should voice an obvious truth.

'Go on. Tell me what's on your mind.'

Lucy's hands paused from the continuous kneading. 'The war was a long time ago. You've shut yourself away for long enough. It's not easy. I understand that, but you need to make the most of what you have. You're intelligent. You have a healthy body. Your mind needs to feed on new experiences. Working in an office, mixing with other people, is bound to be a good thing. I've seen you take big strides since I arrived, but there are more you can take. There,' she said, resuming the massage. 'I've said it. Tell me I'm wrong if you like. Throw a tantrum if you like...'

He'd thrown tantrums when she'd first arrived, but not now.

He lay silently as she resumed pummelling his back. He enjoyed her hands on his skin, enjoyed her closeness, the smell of her, the feminine voice that both ordered and calmed him. He sometimes felt as though her hands were physically hard against his back, pushing him to come out of his shell. As well as a job, he might also return to the world with a lovely young woman hanging on his arm.

16

Frances received a phone call from Lady Araminta Compton-Dixon at around eleven forty-five.

'In view of the increase in patients, the committee have agreed that a new kitchen will be installed at the hospital, staffed by a cook capable of providing nourishing meals for patients. There are too many staff and patients for the custodians of the Hat and Feather to cope. I have invited them to the staff garden party along with the new incumbent – once chosen.'

'That's very good to know. I have been worrying that I might have to give a hand in the kitchen myself. As it is, my nurses step into the breach when the need arises.'

'Indeed. Hodges and Sons have promised to get the old stable converted as quickly as possible. I will hold them to that promise.'

Frances had no doubt that she would. She smiled to herself before expressing her appreciation. Her ladyship had been supportive from the very beginning of her arrival in Norton Dene. So far, everything she had asked for had been agreed and given.

'I will put out feelers immediately. Good cooks are hard to find in this day and age, as are all domestic servants. Another casualty of war. But there must be someone. Good day, Frances.'

'Good day...'

The connection was lost before she had chance to add 'Minty', the personal name that only friends were allowed to use. *And I've become a friend to the gentry*, thought Frances and was slightly bemused.

Susan came into her office with a surprised look on her face and what looked like a cape over her arm. 'That woman's been in. The one who keeps popping in and running away. She brought this.' Susan held up the arm holding the cape. 'It belongs to Sister Harrison.'

Frances got up and on fingering the dark navy material noticed it seemed a bit grubby, but a good clean would soon sort that. She recalled it going missing at the same time as the gardener was missing a pair of dungarees; the same time as the boy went missing. 'According to Nurse Daniels, she's working as a laundress up at Orchard Manor. Did she explain how this came into her possession?'

'She said she took it off a boy named Billy Noakes sleeping rough in an outhouse.'

'My word.' Frances was slightly peeved that Mrs Devonshire had managed to prise the boy's name out of him when she had not. 'Did she ask him if he had family, where he came from? I'd really like to meet whoever beat and starved him face to face.'

'And give them a piece of your mind,' Susan stated. 'Just a suggestion, Doctor, but if you do find out who did it and want to put the terror of God into them, take Sister Harrison.' Susan shook her shoulders. 'She certainly scares me.'

Frances couldn't help but chuckle.

'I take it that, yet again, Mrs Devonshire did not linger.'

Susan declared it was so. 'She shot out of the door but can't have gone far.'

Frances thanked her. Mrs Devonshire was like a will-o'-the-wisp, seen one moment and gone the other.

All the same, she felt a strong urge to go outside and look for her. She cared for the welfare of this woman. She also had an instinct that there was something else going on behind those dark grey eyes – something personal to her.

There was no one in sight down at the gates. If she had gone that way, Mrs Devonshire could already be halfway to town. Where else? Frances thought. Instinct, whether feminine or plain natural, turned her attention to the orchard.

A flagstone path led through the grass and mass of wild-flowers between the trees. At the end of the path was a garden bench of intricate design in a pale cream. Head bent, hands clasped tightly in front of her, sat Mrs Devonshire.

'Mrs Devonshire.'

Her head jerked up.

Frances suspected she might run away again. To her surprise, the dejected stance she'd observed previously had gone, replaced by one she could only describe as exhibiting resolve. The same resolve came to her eyes.

'I understand you found a boy in one of the outhouses up at the manor and that he told you his name was Billy Noakes.'

Mrs Devonshire nodded. 'I did. He was starving.'

'And sleeping under Sister Harrison's cape?'

Mrs Devonshire looked at her bright-eyed as she recalled the good she had done. And it was good. Helping anyone from his background was always a right and charitable thing to do. The sparkle in her eyes continued as she used her fingers to count off everything she and Mrs Fiske had done. 'We fed, washed and clothed him. He's been given a job. We'd been nagging the house-keeper for some help heaving heavy washing for a long time. He's been taken on for five shillings a week all found. Mrs Fiske and me put up a bed for him in the outhouse with proper bedding too.'

Frances sighed with relief. People could be so kind, which helped counteract those who were so cruel. 'That really is very good of you. I don't suppose he intimated anything about where he came from, who his parents were...'

Mrs Devonshire shook her head forlornly. 'There are no parents. He told me that much. Said he was placed in the work-house as a small child. The people on the narrowboat paid for him to be indentured as a boat hand. Worked him like a donkey, they did.' Anger flared in her eyes and stiffened her features. 'I'd like to burn down every workhouse in the land. Every single one of them! The only people they benefit is them that take advantage of them that have fallen on hard times. Even children. Though there are exceptions and I for one am grateful for that.' Her hand flew to her throat as though trying to hold back the sigh of satis-faction.

However, Frances was determined that the people who had treated Billy so badly should be brought to justice. To that end, she asked, 'I would like to speak to Billy about his ordeal with those people. I'm sure you'll agree that they should be brought to book.'

Mrs Devonshire shook her head. 'No. It may surprise you to learn that I don't. They should be buried and not referred to. He's been plucked from harm. Everything will be fine now and for that we should be eternally grateful. Praise God,' she said, closing her eyes as if affirming that it was all down to heavenly intervention.

Frances made no comment. Her opinion on God was still divided. He'd taken Ralph from her, though, more realistically, it was human beings who had done that. So perhaps she should blame the Kaiser, the wartime leader of the Prussian empire.

However, kind words were better than harsh ones any day of the week.

'It sounds as though you are an ardent churchgoer.'

Mrs Devonshire nodded and looked just ever so slightly embarrassed. 'For the most part.' Her voice faltered before regaining its previous strength. 'But there comes a moment when neither priest nor God is enough.'

Not quite understanding what she was getting at but very aware of the depth of feeling being expressed, Frances asked her to explain. 'If you don't mind.'

'No,' she said. A faraway look came to her eyes. Although, in truth, it seemed she was watching a flock of sparrows hopping from branch to branch, Frances perceived there was something else Mrs Devonshire was seeing, something Frances could not see.

Mrs Devonshire took a deep breath before continuing.

'I've been attending the Methodist chapel since coming here. I met a woman there who I want to talk to you about. A Mrs Bascombe.'

Frances searched her mind for the name. She'd heard it somewhere but couldn't recall having met the woman.

'I must warn you that she's dead set against the clinic and dishing out family planning advice. I dislike her so much I've decided not to go to that particular chapel ever again. The woman boasted that seeing as the Methodist minister ignored her, she turned to the Church of England and wrote to the bishop.' Mrs Devonshire shook her head disparagingly. 'Some people take pleasure from making trouble for other people and she's certainly one of them... excuse me...' A coughing fit followed, the severity of the coughs causing her to double over and cover her mouth with both hands.

Frances now knew the name of the person who had written to the bishop. The name meant nothing to her, not that she would confront her if she had recognised it. After talking it over with Gregory she had concluded that it was best to keep a low profile and not draw attention to what she was doing. Her priority was to advise the women who needed her help. Drawing attention from hostile forces to the clinic and the women who attended it was best avoided.

Mrs Bascombe. She etched the name in her memory.

The coughing continued.

Perturbed, Frances thought back to the day she'd first met Mrs Devonshire, the day when she'd refused to be examined and ran out. Was it because she already knew how ill she was and had no need of a second opinion? Or was there some other reason? She couldn't guess what that reason might be. All she could do for now was to be patient and let her unfold in her own good time.

'Talk slowly. I'm listening.'

A pair of luminous grey eyes looked up at her from pale hair that might once have been darker. It was hard to tell. 'I went back to my own kind of church. I was brought up a Catholic, you see. So,' she proclaimed, 'it was like this. I went to church earlier, but no matter how hard I tried, I couldn't go into that box and confess to a priest, yet there's so much I want to say – to explain... But it's not a priest I need to confess to.' She dragged her gaze away from the faraway or the twittering sparrows and gazed with eyes as liquid as an expanse of misted water. 'It's you. I must confess to you.'

Puzzled by this comment and strangely moved, Frances reached out and lay her hand gently on Mrs Devonshire's shoulder. 'I'm not a priest, I'm a doctor, but will do all I can to help.

Whatever you want to tell me will go no further. I am obliged not to betray confidences. Please understand that.'

For a moment, the sun hid itself behind a cloud. Frances felt warning in that sudden change in temperature. She'd never been one to believe in premonitions, but in this moment, she felt that Mrs Devonshire's confession was likely to affect her greatly.

The sun came out from behind the cloud touching her shoulders with instant warmth and a feeling – a feeling that had up until now only tingled somewhere deep in her soul. It was now full blown, or at least about to burst out into words, into a truth she only suspected. Those grey eyes fringed with thick dark lashes, the full pale pink lips, sensually beguiling rather than a Cupid's bow... so much like her own.

Mrs Devonshire met her smile with one tinged with sadness and plagued with regret. 'I am so proud of you,' she said in a small hesitant voice.

The sparrows sounded louder than they had done, their constant litany exploding inside her head, so loud, so intense that she couldn't formalise what she was feeling, what she was expecting.

'I gave birth to a baby before I was married. I was married a few years ago when I lived in Australia, but the less said about that, the better. My story doesn't begin with my husband. It begins long before that, at least the bit I want to tell you about.'

Frances felt as if a cold blanket had been thrown over her. What was this woman saying? She was dancing around the edges. Frances in turn was mentally dancing faster and faster away from details of Mrs Devonshire's life. No matter how fast she attempted to divert her thoughts, they kept bouncing back. What she said next changed everything.

'As a young girl, I worked for the Brakespeare family.'

Frances took a deep breath. 'I see.' The dancing thoughts

which she recognised as suspicions were now firmly caught in the spotlight. 'Did you know Izzy?'

In a way it was a silly question. Izzy had been a daughter of Mrs Devonshire's employer. Izzy had lived above stairs and Mary very much below. They would not have had a close relationship but had likely passed like ships in the night, the servant fading into the wallpaper if they should accidentally meet on the stairs. There was also the question of age. Mary had to be ten or even fifteen years younger than Izzy who had been thirty-five when she'd taken Frances from the workhouse.

Mrs Devonshire confirmed the details in need of clarification. 'She'd left home by the time I worked there and only visited when there were papers to be signed. I don't know what papers, but the atmosphere between her and her father and sister was always chilly. She lived away from home by then, in Carwell Street. She was never there when they had family celebrations, which was just as well because they were always arguing...' Pale pink lips pursed, and a pinched anger came to her face. 'That year I was there she spent a lot of time below stairs talking to the old servants who'd known her. She was genuinely fond of them and they of her. She preferred the company of the servants to her family. I recall Cook asking me to deliver a birthday cake to Izzy over in Carwell Street. On getting there, she insisted I sit down and have a piece with her along with a cup of tea. I did say I had to get back, but she insisted, said there was something she wanted to tell me.' Her face darkened. 'She told me to be careful, to never be alone in the same room as her father.'

Frances felt her blood turn cold. 'Did she say why?' It wouldn't be the first time she'd heard rumours of the master of the house getting a young servant in the family way.

Mrs Devonshire's eyelids fluttered, and she looked away. 'I was only a girl – fourteen years old. I knew nothing about such things.

The servants warned me to watch out for myself. The house-keeper, Mrs Standish, told them not to fill my head with such nonsense and that Mr Brakespeare was a fine man.' Mrs Devonshire sucked in her bottom lip and looked worriedly down at her intertwined fingers.

'You didn't get on with the housekeeper.'

'No. She wouldn't have a word said against Mr Brakespeare, but the other servants...' She looked away. 'One day I heard Mrs Standish tear a strip off one of the under maids. They'd been recounting something about Miss Isabelle being sent away when she was a young girl. Told whoever it was that if she ever heard such wicked talk again, they would be dismissed.'

'Do you have any idea what they were talking about?'

'I... I'd rather not say.'

Frances sat unnerved. There was something she wasn't telling her, something that was making her fidget, twist the handle of her handbag, place the right ankle over the left, then reverse the process.

'Did you like her?'

'What?'

Her eyes flashed wide open like a deer taken by surprise.

'Isabelle Brakespeare. Did you like her?'

She nodded. 'I only met her once or twice. Miss Isabelle was a good person, but... She had...' She clenched her jaw as she searched for the words. 'Issues. That's what her younger sister, Beatrice, used to say. That she didn't appreciate their father, who, she insisted, had doted on Isabelle when she was younger and at home. She made no bones about it that she was glad her sister lived elsewhere, leaving Beatrice as the favoured daughter – not that he seemed to give her that much attention. On the rare occasions Miss Isabelle did come home, his eyes used to light up as though she were a goddess come down to earth. But, as I said, I only saw her a couple of times, though each time she told me to take care of myself.'

Frances sensed that somewhere amongst all this history lay the reason why Isabelle Brakespeare, a well-heeled spinster had suddenly decided to adopt a baby from the workhouse. 'Isabelle was a strong character. I should imagine that even as a young girl she would have found home life stifling. I was brought up by her, you know. She was like a real mother to me.' She smiled at the memory.

'There were rumours about why she was sent away. I think you can guess what those rumours were.'

Frances thought of the birth certificate she'd found for a baby girl born in 1899. It wasn't unusual back then – or now in fact – for a girl of Izzy's social class getting pregnant by the wrong man and being shipped off to give birth away from prying eyes, the father never to be mentioned again. 'I know it was only servant gossip, but do you really think she gave birth to a baby?'

'That's what I heard.'

It was hard to ask the next question. The sound of her heart-beat thudded in her ears. Taking a deep breath, Frances swallowed the trepidation she felt and determined to ask what she must ask. 'And the baby. Do you know what happened to the baby?'

Mary nodded. The expression in her eyes had not varied until now. 'I think she lost it.'

Frances imagined Izzy as a young girl, perhaps in love, sent away by her family to give birth alone, losing the baby... She didn't want it to be true. 'Are you sure?'

Mary shook her head. 'I don't know for sure. But I've never forgotten her kindness, especially when the same happened to me some years later...' She said it in an outspoken manner, her eyes clear, although a deep flush came to her face. 'I was taken advantage of and thrown out onto the streets. I was ignorant of the ways of men, you know. And scared of Mr Brakespeare.'

Frances felt her anxiety and her shame. She could also feel her own, the chaos Mary's words had created inside.

'My real name is Mary Baker.'

Frances's jaw dropped. Mary Baker was the name on her birth certificate. 'You're my mother,' she said softly, her voice barely above a whisper.

Eyes brimming with tears locked with her own. She nodded. 'Yes.'

Frances held her breath. The mix of emotions was unbearable, but she'd started and couldn't stop. She had to know everything. She dared push things further.

'And my father,' she said softly, her throat tight with apprehension. 'What did he do when you told him you were expecting a child?'

'He called me a little tart. I told him I wasn't.'

Frances licked the dryness from her lips and placed a placating hand against her racing heart. 'I take it he was a young man.'

She shook her head. 'Not a young man.' The look she gave Frances was incredibly open, as though she'd come to a decision. 'Mr Brakespeare. It was Mr Brakespeare who forced himself on me.'

Frances was stunned. She had been prepared for a feckless father who had taken Mary's favours and perhaps put to sea. As it turned out, the truth shocked her to the core, although the signs had been there. 'Mr Brakespeare was my father.' She whispered it whilst her blood ran cold. She felt foolish. After all, here was a woman with eyes and colouring so like her own; that she could cope with. The fact that Izzy's father was also her father was astounding.

Another astounding truth hit her like a steam train; it meant that Izzy was her half-sister. Shockingly too, so was Mrs Beatrice Trinder. She wondered if the latter knew the truth or was blind to it, wanted it erased from family memory and history – hence her crazy idea to snatch back the Brakespeare name, to keep it like a trophy. If that was so, it also meant that if Frances did refuse to relinquish her name, it would never get to court.

All these things raced through Frances's mind, along with a mix of emotions and silly thoughts about whether they should embrace, the correct endearments to make to a long-lost mother.

The silence was breathtaking, pierced only by the sound of birds and the rustling of leaves. Somewhere further into the orchard came the smell of woodsmoke.

Frances stared at her hands whilst analysing her thoughts before raising her eyes and meeting a pair just like her own. Mary Baker. This woman was Mary Baker. Her mother.

She had the urge to throw her arms around her, but something held her back. She knew that she should, but spontaneity was difficult to come by. They were strangers. Total strangers. But as for the man who had fathered her... it was much harder to digest.

'And Izzy knew?' Frances asked.

Mary nodded. 'Yes.'

It certainly explained the reason Izzy had refused to go to her father's funeral, thought Frances. Deborah had hinted that he was angry at her adopting a 'guttersnipe' from the workhouse. It seemed he'd had more than one reason for being so. He'd known the child was his.

'You were fourteen when you began work in the Brakespeare household?' Repeating the same thing helped Frances digest the situation.

'Yes. I was an innocent. I knew nothing. I didn't know what he was doing. You must believe me and then, once he learned that I was in the family way, I was forced to give you up and told that the workhouse would place you with a foster family in the country. I was also given money for passage to Australia. He wanted me out of the way, so his reputation was not sullied by my wanton behaviour. Wanton!' Tears spilled from Mary's eyes running down her cheeks and soaking the handkerchief Frances had given her. 'It wasn't until very much later that I learned this was not so. That you'd been left at the workhouse until Miss Isabelle had taken you from there, for which I bless her very much indeed.'

Mary, her mother, wouldn't be the first young woman to be ignorant of the sexual act. The fact had been the cornerstone of Marie Stopes' book, *Married Love*. Imagine, she thought, getting married without having knowledge of sexual intimacy, to the extent that some women had been unaware of where babies came from.

Whilst giving Mary a moment to wipe at her eyes and blow her nose, Frances tried to imagine what life had been like for a young girl, pregnant by her older employer and given money and references on the understanding she journeyed to the other side of the world, away from family and familiar surroundings, leaving her baby behind.

'He did that to you. Had his pleasure then sent you away.' It was hard for Frances to control her anger.

'I'm glad Miss Isabelle adopted you. I'm glad she gave you opportunities the likes of me can only dream of. You sound as though you've had a happy life,' Mary said suddenly.

Sniffing and dabbing at her nose, Mary's gaze once again fixed on Frances in a caring almost awestruck way. Their eyes, mutually grey, held the truth that existed between them.

It should have been Mary to put it into words, but instead Frances had to speak it. Having empathy with a patient was a fundamental skill not taught on the medical syllabus, yet was very important. It was something Frances regarded as imperative and perhaps because it was part of her character, she felt a strong need to express what was in her heart, to state what was an incontrovertible truth. 'You're my mother.' The words came out softly, with a hint of disbelief, with surprise and with kindness.

Mary nodded through tears that dripped from the end of her nose and chin, soaked her cheeks and dropped onto her bodice.

'You came looking for me and for that I'm extremely grateful.'

Again, a series of nods. More tears squeezed from the corners of her eyes.

There was so much Frances wanted to know, including how Mary had managed to find her. Mary was in no fit state to explain just yet, but Frances wished to know how she had found her, how Izzy had known that Mary gave birth in the workhouse. How had she known which baby to choose.

So many questions, which in turn gave rise to answers she badly needed.

Izzy having given birth to an illegitimate child explained the much earlier birth certificate, the one that had confused her, made her think a mistake had been made and that the scribbled date, the ink light blue and very faded, had been difficult to decipher. She'd thought it had said 1899, though could as easily have said 1879 – twenty years before when Izzy had been only fourteen or fifteen years old. The truth was too terrible to face but undeniable.

Pulling herself together wasn't easy, but her professional side won through. A serene expression on her face, Frances smiled and said, 'You went back to the workhouse to search for me.'

Mary looked guiltily away. 'Not at first.' Her voice was small and apologetic. 'As I've already said, I was paid to go to Australia. It's a long way. I got married over there, but when he died, I was all alone in the world. That was when I made up my mind to come back to England and find you. I didn't know where to begin, but decided it had to be the workhouse where you were born, so I got a job there because I wanted to know.' Her brow furrowed at the memory. 'A terrible place. The people that run it don't believe in "coddling" babies. That's what they called it. Coddling!' Mary shook her head sadly. 'Those poor little mites.'

Every little bit of her description turned Frances's blood to ice. Descriptions of the workhouse were interspersed with some of Australia, also of working in the Brakespeare household.

'Did Beatrice know about your situation?'

The woman she now knew as her mother shrugged. 'If she did, she would have believed anything her father told her. She doted on him; wouldn't hear a word said against him.'

It all seemed outrageous and unbelievable, but somehow Frances did believe simply because she'd known and loved Izzy. Izzy and her friends. She smiled at the thought of women who resembled men in their mannerisms, men who wore silk scarves, sported highly plucked eyebrows and made expressive movements with their hands. All wonderful characters.

She forced herself to come back down to earth and fix on the facts Mary had presented to her. 'Do you know for sure? Did you check the records? There couldn't be any mistake, could there?'

Mary nodded again, licking the dryness from her lips as she wrested with the past and the stupendous news she'd gleaned from the workhouse records. 'Yes. It was all there. Miss Isabelle's name was there as having adopted my baby.' Her eyes opened wide in response to the guilt that flooded over her. 'I meant to go back for you, honest I did.'

For a moment Frances felt difficulty in drawing breath. There was a tightness in her breast. This woman was her mother. Was it true? She knew it was. Eyes as grey as her own looked at her now.

She wanted to throw her arms around her. It would be the right thing to do. But she wasn't sure how.

'I've known other mothers with no option but to give their babies away. It must have been terrible for you.'

Her eyes brimmed with tears as she regarded Mary Devonshire who had once been Mary Baker.

A weak smile came to her mother's face. 'I was one of the lucky ones, or rather you were, being brought up by someone who loved you. I'm grateful for that. And proud. So proud of you being a doctor.'

Frances reached across cautiously and clutched the fine fingers, the cool white hand that had once perhaps caressed her head, the head of a baby she was forced to give away.

'Who else knew you were my mother?'

'The dark-haired lady. Miss Isabelle's friend. Miss Goldsmith.'

Frances winced to think that Deborah had known. She'd never uttered a word.

'It seems from what you say that Mr Brakespeare had a reputation for fawning over young women. Is that so?'

'Yes. You do believe me, don't you?'

'Yes. I do.' Both before and after she'd answered, Frances was recalling in her medical capacity several young girls she'd come across who had been abused by older men. There was a trade in London and probably a lot of other places for young girls. Born into poverty there had even been incidents of girls being sold into prostitution. 'You're not the first domestic servant to experience such treatment,' she said softly.

Mary lay a hand on her chest, a beatific expression on her lined face. 'You cannot imagine how wonderful it is to be sitting here with you. It's a dream I've cherished for so many years. So, so, many years.'

Her expression and sentiment gladdened Frances's heart,

though for all that she couldn't yet get used to calling Mary Devonshire 'mother'. Deep down, she knew Mary was waiting to hear the word, but it just wouldn't come, jarring in her throat as though choking on a piece of gristle from a tough piece of meat.

Perhaps Mary sensed some way she might break through the barrier that remained between them. Or perhaps she'd fully intended to present the information anyway. Flicking the clasp on her bag, she delved in and brought out a piece of paper. 'This,' she said, her voice slightly breathless, 'is a copy of the bill paid for by Mr Brakespeare. I took it from the workhouse records. And this,' she said, taking out another piece, 'is the letter he wrote containing the instructions regarding what he wanted done with you and the arrangements he'd made for me to go to Australia. They didn't even give me time to say goodbye. Three days after your birth, two people came to escort me to the ship. They even stood at the bottom of the gangway until it pulled away from the harbour just in case I jumped ship.' Mary, her mother, covered her face as the memory hit her. 'I considered throwing myself over the side, but then realised that's what they wanted me to do.'

Her eyes were big with emotion when she came from behind her hands.

'Please read them,' she said, pointing at the two pieces of paper.

Frances bent her head to read the bill. It accounted for payments to the workhouse for extra services. The second piece of paper detailed those extra services as escorting one Mary Baker to Southampton Docks and ensuring the ship had left the harbour before considering their mission accomplished.

How could anyone be so cruel as to separate a mother from her child to avoid a scandal was callous.

Just to prove she had not misread either missive, Frances read through them again.

'This is my testament.' Mary passed her a third piece of paper. 'I swore it in front of a lawyer who was also a justice of the peace. I worked as his housekeeper for a while, and we became good friends. After I told him my story, he suggested I write a statement of facts – purely for future reference – if I should ever find you.' A sudden smile lit up her face. 'And I did. I found you at last.'

Heart pounding, Frances read that too. Her eyes glittered at the thought of what she would do with it. Her inclination was to travel to London and confront Beatrice Trinder. Gleefully, she imagined a face like thunder as the realisation hit her that her attempt to diminish another human being had failed.

Up until now Frances had managed to control herself, to hold back the anger and angst that was bound to come with a realisation like this. But now she spat out what she was feeling, her eyes dark with contempt. 'That man was a monster.'

She meant what she said. He'd preyed on young girls like Mary with no family to protect them, nowhere to run to and nothing to live on should they lose their job and the attic room at the top of the house. That was where the lowest domestic servants slept, up under the eaves on a cast-iron bed with meagre comforts, but still better than the alternative.

Their embrace came without force and with the gentleness of a mother for a child, a young child for a mother who has been missed and must be clung to.

'You must come and live with me in the coach house,' said Frances. Her mother's frame was thin and bony beneath her fingers. 'I could keep an eye on that cough of yours.'

'It's a bit better now. I think I'm getting better.'

Frances pulled her closer so she couldn't see her sad expression. She knew Mary Devonshire was lying. Her cough would never get better.

17

Mary Devonshire did agree to move into the coach house with Frances, though not until after the garden party taking place at Orchard Manor House.

'I've promised to help with the catering.'

Frances said that she understood.

The garden party promised to be a jolly affair. The weather had improved, and the party was to take place on the first Saturday in June.

She had no intention of telling anyone about Mary Devonshire being her mother. It was a private matter; one she would only share with Gregory and then in private.

Gregory was deadheading flowers and pruning roses when she told him she needed his advice and some soothing words to make her feel better.

At first, he smiled, then on seeing the expression on her face, threw aside the secateurs and took off his gardening gloves. 'I'm all ears.'

'Are you sure you can spare the time?'

'Gardening helps me compose the Sunday sermon. I've been

out here all morning. My sojourn amongst the roses is at an end. They were getting fed up with me droning on anyway.'

'I've heard some news that's shocked me to the core.'

He asked her if she wanted to talk it over inside where they'd be more comfortable.

'No. I prefer being out here,' she said, glad to drink in the cool breeze and have it temper her raging thoughts.

'Are you sure?' He waved at the job in hand. 'It's not entirely a chance to practise my sermon. The fact is, it's usually old Mr Wilkins job to do this, but his hip's playing up. He ordered me to do it, and when Mr Wilkins gives an order, it pays to obey.' His grin widened but was at odds with the questioning look in his eyes. Gregory, bless him, was a perceptive man. He could read people.

Frances heaved a sigh.

Gregory noticed. 'That does sound serious. Have you heard more from the Harpy in London?'

'No. Not from Beatrice. This person is far more important.'

She sighed again, at the same time thinking she would be doing quite a lot of sighing in the coming days, a time of adjustment to the news she'd received.

Gregory's eyes fixed on her before throwing down the secateurs. The gardening gloves followed. 'As one of my most valued parishioners, I need to give you my undivided attention. Let us repair to the rose garden.'

She let him take her hand and guide her to a rustic bench beneath an apple tree.

'Now,' he said, sitting her down, his blue eyes fixed on her grey ones. 'You have my full attention.'

A few seconds ticked by before she raised her eyes and began to tell him about Mary Baker, about being Izzy's half-sister, about the circumstances of her conception and birth. It came with a rush of unbridled tears.

'That's Mary who works as a laundress for her ladyship?'

She nodded, her eyes downcast, her fingers inadvertently squeezing his as she fought to come to terms with what she'd learned.

'Everything confirms that she is my natural mother, but it's come as such a shock. I'm unsure how to behave, how our relationship will develop and what the future might hold.'

Gregory looked into the face of the woman he loved, who he hoped sometime soon to make his wife – when he could tie her down, that was. He knew very well he had to accept her dedication to her profession. 'Has it occurred to you that she might be feeling the same? She abandoned her baby to the workhouse and never went back to claim her. Can you imagine how guilty she's feeling, living with that guilt for all these years. She gave away a baby who is now a grown woman. She'll have difficulty adjusting just as you will.'

Gregory's words rang like Sunday bells across the meadow, crisp and clear, urging the faithful to abandon toil and gather for worship. Only she wasn't going to worship. All she wanted to do was cope, adjust and perhaps in time accept this sudden intrusion into her life with grace and love.

'So, I just carry on with my life?'

He enveloped both of her hands in his. 'It's all you can do. It's all any of us can do. Does anyone else know?'

She shook her head. 'Not here in Norton Dene.'

'Do you mind them knowing?'

'I'm not sure.'

'Have you asked her that?'

She shook her head. 'No.'

He raised her hands to his mouth and one by one began to kiss all ten fingers and thumbs. 'Then perhaps you should.'

Frances sighed. 'I have so much to do. I've been asked to write a paper for the Women's Association of Obstetricians on family planning. They've been a long time coming round to the idea of interception methods of contraception... diaphragms and Dutch caps,' she said in response to the slightly puzzled uplifting of one eyebrow. 'I must do it. It's terribly important.'

Gregory scratched his chin thoughtfully. 'I know she's not a hospital employee, but perhaps you can invite her to the garden party.'

'My...' She paused. It was still difficult to use the name mother. 'She's been asked to help with the catering. I think she's quite looking forward to it. I've asked her to move into the coach house with me once that's over. You don't mind, do you? After all, the coach house rightly belongs to the vicarage.'

'Of course I don't mind.'

'That's good.' She immediately brightened. 'One other thing.'

Less brightly, she told him about the identity of her father.

'I cannot warm to the fact that Mr Brakespeare was my father. What I do warm to is the fact that it means Izzy was my half-sister.'

'Good Lord!' Gregory exclaimed. 'Does this also mean that the dreadful Beatrice is also your half-sister?'

'Yes.'

'Well that certainly puts a new slant on things.'

Their eyes met in mutual understanding.

'It explains a lot.'

'It certainly does.'

Frances looked down at his strong hands clasped so firmly over hers. Gregory had a sense of humour capable of breaking through to the grumpiest parishioner. He was also clear thinking, persuasive and one had to say wise.

'It's come as a bit of a surprise. Pace yourself. She'll be doing the same. It's a milestone in both your lives.'

She looked beyond him at the willow tree at the side of the coach house, which appeared to be nodding in agreement and followed its lead. 'Yes. I agree.'

She continued to watch the fragile branches, knowing that Gregory was watching her. Wondering.

'What will you do now?'

'I was going to post the evidence she gave me to my solicitor, but I've changed my mind. I think I should present these items face to face.'

'Is that the only reason?'

When she didn't answer, Gregory reached for her, his hands seeking hers and clutching them close to his heart.

'Post them.'

Her eyelids flickered. 'I think I should go.'

'You don't need to. You know you don't.'

'But...'

'What would be gained by seeing Izzy's sister and crowing out your victory. Leave her to fume and reflect. Whatever else went on in that house, it seems she was the neglected one. Oh, I know,' he said as she countered that her mother, Mary Baker – now Devonshire – had been the abused one. 'But think about it. Beatrice wasn't her father's favourite daughter. She was bereft of affection. Imagine how that is for a child. Leave it. Give the evidence to Gunther. Let the solicitors battle it out. It's going to come as shock to her that you're her half-sister and have every right to the Brakespeare name without rubbing it in. Anger eats at the soul, and you know me, I'm the man whose business is knowing about souls.'

'My soul wants to confront Beatrice on the doorstep and crow that I'm entitled to the Brakespeare name, but you're right. However, there is one other person I need to speak to.' Her expression darkened. 'Deborah knew more about the circumstances of my birth but never told me.'

'Perhaps Izzy made her promise to keep the secret.'

'Perhaps that might have been true whilst she was still alive, but not after she'd died. Surely, she should have told me.'

'Or seeing you happy, she might have thought it best to let sleeping dogs lie.'

Frances shrugged. 'Perhaps. I will write to Deborah, tell her the matter of my name appears resolved and about my natural mother turning up after all these years. Let's see where we go from there. Mary... my mother... said that it was Deborah who told her that I was in Somerset. I wonder why she didn't tell me that either.' She sighed. 'It's been quite a day.'

'I'll walk with you and make sure you get safely home.'

The coach house was almost next door. The walking her home had become their shared joke, but right now she was too distracted even to smile.

The sun shone a golden glow over the coach house interior, warming the old plasterwork and throwing patches of gold over the flagstones.

Gregory kissed her very gently, stroked her hair and told her all would be well. One more hug at the front door, another kiss and she was finally alone.

Once dusk had fallen, Frances lit the oil lamp, took out pen and paper and wrote to Deborah.

Dear Debs,

My world has become quite surreal. Or at least the events in it have become strange. I kept seeing a new arrival in town who seemed to be seeking me out but hesitated to confront me. She initially introduced herself as Mrs Devonshire. I now know her as Mary Baker, my mother.

She mentioned that it was you who gave her my present whereabouts and the name I go under. She gave me much more information which makes me wonder that there are sections of Izzy's life that I never knew. I also understand from her that you knew of her existence. Having been Izzy's long-time friend, I am assuming you might be able to fill in the gaps in my knowledge.

Do get in touch. I'm not so much in a state of shock but a little disorientated and surprised that you never mentioned having known Mary Baker – my mother. I feel there are circles that need closing, outlines that need filling in with some colour. I need to speak to someone who can finish that circle and fill in those colours. I understand that that someone is you.

With kind regards, Frances.

18

Before leaving the hospital for one of her days at Orchard Manor House, Frances called Lucy into her office.

It surprised Lucy to see her looking a little more nervous than usual.

'Seeing as you're going to the manor house today, I wondered if I could prevail on you to check the laundress, Mrs Devonshire. She has a terrible hacking cough and I fear it's quite serious. Do you think you can do that?'

'Of course I can.'

'And the boy, Billy Noakes. I take it he's settled in well?'

'Very well. He's put on some weight, thanks to Mrs Fiske and Mrs Devonshire. Neither of them would have it any other way, though Mrs Fiske makes sure there's always leftovers from upstairs in the laundry room. There's usually pie and cakes besides three meals a day. They all make the most of it and Billy Noakes being a growing boy...'

A look of what seemed to Lucy to be contentment came to Doctor Brakespeare's face.

Lucy assured her that she would check on both.

'Has Mrs Devonshire allowed you to examine her, Doctor?'

The doctor looked a bit vague before she answered.

'I don't think she's a well woman. Let's leave it at that, shall we? And Lucy...'

Lucy had turned to go but stopped at the door. 'Yes, Doctor.'

Frances smiled. 'I'm looking forward to the garden party. I think everyone is.'

'Then with the help of The Honourable Devlin Compton-Dixon, I will endeavour to organise a day to remember.'

'I'm sure you will.'

* * *

Lucy and Devlin had passed on their lists for items to be sourced and orders for food and drink to the relevant people and shops.

'Finito!' declared Devlin. 'All paperwork is finished for the day – unless I've missed something.'

'We're done.'

'Work is over. Pleasure to come. Now where shall we walk today?'

It pleased Lucy to hear Devlin speak enthusiastically about going out, a far cry from those early days of their acquaintance when he'd not ventured further than the lawn.

'As far as you like, but...' She hesitated. Doctor Frances had asked her to call in on Billy, and to check on Mrs Devonshire. Bearing in mind her bad chest, she believed Mrs Devonshire to be the priority. She explained this to Devlin.

'And from there?'

'Let's not plan,' returned Lucy. She dearly wanted Devlin to venture out more but wished it to be spontaneous on his part, so it would not seem to be remedial. He was gradually getting over his mental drawbacks, but she would not push him. In a discus-

sion with Frances, they had both agreed to let time heal and
recovery thus take its course. Helping to organise the garden party
was a big step in that direction. 'Let's take the day as it comes,
although we could call in on the gardener. He's expecting a visit
from Ma Skittings, my sister's mother-in-law.'

'I've heard of her,' he said with a laugh. 'That fool Simon
Grainger put it about that she was a witch. Grimes was agog when
he told me about it.'

'Methinks your old retainer, Mr Grimes, is worse than any of
the townswomen when it comes to gossip! I can assure you Ma
Skittings is a good soul. She keeps bees and provides the honey
you partake for breakfast. But she is *not* a witch.'

'I don't doubt it, but you have to admit it does make Norton
Dene seem a little less dull than it actually is.'

Lucy laughed. 'She's a healer in the old-fashioned sense. She's
bringing the gardener some embrocation for his lumbago. He'll
no doubt put the kettle on for her and they'll have a chinwag
about old times when they were young and more agile than they
are now. Not that either of them is doing badly for their age.'

Their hearty mood continued as they ventured down the back
stairs to take them past the laundry and out of the back door into
that part of the garden mostly frequented by servants. It was
where the washing was dried and where the path ran across the
expanse of grass to the door to the walled garden.

Devlin used his walking stick to tap his way down. He told her
to go carefully. 'From memory, I believe this staircase is ill lit.'

She confirmed that it was.

'Though you manage very well coming down them.'

'It's the sticks,' he said, waving one of them in the air. 'I used to
ski, and the sticks are very like that. I was a good skier.'

'Do you recall the gardener's shed where the gardener and Ma
Skittings will be supping tea?'

'Yes, indeed! My main memory is the smell of pipe tobacco and pear drops. The gardener of my youth smoked black navy shag tobacco. His wife found the smell of it on his breath disgusting. The pear drops were by way of disguise. He let me dip into the bag and eat a few.'

'I wouldn't have thought it would be that noticeable to the gardener's wife unless they were kissing.'

Devlin laughed. 'I wouldn't be surprised if they kissed quite a lot – if the ten children they had are anything to go by.'

At the very time when they were planning their walk in Devlin's suite of rooms and before they'd ventured down the steps, Billy Noakes was out back turning the handle of the mangle. He enjoyed seeing the water cascading from the sheets and collecting in the zinc bath placed beneath the heavy rollers. When first given this task, he'd been the one turning the handle whilst somebody else – Mrs Devonshire or Mrs Fiske – fed the rollers with carefully folded laundry. He'd been so good at it – possibly because he enjoyed it – that they left him to carry out both aspects of the chore.

So here he was, out here all by himself whilst the two women ate some lunch, after which Mrs Fiske had stated her intention to call in at Orchard Farm for a jug of milk and Mrs Devonshire had made her way home.

Nobody here, all by himself, was the best thing to be. He loved this place and enjoyed helping in both the laundry and garden, not just the jobs themselves but because he enjoyed solitude.

There was a gate between this area where sheets were hung to dry and the walled garden, on the far side of which was another gate leading into the fields. The track through the fields terminated in town, not far from where ordinary folk lived. Sheets billowed on the washing line in a fresh breeze, cracking at times like a shotgun going off.

Engrossed in his work, Billy gave no heed to the squealing of the back gate as it was pushed open. Neither did he notice a figure in dark corduroy trousers, garishly embroidered waistcoat and grey wool shirt zigzagging between the lines of washing.

The boatman, Greville Matthews, was on a mission, driven by a vitriolic anger that could only be placated with a show of brutality. Billy Noakes had played him for a fool. At first, he'd believed him drowned, but canals were shallow, and bodies usually floated on the surface. Billy's never did.

He might never have known his whereabouts if he hadn't dropped in at The Goose and Gander, a scruffy pub on the edge of town where he flogged pilfered items from his loads or vegetables and chickens stolen from canalside farms. Seeing as Billy had fallen into the canal just a few miles away, he'd pretended to be a concerned father looking for his son. His initial plan had been to put on an act, to appear so distraught that more than one pub patron would stand him a pint of cider. As it turned out, he'd got more from his playacting than he'd bargained for. The landlady had told him about the boy being found out back among the beer barrels and taken to the hospital.

He'd used the same tactics at the hospital as he had at the pub, pretending to be out of his mind with worry as to where his son could have got to. A young nurse had taken pity on him and told him she believed the boy was employed in the laundry room at the back of the manor house. She'd even told him how to get there.

Once he had the information, he'd legged it quickly before anyone more senior could ask him awkward questions that he didn't want to answer.

He eyed the happy little figure who was now whistling as he worked, feeding clean laundry through the thick rubber rollers. The fact that Billy was whistling conveyed that he was happy, and Greville much resented the fact.

In a few strides he was through the forest of drying sheets. A heavy hand landed on Billy's shoulder, gripped, hard then banged him against the wall of the building. 'Gotcha!' he snarled.

Billy's jaw dropped. Clawlike, Greville's hands were tight around his neck, making it hard to breathe, let alone speak. Billy felt as though his eyes were bursting out of his head.

'Right. I paid for you, so you're coming with me.'

Billy struggled, enough to say, 'No. I work here.'

Greville slapped the side of Billy's head so hard he cracked it against the wall.

'Like it here, do ya,' rasped Greville, his face full of menacing intent.

'Yes,' Billy managed to say despite the blood trickling from the wound in his head and his fear, his terrible fear, that Greville would kill him.

Greville glanced at the mangle. 'You like that thing, do ya? Women's work?'

Billy decided that whatever he said Greville would twist it or lash out again with his hand, his fist or his boot. Billy didn't want to be on the receiving end of any of it, so he kept quiet, waiting for the first chance to escape.

Greville took a more lingering look at the mangle. 'Dangerous things them rollers,' he said, his eyes sliding sidelong, a cruel twist to his lips. 'You can get yer fingers caught in them. Don't 'alf 'urt, it does. Caught yours in there so far, 'ave ya?'

It felt to Billy as though his stomach was sinking to his knees. He kept quiet, knowing full well that whatever he said Greville would delight in proving his point.

'Time you did,' said Greville, the delight of inflicting pain ingrained in his soul and showing in his cruel expression.

Holding Billy's fingers in a vice-like grip in one hand, Greville began to guide them towards the two rollers. His other hand reached for the handle.

The mangle was big, the rollers ten inches in diameter. Billy watched in horror as his fingertips were forced into the crease between the two rollers. Greville gained a good grip before turning the handle. Billy screamed.

A horrified Lucy saw what was going on and Devlin heard the scream. His voice rang out, a voice of authority that had once rang out over the trenches of Northern France.

'What's going on here?'

Having no idea that the person addressing him was blind, Greville Matthews let Billy's hand drop. The boy immediately hugged his tender fingertips to his chest whilst his tormentor held firmly onto his shirt collar.

'Let go of the boy this minute,' demanded Lucy. She whispered an aside to Devlin: 'The boy's Billy Noakes. He works in the laundry but was in the hospital. Doctor suspected he'd been beaten and starved. I'm guessing this is the man responsible.'

'The boy belongs to me,' declared Greville Matthews. 'I bought 'im out of the workhouse. Gave 'im an apprenticeship, I did, not that I got much thanks for that. Ran away 'e did. Absconded.' He emphasised the last word as though he'd only just discovered it and it had somehow upped his position in the world.

Devlin looked every inch the military man he'd once been, and his voice radiated with the confidence of someone used to giving orders. 'No civilised person should own another,' he barked and waved one of his sticks.

Not aware that he was blind, the sight of the waving stick must have made Matthews think twice.

Even Lucy jumped but didn't take her eyes off this wild-looking man.

'Let the boy go,' she shouted. 'Let the boy go now.'

She knew the man wasn't likely to do so, but her outburst would give Devlin some idea of a situation he could not see. What he was able to do about it was another matter. And she didn't want him hurt.

'And what if I don't,' Greville snarled, his lips constantly moving, like a dog that's baring its teeth, ready to bite.

'Then we call the police.'

Devlin maintained a cool confidence that Lucy had never been privy to up until now. She instantly imagined him in command of a battalion, living with the fear of whether he would live to see another dawn following an enemy barrage. That's how he would have felt, she supposed. Vulnerable but brave.

Greville looked more uncertain than he had done. His eyes stayed fixed on Devlin. No doubt he saw the scar on his face, but from the slight distance between them, he had not discerned that Devlin was blind.

Billy took full advantage of his loosened grip and began backing off towards the gardener's shed.

Devlin shouted at Greville once more. 'My mother, Lady Compton-Dixon, is a magistrate. Be aware, sir, that when you stand before her in court accused of grievous bodily harm – as believe me you will be charged for what you did – she will not be lenient. Now, are you clearing off or do I telephone for the police?'

Judging from his expression, Greville was in two minds about what to do next. The threat of being arrested and spending time in prison did not sit well in his piggy eyes or on his swarthy complexion. Perhaps he might have stood his ground and gone after Billy if the lad himself had not reappeared accompanied by the gardener and Ma Skittings.

'Now what's going on 'ere,' declared Ma Skittings, her ample fists fixed on her equally ample hips, striding over like a prize fighter coming out of her corner at the sound of the bell.

Lucy explained. 'I think I mentioned Billy to you, Ma. He was admitted to the hospital half-starved, with a back scarred with whipping and bruises. This man was responsible for his ill use and now he's here demanding the boy goes with him. We caught him, Devlin and I, threatening to feed his fingers into the mangle.'

Greville Matthews, confronted with more than one person to protect the boy, took on a cocky stance and sneeringly said, 'And who's goin' to stop me?'

'I am.'

He didn't see the blow coming. It helped that he'd backed off from the powerful presence of Ma Skittings, who was quite capable of pushing him to kingdom come all by herself.

Devlin, his sense of hearing so acute he could measure distance with it, sensed when someone or something was close enough to lash out at, he did so now. There was a loud crack as his walking stick struck Matthews on one side of the head, powerful enough to send him flying.

He lay sprawling on the ground, a pool of blood spreading around his head.

'Blimey,' said Jack the gardener, scratching beneath the peak of his cap whilst his eyes glowed with admiration. 'You certainly gave 'im a good 'un, Mr Devlin,' he chuckled.

'Is he dead?' He said it quite evenly, as though not caring one way or the other.

Lucy checked. 'No.'

'Deserves to be,' added Ma Skittings, her large shadow falling over the supine man like a heavy blanket.

Young Billy just stared before suddenly jettisoning his shyness in the company of toffs – people he wasn't used to – and saying, 'Blimey. You certainly hit him a real good one, sir.'

A short discussion followed as to whether they should let him go once he'd come round. Devlin stepped in and gave orders for the police to be called.

'The man deserves to be in prison for what he did to this boy. Tell them to come quickly and take him away.'

The gardener looked a bit worried. 'Begging your pardon, sir, but won't they hold you responsible for cracking his skull? We don't want you going to prison, do we, sir.'

Lucy smiled. She somehow knew what Devlin's response would be.

'It was an accident. I'm blind, was told of what was going on and, fearing I would be attacked, began waving my walking stick in self-defence. It accidentally landed on his skull. Couldn't be helped, old man.'

'No, it could not,' whispered Lucy. 'I'm witness to that. You're a brave man, Devlin Compton-Dixon.'

They didn't wait for the stunned man to come round or for the police to collect him.

They left Ma Skittings with a protective arm around Billy's shoulders. His eyes were wide with delight to see his old master prone on the ground with Jack the gardener standing over him, a garden hoe raised over his head, ready to strike another blow if need be.

'Take my hand,' Devlin said as they made their way into the walled garden, heading for the path through the fields beyond.

'In case you slip?'

'In case you do,' he replied.

A sunny expression lit his face as she took his hand. Nothing to do with the sun in the sky but with what had just happened.

He had made an impression on the world – certainly on the head of the ignorant man who had treated young Billy so cruelly.

'You're a wonderful woman, Nurse Lucy Daniels. The most wonderful I've ever met. Note that I cannot say you are the most beautiful woman I've ever seen, not in the present. But I remember what you looked like as a child, and just by the sound of your voice, your fragrant smell and the softness of your presence, I know that you are.'

Still holding hands, they came to a halt at the stile at the edge of the field where nature took its course.

Lucy felt his breath falling over her lips. Then his mouth was on hers, gently at first, then with more vigour, like a thirsty man unable to quench his thirst. Both breath and lips tasted sweet and soft. She hung onto him, one hand still clasping his, the other around his neck.

The kiss ended, leaving Lucy feeling bereft, as though it was natural for their lips to be forever conjoined.

'I've been longing so much to do that.' His voice and breath were soft against her ear.

'I've been longing for you to do so,' she replied.

'Remember that night we danced on the wet grass?' he asked her.

'Yes. And we've been dancing around each other ever since.'

He laughed. 'I suppose we have. Why was that, do you think?'

'Strangers in the night – but that was then, and this is now.'

'Ah yes.'

As if to confirm it, he kissed her again before, still holding hands, they made their way into the middle of the field and sank into the long grass. Fragile as it was, the grass formed a barrier against the world. One thing led to another, a loosening of clothes followed by their removal, fevered movements dictated by a hunger they both felt. Her nipples hardened beneath his gentle caress, their loins were hot for each other, as belly against belly, they fulfilled what their bodies had lusted after for days, weeks, months. They were together, lost in each other and having faith in whatever the future might hold.

* * *

Later that evening as the sun was setting over the roofs of the town, Lucy met Harry Bascombe. He was waiting for her at the end of the street wearing his best suit, a bowler hat and carrying a bunch of flowers.

'Good evening, Lucy. I brought these for you.'

She hesitated before taking the flowers, then said, 'You really shouldn't have.'

'A chap should buy flowers for his lady friend.'

The words 'lady friend' would be considered old-fashioned by other young men. However, she was glad he referred to her as such. It gave her the opening to state exactly how things were between them. The blush of the day remained in her cheeks. Her breasts tingled with the memory of Devlin's caresses and there was an ache between her legs that was already diminishing. She wanted that experience again, but only with one man and poor Harry wasn't it.

'From one friend to another,' she said cheerfully.

'Oh,' he said with a bashful smile and shake of his head. 'I think we're more than friends. I've talked it over with Mother and she thinks getting engaged in a year's time would be an acceptable arrangement and getting married three years after that. Early days, so no need to make firm plans just yet.'

Feeling slightly guilty, Lucy handed him back the flowers. 'I prefer us to stay as friends, Harry. Just friends.'

His features drooped in folds like those of a bloodhound. He was disappointed. She could see that. However, after her time with Devlin today, she knew her mind. Harry would never be part of her future, but she sincerely hoped that Devlin would.

'But I want us to get married.' He sounded quite surprised.

'I don't want to marry you, Harry. But we can remain friends,' she added brightly, hoping that would be enough to placate his wounded pride.

Harry's normally bland expression turned to thunder. 'You ungrateful harlot!'

Lucy's jaw dropped.

He threw aside the bunch of flowers. 'I hope you become an old maid,' he shouted over his shoulder as he stormed off.

Lucy stood there for a while. Some girls would be thrilled to receive a proposal of marriage and accept without a second thought. Lucy was not thrilled. She knew today that she could never marry someone she didn't love, and she didn't love Harry. She loved Devlin and wished with all her heart that their first tryst would not be their last.

19

It was some days later that Frances received a phone call from Gunther Seeberger confirming that the 'other party' had dropped their action.

Frances breathed a sigh of relief. 'That is good news, though not entirely unexpected. After all, her father was my father, and thanks to my natural mother's testimony, she cannot refute that.'

Gunther cleared his throat before saying, 'Mrs Trinder's loyalty to her father had everything to do with it and so did what she regarded as familial reputation. I'm guessing she was horrified at the thought of hearing her father's good name dragged through the courts and perhaps making newspaper headlines.'

'The power of the press,' Frances said thoughtfully. She felt no sympathy for her half-sister whatsoever. She was mean-spirited, vindictive – completely the opposite to Izzy, a fighter for the underdog and full of love for both herself and her friends.

'Indeed. The matter is at an end. You will receive my bill in the post. Good day, Doctor. It's been a pleasure acting for you.'

'I will use you again should I need to,' she told him.

He thanked her before breaking the connection.

Her experience with this matter somewhat prepared her for a local reporter turning up at the hospital requesting to write a piece regarding the new clinic.

He made himself comfortable in the confines of her office, where she offered him tea and biscuits. She was amiable but all the time on alert. News should be reported accurately, and she had heard of things being misconstrued. So it was that with sharpened wits, she sat across from Mr Nicholas Fox, reporter for the *Norton Dene Herald*. Would his pen depict outraged public opinion or was he enlightened in modern thinking and would depict her clinic with glowing admiration? She obviously wished for the latter.

About thirty years of age, too young to have fought in the war, he had the bright-eyed look of a man keen to make his mark in the world. His hair was parted in the middle and the length at the nape of his neck was perhaps a little too long for traditional tastes. It was a bit foppish, almost girlish.

He asked her at first about her qualifications. She answered honestly and he seemed impressed.

'And when did you come here to live in Norton Dene.'

'Spring, 1930.'

'Quite a memorable day,' he said, taking a sip of tea as he awaited her response, his pen poised in his right hand for further action. 'What do you remember most about it?'

His expression never changed. He kept smiling as though implying that he was of a kindly nature and would like to be her friend. She knew better than that and was on her guard.

She responded that it had indeed been a memorable day. 'Before I had chance to enter the hospital, an accident had taken place at the quarry. I spent that first day dealing with casualties and taking the worst injured of them to Bristol in my car.'

His pen scampered across the page in his urgency to get every detail down.

She outlined for him how she'd reorganised a few things at the hospital which had led to them being able to house more patients. 'And we have a new district nurse to visit those who find it difficult to travel.'

'Very commendable,' he said after jotting that down. 'Now,' he continued, shifting in his chair before sitting up straight and asking the question she knew he would. 'How about this clinic you've set up. Can you tell me something about it?'

'The mother and baby clinic. Yes. Of course.'

She went on to describe its setting up and its merits in great detail. At first, he appeared satisfied. Perhaps he wouldn't go any further, though her instincts told her that he would – that he couldn't resist.

'I understand that women coming here can also obtain advice regarding family planning.'

There. It was out in the open. She had no option but to grasp the nettle and, picking her words carefully, outline the premise for controlling population.

'Too many women give birth to too many children. In the poorer areas of this country, it's not uncommon for women to have six, eight, ten and many more children. You must agree that it's a hard task to bring up so many children. Their health suffers, as does that of the mother. Planning a family with the aid of contraception can make a difference to their lives.'

'I believe Marie Stopes set up the first clinic. In London?'

Frances nodded. 'Yes. She did.'

'That was back in the twenties. Am I right?'

It shouldn't have surprised her that Mr Fox had done his research and, in all likelihood, would throw questions at her that were well founded in fact. However, such questions and the answers given would also influence the angle of his article to praise or condemn.

'You are right, though she was hardly the first to advocate the advantages of maintaining a manageable family.'

'Some people have criticised reducing families, that the Empire needs more British citizens to send out to expand empire. Spread the word, so to speak.'

Frances only just about refrained from grinding her teeth. The same argument had been thrown at Professor Marie Stopes. She'd been accused of eugenics, the erasing of the feeble-minded. It simply wasn't true. Frances gathered up all her courage to make her point.

'What's the point of bringing more children into the world if they're to die within five years of being born? As for the mothers, too many are worn out with health issues connected to child-birth. I've seen many women of thirty look as though they're fifty.' She was getting into her stride, her eyes glowing with enthusiasm for her subject, passion for her cause rising within her.

Mr Fox smiled. 'It all sounds very commendable. There are, however, many detractors as well as supporters. The Church, for instance. What do you say to them?'

Fired with zeal, she said the first thing that came into her mind, the truth she felt with such passion. 'Not all churchmen are against the concept, but too many oppose it, even from the pulpit, but there,' she said with a sardonic smile. 'They are all men.'

Mr Fox wrote it down. 'What do you say to those of a religious persuasion that the birth of children is ordained by God, not by man?'

'God doesn't have to feed and clothe them,' she said bitingly. 'And churchmen have a comfortable lifestyle which many work-ing-class men do not.'

She regretted the statement the minute it was out, but it was too late.

A few more questions, the tea finished, and Mr Fox was ready to return to the newspaper offices and type up his copy.

On the way out, he thanked her for her time. She thanked him for more than one reason. He hadn't asked her for a photograph and for that she was sincerely grateful.

* * *

Susan brought in a copy of the newspaper a day or two later. There on the third page was the article, with the headline, 'Controversial Clinic at the Orchard Cottage Hospital'.

Frances could hardly believe her eyes. 'Oh my God. Her ladyship won't like this.'

'Au contraire,' said Susan, who fancied going to France one day and was learning the language. 'She's already been on the phone whilst you were doing the ward rounds. She said to keep up the good work. Onwards and upwards and all that.'

'That's a relief.' Frances continued to read the article. At first, it listed the facts before relating the opinions of people asked about the subject. One of them was Gregory.

The vicar of St Michaels, the Reverend Gregory Sampson, when asked for church guidelines on the matter, answered that some members of the Church were presently against the control of birth by applied devices, but not all of them.

It was suddenly as if the newspaper was too heavy to hold, falling flat on her desk. Gregory had given much the same response to Mr Fox as she had. There was division in the Church but not outright condemnation. A chink of light was shining through the old dark ways of thinking. Perhaps at last a new dawn was possible.

Susan's voice broke into her thoughts. 'Your next patient is here, Doctor.'

Frances stared at the wall opposite her. 'Yes,' she said when she'd regained her self-control. 'Send her in.'

Mrs Sylvia Selwyn-Frobisher was a tall, elegant woman in her mid-thirties. Her husband was a barrister in Lincoln's Inn, London. She herself had of late been summoned to the bench, a magistrate when still relatively young. She wore a pale green outfit coupled with a cream hat with a checked bow at the side. Her face was unlined, her eyes clear and her face immaculately covered in translucent powder, her lips a deep red.

'Referring to our phone call, Mrs Selwyn-Frobisher. Is your husband in agreement with you being fitted with a contraceptive device?'

Too many women would have nervously responded that no, it was to remain a secret. Mrs Selwyn Frobisher responded that, yes, her husband was in complete agreement.

Whilst her patient prepared herself behind a folding screen, Frances sent for Sister Harrison who would assist.

'Mrs Selwyn-Frobisher is ready.'

Sister Harrison's face was inscrutable. With her usual air of efficiency, she followed Frances back into the room. Mrs Selwyn-Frobisher came out from behind the screen. Frances invited her to lie down on the examination couch, where Sister Harrison made the necessary arrangements for the procedure to begin.

'Just relax,' Frances said to her as she approached. 'You've certainly come on a nice day. It's quite beautiful out there. Summer has arrived. I believe you already have two children. Is that right?'

Their procedure was to keep the patient talking whilst they

did what they had to do in a woman's most private region. Talking helped keep women's minds off things. They hadn't needed to say very much at all in this instance. The patient had come very well informed with her husband in full agreement.

'Yes. I do. Cedric also has a child from his first marriage. His wife died in childbirth, leaving him to bring up his son alone. My husband is a reasonable man and not given to the hysterical rantings of some men. We discussed the matter of having more children in great depth, decided we'd been lucky and should be satisfied with those we have. My husband is also of the opinion that losing one wife was tragedy. Losing a second would be careless. So, we made a joint decision that we would be happy with what we have.' She turned her head slightly, winced as the appliance was pushed into place, then smiled. 'We decided not to tempt fate, which means taking advantage of modern progress.'

And that's what it's all about, thought Frances once Mrs Selwyn-Frobisher was back behind the screen getting dressed. Informed women were unafraid of the procedure, though it also helped if their husbands were also informed. *Education*, thought Frances. *It's all down to education.* Which was exactly what she was intent on providing at the family planning clinic.

Once her patient had left, device inside her and accompanying pessaries secreted in her handbag, Frances sat behind her desk and breathed a sigh of relief.

'You do know that her husband is legal advisor to the Church of England Synod,' said Sister Harrison.

Astounded, Frances flopped back in her chair, mouth hanging open. 'No. Well, that's a result.'

She was unaccustomed to seeing humour on Sister Harrison's face, but she saw it now when she said, 'It's always an advantage to have God on your side.'

Frances burst out laughing. 'God moves in mysterious ways. Thank goodness.'

20

Rummaging through the piles of books, correspondence and Izzy's other things was a diversion, an aid to swallowing how Frances was dealing with Gregory's statement in the paper. He hadn't condemned the clinic, but neither had he supported it. Not that she was too worried about that right now. Mrs Selwyn-Frobisher would probably move the mountains Gregory could not – or at least her husband could.

Frances had been a bit remiss at unlocking the last items from the packing case, but the truth was they hadn't seemed to matter until now. Hopefully she'd find more from Izzy's past, pieces of a jigsaw that was now falling quickly into place following the appearance of Mary Devonshire, Frances's mother.

She found yet another journal detailing her life, from when she'd first been adopted. The details inside were mundane, references to how well the new baby was feeding, sleeping or the day when she'd taken her first step.

Seeking distraction, Frances turned her attention to the birth certificates that she'd scrutinised before. Taking the first out of its crumpled envelope, she unfolded it carefully, the paper crisp, the ink faded. The date of birth had been written in a very pale ink and the writing was thin and scrawled.

In order to see better, she took it over to the oil lamp and held it close to its glowing glass bowl. A small sob escaped from between her parted lips. Faint and scrawled as it was, there was no doubt about the date. 1879. This birth certificate was evidence that Izzy – Miss Isabelle Brakespeare – had been only fifteen years old when she'd been sent away from home to give birth.

The father was listed as unknown, the mother described as spinster and the child's name was given as Frances Isabelle Brakespeare, Izzy having swapped her own name around. As though bequeathing part of herself, thought Frances, tears stinging her eyes. The broken pieces of her life were now coming together, including Izzy's reason for adopting her.

According to Mary, the baby born to the young Izzy had died and she had transferred the name to the baby she'd rescued from the workhouse.

Looking through the rest of the paperwork might just give a clue as to whether this was true. If the child had been stillborn, there might only be a side note or perhaps nothing at all. If it had lived for even a little while, there should be a death certificate.

A thorough search brought nothing of any consequence.

After placing the birth certificate back where she'd found it, Frances took her own birth certificate out of its envelope with thoughtful reverence.

Carefully, she unfolded it and, using both hands, pressed it flat. There were similarities with the older birth certificate. A blank space where the father's name would normally be inserted. Izzy was named as the mother.

'But no father,' Izzy whispered. Poor Izzy. What happened to you? Who was he? Why did he abandon you?

The questions were heart wrenching. Placing it to one side,

Frances delved into the contents of the tea chest, taking out old bits of paper and scrutinising each before discarding it as of no use.

Exasperated, she sat back in her chair. Her eyes wandered over the paper and eventually settled on the journal. What light could it throw on her quandary? She now knew who her mother was, but what about her father?

With a heavy sigh, she picked it up, opened its front cover and slowly began to flick through the pages. They all flowed freely, except for two at the very end which were stuck together. Not only that but there was a square-shaped bulge dead centre.

Her heart quickened at the possibility that she might have found something. Or it could be nothing. Perhaps just something random Izzy had used as a bookmark and promptly forgotten. Either way, her curiosity needled her to continue.

Laying the journal flat in her lap, Frances inserted her thumbnail between the fine edges at the top of the page where the corners curled slightly. With careful precision, she slid her nail down between the gold leaf edges of the high-quality pages. They gave no resistance, parting easily and exposing the item she'd detected inside.

It was folded into four and once she'd caught sight of the name of a firm of solicitors at the top of the paper, she knew she'd found what she was looking for.

The details were there in black and white. Izzy had arranged a formal adoption. She'd also noted in the legal deed signed by both her and the solicitor who had officiated that her adopted daughter, Frances Isabelle Brakespeare, was also her half-sister because her father had raped a young house servant – Mary Baker who was now Mary Devonshire.

Her senses were reeling. But one thing above all else had come out of this. Beatrice could not prevent her from using the

Brakespeare name. Although born out of wedlock, it was hers by right.

She only wished she could have solved the mystery of who had fathered the fifteen-year-old Izzy's baby. There was a birth certificate but that was all.

Gregory was the first person with whom she wanted to share this discovery. Although she had to be up bright and early to meet the hospital committee and calm their fears about the newspaper article and local opposition to family planning, she couldn't wait.

Wet grass flicked against her legs as she ran along the narrow path to the vicarage, banged on the door and almost fell into the hallway when he opened it.

'You're never going to guess what...'

Her excitement evaporated when she saw a figure she knew well, smartly turned out in city clothes and hat at the entrance to Gregory's drawing room.

'Deborah! What are you doing here?'

Dark eyes in a lined face fluttered nervously and there was hesitance in the way she looked, not surprised, but afraid. 'I received your letter. I wanted to speak to you about it.' She looked at Gregory. 'I first wanted to know if you could cope with what I have to tell you.'

'I reminded her that you'd once served on the Western Front,' said Gregory as he pulled out a dining chair from beneath the table and invited her to sit. It was not the comfiest but was the closest.

There was no sign of the perpetual amused expression from Gregory she'd become so used to. Apprehension was one of the feelings she entertained, but also a simmering anger, born of all she had heard from Mary and found in the tea chest and Izzy's journal.

Without bothering to ask her whether she wanted one, Gregory poured her a measure of brandy.

She eyed him quizzically. He knew she never touched spirits. 'I don't...'

'You might need it once Deborah has explained why she's here,' he said softly.

Deborah cast off her doll-like stiffness and became overly animated as she unnecessarily recounted her journey. 'Darling, I had to come down from London. Forgive me for not coming to you direct, but the train was late, and the coaches crowded. The man next to me was reading a broadsheet, which kept flapping in my face. Usually, I enjoy a train journey, but, on this occasion...'

This was not the usual Deborah but one overcome by nerves. Frances lost patience.

'You never told me about Mary Baker. Why not?'

Deborah fidgeted, tried to smile, but couldn't seem to work out quite how to do it.

'Izzy made me promise not to.'

'That was before she died. You could have told me after.'

'I didn't think—'

'No. You didn't think my mother was still alive. You didn't think she would seek me out. Why are you here, now, Deborah?'

Although she was dressed in a modern fashion, there was something about her stiff stance that made Frances think she was wearing a corset – or her nervousness had turned her to stone.

'You wrote to me. I thought the time had come. You wanted to know.'

Frances was aware of Gregory pulling a chair up beside her. The warmth of his body and sympathy was tangible, reaching out, ready to give her support.

Frances opened the dialogue. 'Before you say anything, I will refer you to my letter in which I stated that my mother had made contact. Why didn't you tell me sooner?'

It seemed for a moment that Deborah's face turned white. Her rosebud lips fell slightly open.

'It's difficult,' she managed to say at last.

'You told her where I was. Don't worry, I'm quite happy about that. It's the other matter. It appears that I'm Izzy's half-sister. We had the same father.'

Deborah nodded. 'Yes,' she said softly, eyes downcast. 'Izzy told me.'

'But nobody thought to tell me.'

'Izzy didn't think it wise to do so, though she did leave the journal and papers for you.'

'Yes. She did that, but it wasn't that clear.'

'That's why I came down here. To explain. The Reverend Sampson was about to take me round to see you. He gave me a drop of Dutch courage to help. He's given the same to you and, believe me, you're going to need it before I've finished telling this sorry tale.'

Frances looked at Gregory. There was no trace of a smile on his face, though kindness shone in his eyes as he declared, 'Frances did tell me about Mrs Devonshire – Mary Baker. I'm sure you'll agree that it will take some getting used to.'

Deborah nodded. 'Of course it will.'

Regretting sounding so sharp, Frances pursed her lips. However, the agitation remained. It was like being on the edge of a cliff debating whether the wings she wore would send her soaring or crashing to earth. She'd always liked Deborah – as a child she'd called her Aunt Debbie or Debs. Deborah had basked in her childish admiration.

'Why did you come here now when it seems all has been revealed?'

'Not quite all.'

Deborah smiled in the sweet way she always had when Izzy had accused her of being melodramatic and she'd apologised profusely before doing it all over again. Silence fell over the three people in the room, making the ticking of the mantel clock seem extra loud.

Frances downed the brandy. It burned the back of her throat and did little to help the seething thoughts rocking back and forth between a former time and now.

Deborah fiddled with the bow at her throat, her dark eyes downcast. It was as if she was waiting for Frances to probe some more, to ask a question that would be difficult to answer but all the same needed answering.

'So you've met your real mother.'

'I have.'

Deborah nodded as if well satisfied. 'That's good.'

'I think it will turn out to be good. I know who I am. I know who my real mother is and...' She paused the truth suddenly sticking in her throat. 'I now also know who my father is.'

'That's good,' Deborah repeated, nodding her dark head of curls.

'There is something else I want clarified. I found two birth certificates. My own of course but also that of the child Izzy had given birth to when she was only fifteen years of age.'

Deborah's eyes fluttered. It was easily read that the question was unwelcome.

'I want to know what happened to that baby and also what happened to the father. I would like to know whether he's still alive at least. Him and the baby, though my mother...' My mother. The words seemed gentler now on her tongue. Not so strange as it had been. 'My mother said it died.'

Frances noticed Deborah glance slyly at Gregory from beneath the brim of her hat.

'Of course, but in private if you don't mind. I don't think I can speak of it with a man in the room – even one of the cloth.'

Instantly taking her reluctance on board, Gregory got to his feet. 'As you wish.' He maintained his affable expression, but a shadow of concern darkened his eyes.

'Please excuse my rudeness,' Deborah said suddenly. 'But this is a woman-to-woman personal thing, a rather delicate matter.'

Once they were alone, Deborah took a deep breath and fixed her brown eyes on those of Frances.

'So,' she said, sounding and looking somewhat relieved that it was just the two of them. 'You now know the truth about your parents.'

'And that I was named after the daughter Izzy gave birth to when she was just fifteen years of age. I found the birth certificate and, as with me, there is no father listed.'

Deborah took a deep breath. 'So you know that much.'

'I must admit it came as something of a surprise. It seems I really am a Brakespeare, though quite frankly I'm not sure it makes me proud. That man, Izzy's father, took advantage of an innocent young girl. On the one hand I'm appalled, although finding out that Izzy is – or was – my half-sister explains a lot.'

Deborah patted her chest with a kid-gloved hand and breathed a sigh of relief. 'That's what I wanted to ask you about and wasn't sure your vicar friend knew. I had strict instructions to let you find out for yourself. Of course,' she said, a look of sadness on her face, 'Izzy didn't expect to die. I suppose none of us do, do we,' she added with a hint of girlish laughter, her fine delicate hands flapping like a small bird's wings.

Frances couldn't laugh. The best she could do was a smile. There were still too many questions for which she wanted answers. 'You knew Izzy well. In fact, you knew her better than anyone, even me,' she added. 'I detect a mystery here, one that you might be able to answer.'

The laughter had gone from Deborah's face and the leftover smile slowly faded.

'I found two birth certificates. My own and the one from twenty years before, yet the names were the same. It was the birth certificate for a baby born out of wedlock to a young girl who was sent away to give birth. Am I right?'

'Yes. I didn't know it was there. I didn't know she'd kept it.' Deborah's voice was not much more than a whisper.

'I understand the baby died.'

Again, a hushed acknowledgement and a curt nod that wordlessly confirmed she was correct.

Frances shook her head disconsolately. A young girl had fallen in the family way. She wasn't the first and she certainly wouldn't be the last, hence the urgency to educate women how to use a Dutch cap, how a man might prevent getting a woman pregnant by the simple use of a condom. 'I take it she was in love with the father.'

The look on Deborah's face was difficult to interpret.

Frances concluded the only possibility to make Deborah react as she did. 'Was she raped?'

Deborah seemed to think about it before she nodded, swallowed and uttered a wistful, 'Yes.'

'Oh. Poor Izzy. Do you know who the boy was?'

For a moment, Frances thought Izzy's old friend was going to faint and wondered if Gregory might have a bottle of smelling salts. Instead, she gathered her courage, determined to press on and hear the truth – whatever that might be.

Deborah took her time answering and when she did, there

was a look in her eyes that hinted at pleading for her to understand. 'It wasn't a boy.'

'A man then? An older man who took advantage?' Despite the clearness of her voice, it felt as though a length of barbed wire was wound around her throat.

Deborah stared at her. 'Yes. But more than that... Oh my goodness, I really don't want to say this. It was so unnatural, so... so... As a child, he encouraged her to tell him that she was his little girl and promised to make him proud of her. Her father loved her to say things like that and told her that if she told their little secret he might end up in prison and she would never see him again. She was just a little girl...' Deborah failed to find the rest of the words and tears filled her eyes.

Suddenly Frances knew. Did she want to hear this truth? She recalled Mary being warned by the servants in the household to be wary of Mr Brakespeare. No, she thought. It couldn't be – could it?

In the parish next to St Michael's, there'd been a case of a pregnant adolescent girl whose mother had died having two children. The girl was not known to dally with boys and in time the truth had exploded into the open.

Most people thought such things only happened to disparate families living in dire accommodation. It was not always so. It chilled Frances that she was even thinking the unimaginable, a taboo observed by humanity for millennia.

She felt its presence in the air even before finally, Deborah spoke. 'I'm not sure I want to tell you.'

This was it, hard as it was, she had to hear the suspicion that lurked in the darkest recesses of her mind.

'Deborah, I'm a doctor. I see all sorts and the depravity of human nature crosses the class divide. Do you want me to say it? Would that make it any easier?'

Deborah shook her head and raised her eyes. After a moment of what seemed indecision, she finally stated what Frances was fearing to hear. 'Her father loved her too much. The baby was his.'

Even though she'd been expecting it, Frances felt as though she'd been hit by a tram. 'That wasn't love,' she exclaimed through clenched teeth and sprang to her feet. 'Excuse me a moment.'

She raced out of the room, almost choking on each harried breath. She needed Gregory and instinctively knew she'd find him in the kitchen. By the time she did, sobs were wracking her body.

Without saying a word, Gregory held out his arms, wrapped them around her and patted her back.

Not wishing Deborah to hear her sobbing, Frances buried her face against his shoulder. To his credit, he kept silent and did not pressurise her into telling him what was wrong, what was the terrible truth Deborah had told her.

Once she had raised her head, he dabbed at the tears on her face with his handkerchief.

'We're better go back in,' said Frances. 'I have to face this.'

Looking at Deborah was awkward.

'Quite a night,' said Gregory, 'but thank you for coming. It took guts to tell your story and...' He sighed. 'It took guts to listen to it.'

Both women nodded silently. Frances knew for sure that it would be some time before she ever got used to this news – if at all.

'I need to get to the train station.' Deborah looked at Frances pointedly. Perhaps she was angling for forgiveness.

Frances remained silent. She didn't know how long it would take to forgive Deborah for withholding the truth.

'Would it be possible to take me to the train station?' she asked in an uncharacteristically timid manner.

Frances shook her head. 'I have some thinking to do, besides which I don't think I would be pleasant company. Gregory can take my car.'

Whilst Deborah made her way out into the hallway, Gregory touched Frances's cheek, his expression one of concern. 'Will you be here when I get back?'

She nodded. 'Though I might have drunk all your brandy. The occasion demands it.'

She didn't notice that it was getting dark. Her thoughts were with Izzy and not just about all she'd been through. Memories of those times in the house in Carwell Street, the laughter, the radical views, the unending fight to improve women's lives. She knew now that the adult Izzy had once been a helpless young girl overpowered by a man. And that, she thought, was what made her the woman she became, that and the natural love she'd had for her own kind and for her adopted daughter.

And so it shall pass into the next generation, she thought to herself. *I will continue with my own projects to improve the lot of women. My clinic will go from strength to strength, a fitting epitaph to Izzy's memory.*

21

The garden at Orchard Manor House was wearing the freshness of an early June day. The scent of roses filled the air along with that of freshly mown grass.

Lady Araminta Compton-Dixon watched from the window of her upstairs room. The garden had changed little over the years; there'd always been expanses of green lawn, always rose beds, silver birch, beech and a few unusual varieties brought back from the Tropics by some adventurous ancestor. She also thought of her husband, Devlin's father. Unlike some of his class, he was not a hunting, shooting and fishing man which didn't mean he wasn't any good at any of those sports. The fact was he'd much preferred to go grubbing around in the quarry or a coal mine for fossils, a few of which now formed a rockery beside the pond, which was fringed by a copse of willow at the north side of the garden. Her husband had preferred shady areas of ferns and moss to roses and sunlit lawns. He'd been a good man, though a bit distant.

She moved away from the middle window of the room to another where she had a better view of the gateway between the verdant lawns and the walled garden which wrapped around the house from back to front. She smiled on sighting Devlin, shaking the hands of their visitors. Even from here, she could see he was smiling. How things had changed in such a short time and all because of Nurse Daniels.

A knock at the door of her room was expected. Grimes ambled in to tell her that all was ready for her to make the grand entrance and announce the party open.

She thanked him and asked, 'Is there no music yet?'

'Not yet, my lady. Mr Devlin won't let anyone touch his gramophone and he's otherwise engaged at the gate welcoming everyone personally.'

'And Nurse Daniels?'

'I believe she's overseeing the catering.'

'A young woman of many talents,' murmured Araminta. She picked up her shawl and her sunshade. 'If you could carry these down the stairs for me, Mr Grimes.'

'Certainly, my lady.'

'Do you happen to know if Doctor Brakespeare has arrived yet?'

'I believe she has, though I cannot pin down exactly where she is at present.'

'Thank you, Mr Grimes. If you see her before I do, tell her I'd like a word.'

* * *

'Your hand must be aching with all that handshaking,' said a bemused Lucy.

'That's the lot, I do believe,' Devlin said, smiling as he turned to greet her. 'I want to take you down to the pond later. There's something I want to say to you.'

'If we can get away,' Lucy returned. 'Goodness,' she added on spotting a familiar figure. 'Isn't that Mr MacDonald, the under-taker? What's he doing here?'

'Transport,' said Devlin, taking her arm. 'Doctor Brakespeare's car only takes four people, five at a squash. It's surprising how many people you can crowd into the back of a hearse.'

Their laughter was shared but subdued on account of not wanting to upset anyone.

'You must be hungry by now. Let me take you to a groaning table.'

'A table that complains?' Devlin's comment was accompanied by more laughter.

Lucy gave him a dig with her elbow. 'You know very well what I mean.'

She'd barely slept the past few nights, her mind occupied with what had passed between them in the long grass between the manor and the town. Nothing could be gained from feeling guilty that she'd abandoned herself to a man she'd once thought was unattainable. Devlin was very attainable. She knew that now.

'The ham sandwiches are good.' Billy Noakes was standing next to them, eyeing their empty plates. 'I made them,' he said with obvious pride.

'Then I cannot resist. And I'm guessing they're right there in front of me.'

Lucy looked at Billy whilst jerking her chin at the pile of sand-wiches. He instinctively pushed the platter of ham sandwiches within Devlin's reach. She smiled and mouthed a silent thank you. At the same time, she thought what a kind-hearted boy he was, certainly not deserving of the harsh treatment he'd had in his young life.

Heads turned as Lady Compton-Dixon appeared at the top of the stone steps leading down from the balustrade to the lawn.

Lucy whispered to Devlin that his mother had arrived.

'Making the grand entrance, no doubt,' he replied.

Mr Grimes called for silence. 'Her ladyship wishes to say a few words.'

Grimes had a resonant voice for an old man. The crowd fell to silence.

Her ladyship cast her gaze over the assembly before extending a few welcoming words. 'It is with great pleasure that I welcome you here today. It is some time since a member of my family established the Orchard Cottage Hospital. It was small back then and medicine was primitive. We have come a long way. However, progress continues. To that end, I have made the decision to build an extension to the hospital. This extension will contain a new mother and baby clinic, plus a maternity ward. The present clinic will be converted into a children's ward. As yet, none of this is firmed up. It's just a dream I suddenly had that I believe can be turned into reality. Now, enough of me deliberating on my intentions. Please enjoy yourself. There's plenty of food and my son has brought his gramophone. You are welcome to dance – in fact, I order you to dance. I only wish my old legs would allow me to do the same.'

The ensuing laughter was followed by a ragtime number, the record already in place, Devlin passing his plate to young Billy Noakes, who had taken to being his guardian, making sure he had everything to hand, sliding between him and Lucy, who was somewhat bemused by the boy's loyalty to the man who had bashed his tormentor about the head.

Lucy smiled as she watched them, the young boy and the man who she loved. It didn't matter about his eyes – not to her. She could see into his soul regardless.

She was still smiling and watching the pair of them when she realised that her ladyship was standing beside her. Like her, Lady Compton-Dixon was eyeing her son and the enthusiastic young man who was trying to copy the dance routine Devlin was showing him.

At first, they said nothing, just an older woman and a younger one entertaining their individual emotions, both of which were based on love.

'You have my permission, my dear.'

Lucy's head jerked round. She was shorter than her ladyship, so had to look up into her face. Even so, she saw the watery eyes, not watering from sadness but from contentment, even happiness.

'You have my permission, my dear,' her ladyship repeated. 'Please tell my son that my only wish is for him – and you – to be happy. My best wishes for your future together. Now,' she said as though she'd just got something quite heavy off her chest. 'Where is Doctor Brakespeare. Quite extraordinary. I haven't seen her. Doesn't she know this event is not just about the hospital, it's about her. She's responsible for its success. Where is the woman?'

'She's otherwise engaged at present.' The vicar, Reverend Gregory Sampson, held out his arms. 'Perhaps you would like to partner me in a slow waltz?'

'What?' Her ladyship looked flabbergasted, but on seeing the humour lurking in Gregory's eyes, decided to play him at his own game. 'A very slow waltz.'

'Your wish is my command. Devlin,' he shouted across to where her ladyship's son was standing by his gramophone in a rather possessive manner. 'Your mother requires you to play a waltz. A very slow waltz. Only then will she deign to dance with me.'

* * *

The area around the pond in the northern part of the garden was scattered with moss-covered rocks. Some were big enough to sit on.

The effort of preparing and bringing out platters of sandwiches, pies and cakes had proved a little too much for Mrs Devonshire.

Embarrassed to be coughing in the proximity of food, she'd taken herself off, running to the hidden pond where damsel flies skimmed over the silver surface.

Unseen by her mother, Frances had followed and found her sitting on one of the large rocks, head bowed and coughing into her handkerchief.

On realising that Frances was with her, Mary attempted to get up.

'No,' Frances ordered, one arm stretched, one hand directing her to remain sitting. 'Be still. Take deep breaths.'

She sat down beside her, reached out and placed her hand on her mother's shoulder.

'I think you need to tell me what's wrong with you. I want to help you.'

Her mother, who she still thought of as Mrs Devonshire, trained her eyes on the placid waters of the pond.

A pair of mating damsel flies fluttered just in front of her when she shook her head.

'There's nothing you can do. I've got growths in my lungs. Not just one growth, but two. It's too late to do anything – so I've been told.'

Frances felt a choking sensation in her throat. 'How long have you got?'

'They told me six months, but that was ten months ago. I couldn't have found you in six months, but ten months has just about given me time.' She turned her head and looked at Frances with tear-filled eyes. 'But I did find you.' She smiled through her tears. 'I found my baby. My only baby.'

When faced with delivering a damning prognosis, Frances usually managed to maintain a professional manner, holding back on emotions and showing the strength of a person the patient and relatives could lean on. But this was her mother. She attempted to blink away the tears, but it did no good. A trickle of saltiness ran down one cheek.

'This is so unfair.'

Her mother's smile was sad. 'Life is unfair, but I found you before I die and for that I'm grateful.'

This time when they embraced there was no hesitation. Their heads were together, their arms tight around each other.

Frances made an instant decision. From that moment on, she would call this woman by the name she rightly owned – just as she owned the name Brakespeare. Both had value in her world.

'We'd better be getting back now. I've a suspicion that Minty – her ladyship – will be looking for me. Will you take my arm? We can walk back together.'

The leaves on the trees rustled. The smell of roses filled the air. There was dancing on the lawn.

Fanning herself with a black feather fan, her ladyship was sitting red-faced and puffing on a garden seat. On seeing Frances, she beckoned her over.

'Doctor. Where have you been?'

Frances had known this would be the first questions answered and had planned her reply.

'I've been talking with my mother. My natural mother. This is she. Mrs Mary Devonshire. She hasn't long come back from Australia.'

Her ladyship gave no sign of being surprised but nodded her head in greeting. A quizzical look appeared then disappeared from her eyes. 'Haven't I seen you somewhere before?' she asked.

'I'm a laundress. Your laundress.'

'My word. How amazing. Though I'm guessing you won't be working for me for much longer. I understand from Cook that you had a hand in preparing this sumptuous feast and seeing as the hospital is in need of a good cook, the good doctor here – your daughter – is bound to snatch you from my employ. Not that I can hold that against her, of course. The hospital wouldn't be the same without her.' She looked directly at Frances. 'Both your mothers – natural and adoptive – deserve you. You are a credit to them both. That is why I've decided to name the new children's ward of the hospital the Isabelle Brakespeare ward. I think it very fitting, don't you?'

Frances fought for the right words. Her gratitude was limitless, but something deserved to be said.

'I think given Izzy's beliefs in the rights of women, the name is very apt. I thank you very much – from the depths of my heart.'

Araminta smiled, her old hands clasping the ebony handle of her walking stick.

'She deserves it. You deserve it.'

The meeting finished; Frances walked off with her mother, enjoying their closeness even though their time together was limited.

'I'm going to examine you and see what's to be done,' Frances said determinedly. 'In the meantime, I'm going to spend all the time with you that I can, and to that end you're moving into the coach house with me.'

'I can't do that. I need to keep my job at Orchard Manor. I need to earn a living.'

'And I need a new housekeeper, someone to take care of me

and you're the best person to do that. Only the lightest of tasks. Do you think you could do that?'

Frances waited for her response. In the short time since she'd known her mother, she'd detected a sense of pride. She'd had a hard life but wouldn't accept charity. Ma Skittings already had the job and once she had the facts would make sure her mother would not overtax herself. Frances was adamant that they wouldn't be parted again, that she would make her mother's life as easy and as happy as possible for as long as it might last.

Her mother responded instantly. Her face shone like the sun that now dappled the lawn through the leaves on the trees. 'That would be heaven. No matter how long I last, each day will be a bonus, and who knows, I might beat this thing and be with you for a very long time.'

Her words brought back a memory from the Great War when she and Ralph had lain in a field of golden corn and red poppies. 'In war or peace, every day is precious.'

And so it was.

ABOUT THE AUTHOR

Lizzie Lane is the author of over 50 books, including the bestselling Tobacco Girls series. She was born and bred in Bristol where many of her family worked in the cigarette and cigar factories.

Sign up to Lizzie Lane's mailing list here for news, competitions and updates on future books.

Follow Lizzie on social media here:

 facebook.com/jean.goodhind

𝕏 x.com/baywriterallatı

⊙ instagram.com/baywriterallatsea

BB bookbub.com/authors/lizzie-lane

g goodreads.com/lizzielane

ALSO BY LIZZIE LANE

The Tobacco Girls

The Tobacco Girls

Dark Days for the Tobacco Girls

Fire and Fury for the Tobacco Girls

Heaven and Hell for the Tobacco Girls

Marriage and Mayhem for the Tobacco Girls

A Fond Farewell for the Tobacco Girls

Coronation Close

New Neighbours for Coronation Close

Shameful Secrets on Coronation Close

Dark Shadows Over Coronation Close

The Strong Trilogy

The Sugar Merchant's Wife

Secrets of the Past

Daughter of Destiny

The Sweet Sisters Trilogy

Wartime Sweethearts

War Baby

Home Sweet Home

Wives and Lovers

Wartime Brides

Coronation Wives

Mary Anne Randall

A Wartime Wife

A Wartime Family

Orchard Cottage Hospital

A New Doctor at Orchard Cottage Hospital

Family Affairs at Orchard Cottage Hospital

The Kowloon Series

Doctor of Kowloon

Escape from Kowloon

Standalones

War Orphans

A Wartime Friend

Secrets and Sins

A Christmas Wish

Women in War

Her Father's Daughter

Trouble for the Boat Girl

Sixpence Stories

Introducing Sixpence Stories!

Discover page-turning historical novels from your favourite authors, meet new friends and be transported back in time.

Join our book club
Facebook group

https://bit.ly/SixpenceGroup

Sign up to our
newsletter

https://bit.ly/SixpenceNews

Boldwood

Boldwood Books is an award-winning fiction publishing company seeking out the best stories from around the world.

Find out more at www.boldwoodbooks.com

Join our reader community for brilliant books, competitions and offers!

Follow us
@BoldwoodBooks
@TheBoldBookClub

Sign up to our weekly deals newsletter

https://bit.ly/BoldwoodBNewsletter

Printed in Great Britain
by Amazon